S0-BNJ-091

ALSO BY MAX EHRLICH

THE CULT
THE REINCARNATION OF PETER PROUD
THE EDICT
THE SAVAGE IS LOOSE
DEEP IS THE BLUE
THE TAKERS
FIRST TRAIN TO BABYLON
SPIN THE GLASS WEB
THE BIG EYE

MAX EHRLICH

Reincarnation in Venice

SIMON AND SCHUSTER

NEW YORK

COPYRIGHT © 1979 BY MAX EHRLICH
ALL RIGHTS RESERVED
INCLUDING THE RIGHT OF REPRODUCTION
IN WHOLE OR IN PART IN ANY FORM
PUBLISHED BY SIMON & SCHUSTER
A DIVISION OF GULF & WESTERN CORPORATION
SIMON & SCHUSTER BUILDING
ROCKEFELLER CENTER
1230 AVENUE OF THE AMERICAS
NEW YORK, NEW YORK 10020

DESIGNED BY ELIZABETH WOLL
MANUFACTURED IN THE UNITED STATES OF AMERICA

1   2   3   4   5   6   7   8   9   10

LIBRARY OF CONGRESS CATALOGING IN PUBLICATION DATA

EHRLICH, MAX SIMON, DATE.
REINCARNATION IN VENICE.

I.   TITLE.
PZ3.E334RC [PS3509.H663] 813'.5'4 78-15241
ISBN 0-671-22689-4

All of the characters in this book are fictitious, and any resemblance to actual persons, living or dead, is purely coincidental.

FOR MARGARET

1954

ON a balmy evening in early September, a man came out of a palazzo overlooking the Fondamenta Narisi, just off the Grand Canal.

He was young, perhaps no more than twenty-five, with a darkly handsome patrician face, and was, like most Venetians of his class, exquisitely tailored. He paused for a moment, in front of the great doors of the palazzo and looked up. His wife was at one of the upper windows. He smiled at her and blew her a kiss. She waved back at him.

But even from here he could see that she was still disturbed.

About exactly what, he did not know. Bianca was a young mother. His son was only a month old, and perhaps it could have been that. He had kissed her goodbye and told her he would be back early, but suddenly she had clung to him, he had felt her body trembling and she had begged him not to go, to cancel his appointment with Teodoro, to stay home with her. Naturally, he was puzzled. There was nothing about this particular evening that would upset her.

Actually, Teodoro Borsato, his good friend, family counselor, and legal advisor, had phoned and asked him to stop at his, Borsato's house. After he picked up his friend, they would walk the short distance to the Piazza San Marco, and there spend an hour or two. There were some business matters to discuss—additional taxes on the palazzo, some developments on his investments in Milan, and so on. They would have a drink at Florian's, as they always did, listen to the music, stare in amusement at the tourists, as they talked. He would be home early, before eleven at the latest.

Still, seeing her so upset and putting it down to some mysterious feminine insecurity, he had told Bianca that the meeting wasn't important, that it would wait until another day. And he had gone to the phone to call Teodoro . . .

It was then, abruptly, that she changed her mind and told him to go after all. He repeated that he would be glad to stay, but she replied that she had been foolish, that of course he should keep his appointment. She insisted on it. It would be silly for him to stay, just to humor her.

He began to walk along the canal toward the Ponte del Pestrin. When he reached the little bridge, he turned to look back again.

She was still in the window, watching him.

Still puzzled, he crossed the bridge and walked up the *calle* toward the Campo Francesco Morosini. He had told the family gondolier, Bruno, that he would not need him that night; he preferred to walk. He was one of the last in Venice to employ a personal gondolier; of course, it was an extravagance, as there was a family speedboat moored in front of the palazzo for use on the canals. But the idea had a certain flair, it was very Venetian, it was a touch of past glory, and a luxury he could easily afford.

Always, he enjoyed this particular walk. A vagrant breeze sneaked through the *fondamenta* from the Grand Canal, ruffling the curtains in the windows. Although he was now engulfed in the dark shadow of oncoming night, the last of a spectacular sunset still gilded the roofs and set fire to the laundry hanging high on lines between the balconies of adjoining houses. In the distance, a dog barked. A gondola passed him, with a white cat, one of the justly famous cats of Venice, sitting high on its prow. The gondolier, in blue-striped jersey and red-beribboned straw hat, guided it skillfully into a marble-surfaced landing between candy-striped mooring poles. The cat sat unmoved, its unblinking eyes critically watching the performance of its master. The gondola had left a small wake, slapping the water against the mossy sides of the canal and stirring the green weeds beneath the brackish surface.

This was his city, the city he loved, and all these were familiar sights. His step was springy, he looked forward to the evening, it felt good to be young and alive.

He did not know, he could not know, that this was to be the last hour of his life.

The Campo Francesco Morosini was buzzing, alive with people. He was a little early, and he took a table at a cafe and ordered an espresso. From within the cafe, a radio blared the evening news. He listened with half an ear. The first atomic-powered submarine, the *Nautilus*, had just been commissioned and had joined the Atlantic fleet. In Cuba, Major General Fulgencio Batista had again been elected president without opposition. The Swedish Academy had awarded the 1954 Nobel Prize for literature to Ernest Hemingway. And, most importantly for Italians, especially for those living in this corner of the country, Trieste had finally been formally turned over to Italy.

To the man lingering at his table, all this seemed very far away. Venice, he reflected, was a world unto itself, immune to all this, an enchanting womb, where the past was everywhere visible, overwhelming the present. It was vulnerable only to time and to the slow and relentless erosion of the sea. Some day it would all be gone, but not in his time, *grazie a Dio*, not in his time.

He watched a pigeon, perched on the head of the statue

15

of Niccolo Tommasseo, which stood in the *campo*. It ruffled its feathers a little and then, with fine irreverence, settled down to pass the night. A vendor came into the *campo*, selling illuminated yo-yos, flashing them back and forth, one in each hand, to illustrate his wares. A mob of shouting children, who had been playing one of their mysterious games in the center of the *campo*, quit and gathered around him. Lovers strolled arm in arm in front of the Church of San Stefano, and from the windows of the music conservatory came the piping of an oboe, the scraping of an amateur bow over a fiddle, the plunk of a piano, and the uncertain trilling of some aspiring soprano.

It was dark when he finally left the cafe. He had enjoyed this small interlude. He reflected that the poets had been all wrong about this city. They had portrayed Venice as a sad and brooding place, with a tradition of melancholy, preoccupied with the drama of death. But he knew better, and so did all Venetians. The real Venice merely accepted this canard with a sly wink and laughed softly behind a polite hand.

He walked down a street and then strolled through the Campo S. Maurizio. His mind drifted back to his wife. He wondered why she had seemed so disturbed lately. She was so young, only twenty, and there was this postnatal depression he had heard women talk about, after they had borne a child. Perhaps he ought to take her up to the villa in Cortina d'Ampezzo for a week or two. It would be a change, and the mountain air might do her a world of good.

He came into a *salizzada* now, little more than a paved alley. It was dank and dark, sparsely traveled, a shortcut he always took whenever he walked to the Piazza. At the moment, he was the only pedestrian. He was startled by the sudden screeching of two cats just ahead, as they tangled into each other, snarling, biting, scratching. He hadn't seen them at all, and the sudden noise startled him. They looked up to see him coming and broke and ran.

He stood there for a moment, watching them go. Both of

them were black cats. He grinned mirthlessly. My luck, he thought.

Now, the only sound breaking the silence was the footsteps of some lone pedestrian coming from the *fondamenta* just ahead. They rang rhythmically on the stone, echoing resonantly, then changed pitch as they walked up and then down the steps of the bridge crossing the canal. They became fainter and fainter and finally faded away.

He came into the Fondamenta de la Malvesia Vecchia. It was dark here, as well, and deserted. At this point, the street itself became a *sottoportico,* a narrow walk running underneath the overhang of a building.

He had taken only a few steps along it when he saw the two black figures crouched in a recessed doorway.

The hackles rose on the back of his neck. For a moment, he debated whether to try to pass them or turn around and run. But before he could move, they were upon him.

He fought like a madman. He was strong, and he wrestled them out from under the *sottoportico,* to the edge of the canal itself. But they were too much for him. One of the assassins got behind him, threw an arm around his windpipe in a stranglehold, and started to squeeze. He squirmed and wriggled, fighting for air, trying to break free. He saw the other man close in from the front and brought his knee up into his attacker's groin. He heard the man grunt in pain and swear viciously.

"Bastardo!"

The man holding him from the back continued the relentless pressure on his windpipe. His lungs screamed, he fought for air. His vision began to blur and swim. The black-draped man in front of him raised his arm. He saw the knife glinting in his hand. At this moment, he caught his first full view of his assassin's face. The eyes glared madly, the face was contorted into a twisted smile. Spittle drooled from the sides of his attacker's mouth.

The arm came down hard, and he felt the impact of the knife, felt the blade enter, felt it turn in his flesh, rip and tear. Strangely, he felt no pain. An immense drowsiness overcame him. He started to fall back. As he did, his assassin's face fell out of view. His eye caught something else, over the man's shoulder. It was a small head, carved out of stone and set in the roof of the *sottoportico*.

The stone head was human, but it was attached to the curling body of a snake. The face had big round eyes and an ugly, squashed pug nose. But instead of a tongue, the open, lewd mouth showed fangs. The face smiled insolently down at him, the fangs darting out obscenely from between the thick lips.

It was the last thing he ever saw.

Darkness engulfed him, but he was still alive, still conscious, barely breathing. Dimly, he was aware that he was being dragged across the narrow walk. He felt himself lifted and then lowered into a gondola moored at the edge of the canal.

He felt the gondola drift away a few feet, under the impact of a shove. He guessed they had simply propelled it to the center of the canal so that they could more easily conceal what they were doing, in case some passerby appeared. Strange. He felt no fear now, knowing death was certain. Only curiosity as to what they would do next.

He heard the clink and rattle of heavy chains. His assassins began to wrap him in the chains. He felt the chilling embrace of the cold iron on his flesh. They worked hard and swiftly, breathing heavily. He was aware they were attaching heavy weights to his feet, as well.

Then he felt himself lifted, one man holding him by the shoulders, the other by the feet. With the addition of the extra weight, he had become a heavy burden, and his murderers grunted and wheezed in their exertion. The gondola swayed precariously, almost tipped over.

They snarled at each other like animals, each warning the other to be careful, as they desperately tried to keep the gondola steady. He could smell the stink of their sweat as they labored to drop him overboard.

18

Suddenly, he was released. He hit the water with a slight splash and sank like a stone toward his cold and scummy grave, and his last conscious thought was one of wonderment.

Dio mio, why me? Why have they done this to me?

PART ONE

I

The time was the present.

The man's name was David Drew. He was twenty-five years old, a bachelor, and he lived in a one-bedroom apartment on East Fiftieth Street, in the city of New York.

He was a systems analyst and operations research specialist for Datafax, a major and worldwide supplier of digital-stored computers, and his salary was twenty-seven thousand five hundred dollars a year. On this particular muggy evening in late September, as he rounded the corner of Fiftieth and proceeded to walk north on Third Avenue, he was feeling good, very good indeed.

For two reasons.

First, he had been given a raise just last week, along with a large pat on the back from his boss and a prediction that in a year or two he had a chance to become the youngest man at Datafax ever to become a senior systems analyst. And, second, he was on his way to pick up a lovely redheaded girl named Cassie Knox, who was a reporter-researcher at *Newsweek*.

He grinned when he thought of the way they had met. It had been at a singles bar on Forty-ninth Street, some two weeks ago. One of those noisy and lively little places where you stood three deep, where everybody seemed to know everybody else, and where nobody talked, everybody shouted to each other. He had happened to stand next to her. She had a high forehead, cool and intelligent blue eyes, a provocative mouth, and very white teeth. He introduced himself and she responded in kind. They chatted a little and found each other interesting. And finally, he had shouted:

"Let's get out of here."

"And go where?" she shouted back.

"There's a nice little French restaurant just up the block. Place called Antoine's."

"Oh, yes. I know it."

"How about dinner?"

The blue eyes studied him for a moment. In a singles bar like this, it was SOP—standard operating procedure. If you were really interested in a girl, you not only bought her a drink, you invited her to dinner, and there was a chance you might go on from there. If not, you simply bought her a drink, period. She knew the ritual, and he understood her hesitation. After all, if she accepted his invitation, it was a kind of commitment on her part.

Finally, she smiled, approving him, and shouted:

"I'd love it."

At dinner, where it was quiet enough to really talk, he told her that he was originally from Canton, Ohio, and had graduated from Ohio State, with majors in math and engineering, and she told him she had come from a little town in northern Vermont called Wells River and had graduated from Radcliffe. Then she had asked him:

"What do you do, David?"

"I'm a systems analyst."

"I know that, for God's sake. You told me that back at the bar. But what do you actually *do?*"

24

"It's hard to explain."

"Try."

"Well," he said, his face deadpan. "My job is really operations research. I'm supposed to formulate mathematical models of management problems by the application of advanced mathematics and research methods to provide quantitative bases of planning, forecasting, and making decisions. After the problem is defined, I have to figure out ways to get maximum probability of effectiveness in relation to the cost or risk involved. In short, I gather, relate, and identify information with the variables in my model by applying personal judgments and certain mathematical tests."

She looked at him for a long time, and then she said: "Oh, shit."

"I *told you* it was hard to explain."

He couldn't help grinning. She stared at him, disgusted. "Look, Cassie, nothing I do makes any sense unless you know what a computer is."

"I know what it is."

"Yes?"

"It's a machine with all those flashing lights and it turns out these punched cards and it screws up everything by making all these godawful mistakes, and when you call the charge account section at the department store or the bank and complain, they keep blaming it on the computer, but you can't *talk* to the damned thing, and so it keeps right on making the same stupid mistake and they keep sending you the wrong bills, until you go crazy."

He laughed and they went on to other things. She asked him what his favorite sport was, and he said tennis. He asked her what hers was, and she told him it was jogging. He stared at her.

"Jogging?"

"Some people hate the word. So they call it running. But it's really the same thing. I love it. It's marvelous." She noted his stare. "You seem surprised."

"I guess I am."

"Why? Everybody's into running these days. It improves

skin and muscle tone, sheds water weight, eats up calories."
She smiled slyly. "Besides, it's supposed to make you feel
very sexy afterward."

"It does?"

"So I've been told. You ought to try it, David."

"Maybe I will," he said weakly. "Where do you do all
this running?"

"In Central Park. If you're interested, I jog every morning at seven o'clock. And I always start at the monkey house
in the zoo."

He had decided that he was not about to get up that
early in the morning and run through the park. Somehow,
the whole thing seemed slightly ridiculous. He held out for
two days, then he bought himself a jogging suit and some
special running shoes and joined Cassie. They jogged along
the roads and walks and around the reservoir, and he finally
got to like it.

He learned that Cassie also played tennis, so he took her
to the Gramercy Racquet Club and Bobby Kaplan's East
River Bath and Tennis Club and found that she played
a good game, a very good game indeed. In the two weeks
he had known her, he found her very difficult, very attractive and sympatico, a lady of no nonsense who seemed to
know what she wanted, and he had reason to hope this
might be himself. They both sensed that this was something
special, not just a casual relationship, the kind of in-and-out
thing you ran into so often in the city of New York.

Anyway, Cassie lived on Fifty-sixth just off Third, and
tonight he was on his way to pick her up, and after that,
they were going to dinner, this time at a small Italian restaurant he knew called Alfredo's, and after that . . . ?

Well, he had known her two weeks. That was a respectable amount of time, even for the most respectable lady.

He was walking up Third, between Fifty-second and
Fifty-third, when something caught his eye.

It was a gold medallion in the window of a pawnshop.

26

The window was cluttered with a variety of articles for sale—guitars, typewriters, tape recorders, clocks, golf clubs, and a hodgepodge of jewelry, rings, necklaces, bracelets, and earrings. The medallion itself was large in size, about two inches in diameter, and hung on a gold chain. Mixed with the rest of the jewelry in the window, it was rather inconspicuous. Yet, somehow, it had drawn his attention.

Inscribed on it was something he took to be a family crest or coat-of-arms. A big male lion, heavily muscled and richly maned, standing on its hind legs, paws upraised, clutching a scroll in each paw. He continued to stare at it. The more he did, the more interested he became.

Normally, he cared nothing about jewelry. He had friends who wore gold chains around their necks, amulets, signs of the zodiac, shark's teeth, medallions, and beads. But it was not his style, he wasn't into male jewelry. He could pass a hundred shops like this without a second look. The medallion had a rich look, it had a certain distinction. But there were others scattered here and there behind the window, richer looking, more flamboyant, more interesting visually.

He hesitated for a moment. Then he decided to take a closer look at it.

He walked into the pawnshop. A bell rang as he closed the door. The proprietor came out from behind a curtain leading to a back room. He was a bald man with a straggly beard, and he chewed on a ragged and limp cigar. His shrewd eyes took in David at a glance. This is a man, they decided, who has come to buy, not to sell or hock. He does not look the type, and he carries no package.

"What can I do for you?"

"I'm interested in something you have in the window."

"Show me."

David pointed out the medallion. The owner reached in, brought it to the counter, and laid it on a piece of black velvet.

"This is a very nice piece," he said. "Very nice. First class." He lifted it by the chain, hefted it. "Solid gold."

He handed it to David. The feel of the metal made his skin tingle. Now that he was able to study it close up, he saw that the lion was beautifully etched; it looked extremely lifelike. Even in miniature the artist had managed to finely detail the rippling muscles of the animal, the fall of the thick hair of the mane.

"This is an antique?"

"Sure is."

"How can you tell?"

The man smiled condescendingly. "Mister, I've been in this business a thousand years. Take my word for it. I know an old piece when I see one."

"Any idea where it came from?"

The proprietor took the cigar from his mouth, spat out a bit of tobacco, and shook his head.

"No way I could tell you. I just bought this shop recently. This was part of the inventory I took over, along with everything else. It could have been bought at an auction. Or maybe some G.I. picked it up somewhere abroad in the last war and hocked it later and never came back for it. In this business, you have stuff like this laying around for years. Most of it came from somewhere, but where it came from, nobody really cares. You go to an antique jewelry shop, where they sell expensive stuff, maybe people care about the pedigree. But this is a pawnshop, and my customers couldn't care less."

"How much do you want for it?"

The proprietor checked the tag, on which was written some kind of code.

"Four hundred dollars."

David stared at him.

"Four hundred?"

"That's the price. This is a very fine item. And I'm throwing in the chain, which is fourteen-carat gold."

"I like it. But you'd have to come way down..."

"No way. I figure my profit by pennyweight. What I mean is, there's so much gold in this piece by weight, and it translates into a retail price of four hundred. Just as simple as that. As I said, I don't know where this item came from, or who owned it. Personally, I couldn't care less. All I know is what I have to get for it. Okay?"

"Okay," said David. "Thanks for showing it to me."

The man shrugged. "You're missing out on a good buy. This is a quality item. Take my word for it."

David walked out of the shop. He paused in front of the shop, watching the owner carefully replace the medallion in the window. This time, he placed it in a more prominent place, setting it aside in a little area all by itself. If he knew David was watching him through the window, he gave no sign of it. He simply turned and went back into the shop.

There was a flashing-on-and-off billboard sign across the street. The light glinted on the medallion. He asked himself why he should care for this thing. Why should it turn him on? It was crazy. It was only a piece of decorated gold, hanging on a chain.

And four hundred bucks?

The hell with it.

He continued to walk up Third. Idly, he wondered where the thing had come from. The lion, he knew, was a very common symbol. The king of beasts. It symbolized strength and courage. It was inscribed on hundreds of family crests all over Europe and was admired just about everywhere else in the world, from the Lion of Judah to you name it. He had seen it in the trademarks of industries and in the logos of honor societies everywhere. Clearly, this particular lion with the scrolls in his paws was holding up the law, or perhaps learning. But there was no particular clue in that.

The medallion seemed to haunt him. He couldn't get it out of his mind. He became annoyed with himself, then angry. If he were going to spend four hundred bucks, he had other ways to spend it, ways that made a lot more sense. There was that pair of new ski boots he wanted, and that cashmere jacket he had always wanted to own some day, beautiful and as soft as butter. With the price of that medallion, he could buy them both. With that amount, or with much less, he could buy a new suit, a typewriter, a radio or small television set. Or he could run amuck in some music shop, buy records for his hi-fi. Four hundred dollars would pay for a series of lessons by a tennis pro; he could practically buy a new backhand for that. And it would be more than enough to buy him an air ticket to some distant beach and tropical sea, where the scuba diving was something you dreamed about.

Tomorrow was Sunday. The shop would be closed. If he still wanted the thing he could come in Monday after work and pick it up. But he knew he wouldn't. By tomorrow, he'd have his head on straight and forget the whole thing.

Still, it was possible, not probable, but just barely possible that while he was standing here thinking about it, somebody might, just might walk into that place and buy the medallion right out from under him. Or some time on Monday, before he got there. In that case, he told himself, he wouldn't have any decision to make. Right? He'd have no further problem.

He turned and walked rapidly back to the pawnshop.

The proprietor did not seem surprised to see him again. And David said, almost angrily:

"All right. I'll take that medallion, after all."

"Okay."

The man started toward the window and David said:

"Do you take Master Charge?"

"Sorry, mister. No credit cards. This is strictly a cash business. But if you want to put a little something down, I'll be glad to hold the item for you."

"Would twenty-five do it?"

"Good enough."

"I'll come in Monday with the rest of the money and pick it up then."

The proprietor nodded and gave David a receipt for his deposit. Then he tucked the medallion into a box and put it in a drawer. David went out in the street, a little dazed, and began to walk up Third Avenue again.

Crazy, he thought.

Still, no crazier than some of the other things that had happened to him lately.

Alfredo's was one of those small restaurants on the East Side that was good but not pretentious. It had the traditional red checkerboard tablecloths, low table lamps set on plastic dripping candles, a ceiling covered with empty Chianti bottles hanging upside down, and some bad paintings of Portofino, Rapallo, and other resorts along the Italian Riviera. But the food was delicious and northern Italian, the chef took great pride and pleasure in his work, and the prices were reasonable. It was a homey kind of place, patronized almost exclusively by people in the neighborhood, and it was one of David Drew's favorites.

He led Cassie to a table near the window. The waiter came over, a broad smile on his face.

"Buona sera, Signore Drew."

"Buona sera, Guido."

"Piacere di rivederla."

"Grazie."

"Un aperitivo per incominciare?"

David nodded and looked at Cassie. "Would you like a drink?"

"Please. A daiquiri."

"Per me un gin martini senza ghiaccio e con la buccia di limone. E del vino piu tardi."

"Se vuole che le suggerisca qualche cosa per stasera?"

"Va bene."

"Scallopini marsala sono eccellenti stasera, i funghi sono freschi, e la carne è molto tenera."

"Mi sembra che andiamo bene. Discuteró con la signorina."

The waiter nodded, and left. David was aware that Cassie was still staring at him.

"You really *are* something, darling."

He grinned. "Am I?"

"Surprise, surprise."

31

"Just trying to impress you."

"Oh, you have, you have."

"Of course, Guido speaks English. But we have a deal. Whenever I come here, we speak only Italian. *Solamente*. Gives me a chance to practice."

"You know, it's funny. I mean, I wouldn't have really been surprised if you suddenly broke out into French, or Spanish, or even German. I've been out with men who have. But Italian? Somehow, it's different. Outside of Italians themselves, I don't know anybody who can speak the language. I mean, it's the last thing I'd expect from a nice WASP who was born and brought up in Canton, Ohio. Unless maybe you lived in Italy for a while."

"Never been there in my life."

"Then you took it in school."

He nodded. "Had four years of it."

"But why Italian?"

"The truth is, a girl turned me on."

"I don't understand."

"It's a pretty silly story."

"Tell me."

"You'd never believe it."

"Tell me anyway."

"Well, in my freshman year at the university, we had to take a foreign language. You know, it was required. I tossed it around for a while, nothing about any particular foreign language turned me on, and I finally decided to take Spanish. Not for any real reason, except I'd heard it was the easiest language to learn. Anyway, I was standing in line at the registrar's, one of those long lines you always stand in when you're entering school as a freshman, and among other things, we were supposed to indicate which language we'd chosen. Well, there was this girl standing in line just in front of me. She was beautiful. Really a knockout. I just kept staring at her. Couldn't help it. When we got up to the registrar's window, I heard her say her name was Delevan. Barbara Delevan. And that she elected to take Italian."

"So?"

"It hit me suddenly that they usually placed people in classes alphabetically. If her last name started with a D, the same as mine, I could end up in the same class with her. Maybe even in the next seat."

"So quick as a flash, you decided to take Italian."

"That's it. I told you it was pretty damned silly."

Guido brought them their drinks. Cassie sipped her daiquiri and then said:

"You haven't told me the rest of it."

He laughed: "We never ended up in the same class. And, as it turned out, she was the girlfriend of somebody on the football team. Which, at Ohio State, is a very sacred commitment."

After that, they talked of many things. She liked her job at *Newsweek,* at least for now, but the milieu was somewhat too frenetic, too hypertense, and some day she'd like to get a job as a children's book editor in some nice, quiet publishing house. He told her about the raise they had given him at Datafax, and she was delighted. He found her not only highly sexual, but very intelligent and easy to talk to, and he had a distinct feeling that this one could last a while and might even be serious, and he was sure she felt the same.

The veal marsala turned out to be fabulous, and they ordered extra wine and lingered a long time over their coffee, still talking a little but, for the most part, simply looking and smiling at each other. He had been tempted to tell Cassie about his purchase of the medallion, but somehow he did not, because he saw it as a private nonsense and still felt a little foolish about it. Sitting here now, he had already decided to go back and tell the owner of the shop he did not want the medallion after all and, if necessary, to forfeit his deposit. Right now, he had more important things to think about.

They walked out into the New York night and, without speaking, went directly to her apartment.

2

They stayed in bed late the next morning, luxuriating in the fact that this was Saturday and neither of them had to go to work.

She snuggled close to him and said:

"My dear Mr. Drew."

"Yes, Miss Knox?"

"This is to inform you that it has been quite an adventure to have you in my bed. You will do. Speaking as a primitive, as a vital and lusty female, you will most definitely do, sir. You are what we call a very macho man. Very."

"There happens to be a reason for that."

"Yes?"

"You are a very female female."

She laughed and kissed him for that. "You know, we could stay in bed all day."

"We could."

"Except that would be just too decadent. I mean, even us sybarites have to take time out to eat. Why don't we make a supreme effort? I mean, get out of bed while I make us some breakfast. After that . . ."

She had started to get out of bed when he stopped her.

"Cassie, can you wait a while?"

"What for?"

"I've got to meditate. It'll take me about twenty minutes."

She stared at him. "You're into TM?"

He nodded. "Just began it about two weeks ago." Then, half-apologetically, "Everybody's into something. Biofeedback, scientology, gestalt therapy. I just happened to get into transcendental meditation."

"Does it do something for you?"

"I think so. It's a little early to tell, but it seems to relax me. Maybe you ought to try it, Cassie."

"I? No way. When I was in college, I lived with a boy once who was into TM. Seemed kind of boring to me. I mean, sitting in a chair twenty minutes before breakfast and twenty minutes before dinner. Just sitting there, with your eyes closed, trying not to think. I like something with body action, like Rolfing, for instance. Or something more sexy, like Reichian therapy, where the answer to everyone's problem is supposed to be a good orgasm." She paused. "Can you meditate right here in bed?"

"If I'm alone."

"Okay. Tell you what. I'll go into the kitchen and start to hustle up some breakfast. When you've finished, come out. By that time, everything should be ready."

When she left, he propped himself into a sitting position against the pillows.

He rested for a moment before closing his eyes and beginning his meditation. He looked forward to it now with a mixture of fascination and apprehension. He wondered if the same weird thing would happen all over again, just as it had happened the night before, and the last few sessions before that. . . .

35

He had gotten into TM through a friend, Allan Fischer, an LP, or lead programmer, at Datafax. Fischer was a TM teacher, or, as he was sometimes called, an initiator. But like so many TM teachers, he had to moonlight on other jobs to make a living. He had kept at David, stressing that through transcendental meditation he would discover energy he had never known he had and reduce tension. Everybody was into it, including astronauts, Wall Street brokers, Pentagon generals, artists, scientists, big-name athletes, housewives, students, and thousands of other just plain people.

Finally Fischer had persuaded him, and he had paid the fee of a hundred and sixty-five dollars, which entitled him to lifetime tuition and periodic personal instruction. He had gone through the four days of instruction—since Fischer had been busy elsewhere, his teacher had been a young girl of nineteen—and then the time for the Ceremony of Gratitude had come. He had brought her fruit and flowers, as instructed, and there had been this gentle little ritual, the *puja*, where she had chanted before an icon of Shri Guru Dev. He had found all this strange but quite touching, and it was then that she had given him his mantra and told him that it was his, and his alone, and it was a secret never to be spoken or revealed to anyone.

He hadn't really bought the more exotic part of transcendental meditation, the exaltation of Maharishi Mahesh Yogi and *his* teacher, Guru Dev. Still, he understood it and could appreciate it, because Maharishi, although himself a Hindu monk, was also a scientist, and his great contributions were actually scientific and not religious. Again, David had been at it less than a month, but he had already become aware of its benefits, he did feel more rested and relaxed.

Until the last few days . . .

He closed his eyes, rested for a moment, then began to hear the beat of his mantra, in his head.

Shoom.

Shoom, shoom, shoom, shoom . . .

The mantra was not really a word, it was a *sound*, some-

36

thing you heard. The mantra continued to beat steadily. Vagrant thoughts crossed his mind. Nothing profound. Just ordinary, everyday thoughts. He thought of Cassie's mouth, its taste, the exciting feel of her body, the ways she had of exciting him. He thought of his dentist, and the card he had sent, reminding David that it was time to have his teeth examined and cleaned. He thought of a couple of the problems he had had to deal with at the office during the past few days, involving binary coded decimals, and the systems design of a new third-generation microcircuit computer, operating in nanoseconds. And again, the incident of the medallion drifted across his mind. And he thought of its mystic attraction for him . . .

Shoom, shoom, shoom, shoom . . .

The mantra began to recede a little, he began to hear it from a distance. He sat unmoving, his body totally relaxed. His breathing became much slower, since in his deep rest, his oxygen requirement became much less. His mind was alert, coherent, totally conscious, but his body was resting more deeply than even in deep sleep.

Shoom, shoom . . .

The mantra was becoming even fainter now. He could hardly hear it. He was approaching what was called the state, or level, of "pure awareness." This consisted of nothing more than being wide awake inside without being aware of anything but awareness itself. Here, the mind seemed silent. Empty of all content, all thought. It was a state David had managed to achieve most of the time.

Shoom. Shoom . . .

The sound of the mantra was barely audible now. Like a very faint echo from very far away.

Then, it disappeared.

David drifted now, in the stillness of nothing. His mind was totally devoid of all thought, an empty vessel. He was at the desired level now, he had transcended. He was in a strange and euphoric state, he seemed to be floating. Yet, he was completely conscious, acutely alert. He could hear the muffled traffic in the street below, the faint tinkling of pots and pans coming from the kitchen, the tiny vibration of Cassie's steps on the kitchen floor.

He was empty, empty, drifting, completely and totally at rest, relaxed.

Then he began to see them again, as he had before.

The faces.

Slowly, they began to invade the empty realm of his mind. They appeared blurred at first. Then they came into focus sharply. The heads, or faces, flicked by swiftly, with a strobelike effect, almost subliminal. None of them seemed human, alive. All of them seemed made of stone. Carved and sculpted. And all of them seemed ancient, stained and weatherbeaten. On some, parts of the features were heavily worn, noses and ears had chipped off.

Some of the stone faces were small, and some were larger than life size, set in egg-shaped heads and spherical heads. Some had bulging eyes and wagging tongues. Some were belligerent and some were bearded. There were female faces of classic and exquisite beauty, the faces of fierce and truculent and sneering Amazons, of angry and vicious hags and harridans. There were saintly and pixie faces, grotesque and monstrous faces whose eyes winked lasciviously, as though relishing some dirty joke, twisted faces that snarled and stuck out their tongues, saintly Christlike faces, stern and just prophet faces.

But there was one face that fascinated David and at the same time repelled him.

He gave it a nickname: Fat Face.

Fat Face was set into a huge, giant-sized head. It was evil and obscene, it leered at him with such an inhuman expression that David was revolted. The eyes were vicious, the mouth lewd, the entire face sickly fleshed, fat, and jowly; it was a face that sneered and mocked and spat at the world.

Most of the faces were carved in the human form, but there were also the stone heads and faces of lions, cats, foxes, and birds. David was conscious, too, of other sculpted figures, dryads and nymphs and satyrs, some laughing, some embracing each other or set in a dance tableau, and one, in particular, showing a group of headless girls with perfect, symmetrical stone torsos.

But it was the faces in human form that interested David most of all. They all seemed to be trying to tell him something from their stiff stone mouths.

It was a parade of strange, sick imagery. It lasted only a few seconds and then faded.

Moments later, David began to hear the beat of the mantra again, and he came out of the level of pure awareness, or, as it was sometimes called, the PA stage.

Now, the mantra grew, and became louder and louder, and across it intruded and drifted this thought or that as it popped into his mind, ordinary routine thoughts, the kind that Allan Fischer had once called "garbage thoughts." Finally, David came out of his meditation altogether. He no longer heard the mantra, and he sat there and rested a while, keeping his eyes closed. His breathing became normal again as his body once again demanded its usual supply of oxygen, his concentration of blood lactate increased to its regular level, and, in his brain, his alpha and theta brain-wave production decreased.

He opened his eyes and looked at his wristwatch. He had been meditating exactly twenty minutes.

He sat there for a few moments. He felt rested, but still he was disturbed. What the hell were all those heads, anyway? Where did they come from, why did he see them, what did they mean?

As a virtual TM neophyte, he was supposed to check routinely with his teacher once a week for the first month, just to see if he was using the technique correctly. For the last week, Allan Fischer had been in Cleveland, where Datafax had one of its branch offices. He had been conducting a seminar for junior programmers on flow charts and block diagrams, and he was expected back on Monday.

39

The first thing he intended to do when he came into the office on Monday morning, the very first thing he intended to do, was to call on his initiator and yell for help.

He met Allan Fischer for lunch at a restaurant called the Input. It was located on the ground floor of the building in which Datafax was located. There were several other computer organizations in the same building, and the clientele of the Input consisted mostly of personnel who worked in these firms.

As they made their way to a table in the rear, the buzz of conversation sounded like a language from some other planet. The patrons spoke of alphanumerics and analogs, binary numerals and black boxes, COBOL and CPU's and CRT's, formula translators and game theories, flowcharts and microseconds, peripherals and parity bits, software and third-generation microcircuits. Finally, David and Fischer were seated and gave their orders to a harried waitress.

Allan Fischer was a year younger than David. He had a great, bushy beard, which almost totally obscured his face, a hairy forest through which peepholes seemed to have been cut to allow room for his mouth, the tip of his nose, and two bulbous, nearsighted brown eyes, which peered through his thick, rimless glasses. Aside from this, he had a mind that was a storehouse of information. He seemed to know everything about anything. To David, Allan Fischer was a kind of walking computer. Once he had asked his friend about it.

"I never told you?"

"No."

"It's very simple. When I was a kid, I caught rheumatic fever. Had to stay in bed or in the house for a year. My father bought me a set of the Encyclopaedia Britannica. Wanted to improve my mind, I guess, since I didn't have much of a body. Anyway, I read the whole set, word for word."

"Every word?"

"Every goddamn word. After that, I went through the dictionary. Then I guess I read every book they had in the stacks at my branch library. Hence, the myopia. Besides, I have a retentive memory." Then he added: "Of course, it helps that I happen to be a genius, as well. I mean, I don't want to get into my IQ—but there it is." He shrugged. "Of course, most of the factual stuff I've retained is pretty exotic. Totally useless. File and forget. But sometimes it comes in handy."

The waitress brought them menus. They knew what was on the bill of fare by heart, but they took them anyway. David noted that Allan looked tired.

"How'd you do in Cleveland?"

Allan looked pained. "My God, this group of programmer trainees drove me up a wall. They weren't bad on analysis and flowcharts, but when it came to coding instructions and debugging, Jesus . . . you wouldn't believe it! I mean, the way they freeze when they first look a computer in the eye."

"That's nothing new. I got stage fright myself when I first stood up to Big Daddy."

"Yeah," said Allan. "I guess we all did. But now, David, let's get down to more important things. Let's run a check on your meditation. We're a little overdue on it now. You said you had a problem."

"Yes."

"Okay. Tell teacher everything, and we'll straighten it out."

"This one is crazy, Allen. I don't think even the Maharishi could figure it out."

"You never say *the* Maharishi. That's a no-no. You always say Maharishi alone. Anyway, he isn't available at the moment. So try me."

He told Fischer what had happened when he reached the PA stage. His initiator listened, fascinated. When David had finished, Fischer looked astonished.

"Stone heads? Faces?"

"All kinds of them."

41

"David, you've got to be kidding."

"I'm telling you exactly what I saw."

"How long did you really see these—these images?"

"Well, as I said they all flashed by. But the whole sequence took maybe thirty seconds. Maybe a minute. I don't know. It's hard to tell time in that stage. Anyway, there it is. What do you think?"

Fischer shook his head. "I don't think anything. Because I don't know. This is the first time I've heard anything as wild as this."

"Maybe they could be distortions. Dreams."

"No," said Fischer, firmly. "Transcendental meditation is totally a state of wakeful consciousness. The mind doesn't create dream distortions, as in sleep."

"But I've never seen those damned stone faces before."

"Yes you have," said Fischer, patiently. "You don't remember now, but you've seen them—"

"Damn it, Allan, I'm trying to tell you—"

"Look. Look at it this way. The brain is still the greatest mystery of our universe. We can't conceive how complex it is. It's supposed to have something like thirteen billion interconnected cells, through which consciousness functions. It would make a tenth-generation computer, if we ever get to that, look like a primitive toy. Maybe, for reasons we don't know, one of those cells popped open and dumped these stone heads in your lap. If I'm sure of anything, it's one thing."

"Yes?"

"This stuff came out of your silent world."

"Now what does *that* mean?"

"As Maharishi explains it, the mind is similar to an ocean. There's wave activity on the surface, but way down in the deep, there's nothing but absolute silence. Okay? Now, when you talk about conscious thoughts or emotions, or perceptions of visual images, you can compare them to the surface waves on the ocean. But these thoughts originate first on the silent ocean floor and then rise upward like bubbles. The bubbles grow larger and larger, until by the time they hit the surface they become clear and distinct experiences. If you tell me you saw these stone heads only at the PA stage, then that was the silent floor of your ocean. Maybe they haven't bubbled to the top, as yet. But they're still experiences you've undergone, somewhere."

"I made the point before," said David, doggedly. "And I'll make it again. I never saw those crazy heads or faces before."

Allan thought for a moment. Then he said:

"Look, did you ever hear of cryptomnesia?"

"Crypto—what?"

"Cryptomnesia. It's a term used by parapsychologists. It means an honest forgetting of the actual source of information that you later mistakenly credit to another source. In a peculiar kind of way, you may be experiencing it. Let's just try it on for size. Okay?"

"Okay."

"You could have gone through some museum and seen these stone faces, for instance. Ever been to the Metropolitan?"

"Yes."

"All right. You might have seen them there. They've got all kinds of sculpture there, Greek, Roman, Egyptian, African, you name it. Or you may have seen them in some travel or picture book when you were a kid, or in some film you saw. All I'm saying is, you've *seen* them. In TM, you transcend thinking, and the mind comes into direct contact with the source of thought. Maybe you dredged up those images from the source itself, but they're *real*. Okay?"

David shrugged. "If you say so."

"I do say so. Jesus, I wish that waitress would bring our food. I'm starved."

Five minutes after he had come back from lunch, David's phone rang. A secretary was on the other end:

"Mr. Boyce would like to see you at once, Mr. Drew."

43

"Mr. Boyce?"

"He says it's important and to come right up."

David hung up, puzzled. He'd never worked for this particular executive before and knew him only casually. John Boyce was projects director for the International Division of Datafax. He was rarely found in the New York office. Most of the time he was flying jets from one country to the other, all over Europe and the Orient.

"Come in, Drew, and sit down."

Boyce was a big, bald man with a huge, military-type mustache and hard gray eyes. He clamped a cigar in his mouth and studied David for a few moments. Then he said:

"Got a job for you."

"Yes, sir?"

"It's in Iran."

David stared. "Iran?"

"Teheran, to be exact. Iranian National Petroleum's bought our new 384D computers, and we have to be careful nothing gets screwed up going in. The shah is very rich, and he doesn't like fuckups, and you'd be surprised how fast he can cancel an order, if he's suddenly unhappy. Now, I've already got a team over there—a systems engineer, research analysts, and the rest—working on problem analysis and solution outlining. What I need is a systems analyst to set up a feasibility study. And you're it."

David was confused and looked it.

"This is something I didn't expect. I mean, I don't know what to say."

"Nothing to say. I'm told you've never been on a job overseas. That right?"

"Yes."

"Well, it'll be a good experience. And you'd better be good on this one. I had a hell of a time getting you away from your EDP director. He said you were up to your ass in work here. Called you a boy genius. I had to go all the way up to the thirtieth floor to spring you. I hope you live up to your billing. If you don't, we're in trouble."

"I'll do my best."

"Okay. Now, you'll go to Iran via London. I want you to spend a few days at Stevens Industrial there. They're using our 318's, and they've got a few system bugs they need to iron out. Shouldn't be any great problem. After that, you go right on to Teheran."

"When do you want me to leave?"

"Tomorrow?"

"*Tomorrow?*"

"Okay," said Boyce. "The day after tomorrow. The sooner we get set up, the better." Suddenly, he paused. Then, a little worried: "By the way, you *do* have a passport, don't you?"

"Yes."

"Good. We've already expedited your visa. The travel office has your tickets and itinerary. One of our people, Joe Lassiter, will be there to meet you at the airport in Teheran. He'll show you where you'll live, get you a guest membership into the American Club, give you an early briefing on the project."

"How long will I be in Iran?"

"Depends. Besides the problem analysis and the solution detailing, there'll be program coding, testing, and debugging. May take six weeks or six months. Who knows? It all depends. Which reminds me. I'll need a good programmer to go along with you. Got anyone you could recommend?"

David did not hesitate. He suggested Allan Fischer. Boyce immediately got on the phone and talked about making special arrangements for another visa, name of Allan Fischer, and quick, quick. Then he hung up and said to David:

"I might as well send Fischer to London with you, as well. I hope to hell he's got a passport."

"I'm sure he has. He travels a lot, on his vacations."

"Okay. If he doesn't, I'm sure we can expedite that, too. I'll talk to your boy Fischer and have a preliminary report on all the problem details on both your desks in an hour.

45

Better read the stuff on the plane or something; you ought to have it down cold going in."

"Yes, sir."

"Okay," said Boyce. He stretched out his hand. *"Ciao,* and good luck." His smile was chilly. "I'll be in Teheran a little later, to sit on the project and to check all personnel performances. So hang in there, Drew, and give me the best job you can."

On Sunday, the day before, he had definitely decided not to buy the medallion.

And through most of this working day, he had stuck to this decision. He kept telling himself that four hundred dollars was a lot of money, and who needed it? Again, he wasn't the type to wear this kind of jewelry.

Shortly after his interview with John Boyce, he looked at the clock and realized that he had very little time; the bank would be closing in just five minutes. His bank was on the ground floor of his building, and he raced down the corridor to the elevator. The elevator was slow in arriving, and he just made it into the bank.

He drew the cash he needed, and after work he went to the pawnshop and picked up the medallion.

When he came home, he took off his shirt and hung the medallion around his neck. It felt strange at first. His flesh tingled with the touch of the cold metal, but only for a moment. Then, suddenly, it felt warm and snug against his chest. It felt good there. As though, somehow, it belonged. The owner of the pawnshop had polished and buffed the medallion, and now it shone bright yellow against the light tan of his skin. He liked the look of the big golden disc and the solid weight of it.

He had made a date with Cassie Knox for dinner. He would, of course, have to tell her of his assignment to Iran, and that he would be away from New York for some time. He regretted this. He knew he would miss her. It had been, as he saw it, the beginning of a solid relationship. He knew, too, that it was likely that when he returned he would find that he had lost her. Cassie Knox was a very attractive woman, and she was not the type to wait for anyone.

He shaved, showered, and then sat down for his usual twenty minutes of meditation.

Once again, when he transcended into the stage of pure awareness, he saw the same carved heads, the same faces. This time they did not flash by so quickly that he could barely make out their detail. This time they were like a series of stills, each one lingering long enough that he could really see it.

And this time, something new had been added to this strange gallery.

A stone lion.

It stood upright on its hind legs, and in each raised paw it held a scroll. He had a vague impression that it stood on some kind of pedestal and was framed against a wall.

It was the same lion, down to the smallest detail, as the one inscribed on the medallion.

3

THE stewardess had a British accent. Over the loud-speaker, she asked the passengers to fasten their seat belts, straighten the backs of their chairs, and observe the no-smoking signs.

Flight 316 leisurely taxied down the runway at Heathrow Airport, turned slowly at the far end, and took its place behind two other planes waiting for takeoff. Finally, its turn came, and the 747 was airborne. Destination: nonstop to Teheran.

Allan Fischer took the aisle seat, giving David the window. He explained that on long trips he liked to get up frequently and walk up and down the aisle. He had done a lot of traveling and couldn't care less about the scenery from some thirty-five thousand feet up. David settled back and watched the city of London slide by under him. In a few moments it vanished as the plane plunged into a heavy cloud cover.

The job at Stevens Industrial, Ltd., had taken only three days. The Datafax digital 318 used a symbolic machine language called Common Business Oriented Language—or COBOL, as it was known—which was comparatively uncomplicated. There had been some problems with the code translations and compiler routines, but he had easily managed to straighten these out. He and Allan had been entertained royally by their hosts, had seen a couple of plays, and had even found a few hours to walk around London. Since he had never been to Europe before, he had found it all fascinating.

Allan leaned across David's chest, peering through the thick clouds outside the window. Then he sighed.

"Jesus," he said. "I wish we could have stayed a couple of more days."

"So do I."

"I love London. This is the third time I've been there, and I never get tired of it. It's civilized, you know? It isn't just the people, it's the *feeling* you get." He sounded suddenly disgusted. "And where are *we* going? Iran."

"You make it sound like a terrible place."

"In some ways, it is."

"In some ways?"

"Well, I've never been there personally. But after I got tagged to go, I checked it out with some of the people who have."

"And?"

"And they tell me it can get pretty boring for handsome young studs like you and me. The Iranians are exploding industrially, but in other ways, the more important ways, they're still a little old-fashioned. I mean, they don't like foreigners fooling around with their women. Most of the married guys who are over there for any length of time get desperate enough to even send for their wives. But you and I, my friend, have no wives. So where does that leave us?"

"Maybe the job will be over in a few weeks."

"Maybe. But I doubt it. We are dealing with Persians, remember, who are very good at weaving Oriental rugs but may be slow learners when it comes to handling our bright new Nth-generation computer, the 384D, using Formula Translator for its machine language. You really think they're going to dig FORTRAN in just a few weeks? Man, we're not playing with simple building blocks here. You're going to have to design a whole different overall procedure for the 384D. And that should be a lot of fun, especially with John Boyce up your ass at all times."

David leaned back and thought about this. He hoped that Allan was wrong but suspected he was right. He began to speculate on what would happen if, when he really got fed up, he sent a cable to Cassie Knox, asking her to join him for a couple of weeks. But the truth was, he didn't really know her that well. This wouldn't just be a weekend together somewhere. An invitation like that would mean something more serious. Anyway, it was something to think about. Later, he could make up his mind.

He glanced over at Allan Fischer. His companion's head was back against the pillow, his eyes were closed, and he was dozing. It was morning, but they had been up half the night in London, and they were both tired. Allan was an old traveler, and he could sleep on planes. He had slept through practically the whole flight across the Atlantic. David envied him. Allan had come into some family money, and before he had joined Datafax, he had been around the world twice.

David took out the orientation material on the 384D, but inside of a half hour he became bored with it and stuffed it back into his briefcase. There was nothing to see outside. They were flying through a solid wall of gray cloud; he could see a little beyond the wing tips, and that was all. He felt not only tired and listless but a little tense. He was always a little tense when he came onto a new job, and he knew this one would really try him.

He leaned his head back and tried to sleep.

But sleep would not come. He knew he was not relaxed enough. He decided to meditate instead. It might cut his tension. Allan had told him that, though you meditated twice a day, once before breakfast and once before dinner, this did not exclude other periods. And it did not matter where you were at the time. If you were into TM, you could meditate anywhere. In an easy chair, in bed, in airport waiting rooms, on planes and ships at sea, anywhere.

He closed his eyes and began the mantra.

Finally, the sound of the mantra faded completely. He drifted deep into the PA stage, a silent world, his mind empty of thought. Then the stone heads and faces began to come in, as before.

Up to this point, he had seen them all in limbo, like close-ups on a big movie screen, with no point of reference.

Now, as in the case of the standing lion, they all suddenly seemed to have acquired a sense of *location*.

Dimly, he could make out one of the gargoyles, with stub nose and a leering smile, resting on a pole of some kind. A series of bearded faces protruded on what seemed to be archlike structures. The face of a wizened and toothless old man grinned down at the world from some kind of roof or eave. He saw a series of lion heads, seemingly moss-stained, protruding just above the surface of a body of water of some kind. In the next image he saw, the heads of the same lions were half-sunk below the level of the water.

As for Fat Face, he seemed to be embedded in a wall, or possibly some kind of curved surface, the monstrous, obscene image leering at the world from some eye-level position.

Suddenly, there was a jar. The plane seemed to buck a little. Then, there was a short, sickening drop.

David, rudely shocked out of his meditation, was half-thrown out of his seat.

Some of the passengers screamed as they were thrown forward. A few who had been standing up or walking in the aisles were knocked off balance and fell. When the passengers recovered their seats, they sat mute and white-faced, staring at each other.

51

The "Fasten Seat Belt" sign went on.

Two of the stewardesses hurried forward. They looked the way they were not supposed to look. Concerned. A couple of the passengers tried to stop them, ask them what had happened. The stewardesses brushed aside the delaying hands, ignored the questions, and almost ran into the pilot's compartment.

David sat rigidly. It was a shock to be suddenly wrenched out of meditation, especially for something like this. You were supposed to come out of it gradually. Let the mantra come up again. Rest a while, with your eyes closed. He could feel the blood rush suddenly to his head. His temples throbbed violently.

He looked at his seatmate. Allan sat stiffly. It was impossible to tell behind that beard, but David imagined he was pale. The brown eyes peering through the rimless glasses were apprehensive.

"Allan, what do you think happened?"

"I don't know."

A matronly woman in the seat in the front of them turned. There were beads of sweat on her face.

"I saw this flash," she blurted. "Just before the bump."

"What flash?"

"This flash of fire. It came from one of the wings, I think."

Suddenly, a voice came over the loudspeaker.

"Fasten safety belts. Please fasten safety belts."

That was all.

The smell of fear was heavy now. It was almost a definable odor, unpleasant and sweaty and sour. It seemed to actually exude from the pores of the passengers themselves. Immediately after the initial shock, there had been startled and excited exclamations. Now, it was silent in the huge cabins of the 747. The passengers sat stiffly, like wax figures, waiting tensely, apprehensively, waiting in dread for something to happen, waiting pathetically for someone to tell them what had gone wrong.

The announcement came over the public address system again.

"All passengers please fasten safety belts."

They continued to wait for more, but nothing came. It was not an announcement calculated to comfort anyone.

"Oh God, oh God," said the woman. "Why don't they tell us what happened? Why don't they tell us *something?*"

Allan was peering out of the window. "No sign of any fire. Not as far as I can see. Not on this side anyway." He looked toward the windows on the other side of the aircraft. There was no red glow through them. "So far, okay. I mean, if there's no fire, there's a lot less to worry about."

"But that flash. That big bump . . . "

"I'm no expert," said Allan. "But it could be one of the engines blew. If so . . . "

"If so, what?" David wanted to know.

"No problem flying the aircraft. You can feel that . . . "

"The problem is landing it."

"Yeah." Allan tried to put up a nonchalant front. But he was disturbed. And incredulous. "You know, I've flown thousands of miles on these things. Hundreds of hours. And nothing ever happened. Not one damned thing."

"My daughter married an Iranian," said the woman. "They were going to meet me at the airport . . . "

She stopped. It was as though the bile had come up in her throat and choked off her words. She could say no more. She reached into her purse and fumbled for a cigarette. Her hand shook as she tried to light it with her lighter. She kept turning the wheel on the lighter, which was supposed to strike a flame from the flint. She couldn't make it work. Her hands trembled violently.

David took the lighter from her and lit her cigarette. She looked at him gratefully. He returned her lighter. She took it in her hand and then dropped it. She did not even bother to pick it up.

Funny, he thought. What the hell am *I* so calm about? And then he thought: Jesus, I'm too young to die.

Suddenly, the plane reduced speed and then banked. Slowly, it flew in a long, lazy circle. To David, it seemed close to stalling. It completed the circle and started a new

53

one. It seemed to sail, almost in a hovering glide, like some great hawk high in the sky. It completed the second circle. Then it continued to stay banked, repeating the same circle all over again.

"*Now* what the hell are they doing?" he said to Allan.

"I wish I knew."

There was nothing to be seen below. The earth was covered by a heavy bank of clouds. They seemed to roll angrily upward, trying to reach for the underbelly of the plane. The 747 continued to sail slowly in its great circle. It was as though it was waiting. Waiting for something to happen.

Probably, thought David, the pilot had put the plane in a holding pattern while he was making up his mind about something, trying to come to some decision. Or he might be on the radio, in consultation with the ground, telling them of the emergency, asking for clearance, for ambulances and crash crews, for God knows what.

Now, David began to sweat. It was really getting to him now. Suddenly, he was angry. As angry as everyone else.

For Christ's sake, why don't they tell us something?

Almost in instant response, the voice of the captain came over the loudspeaker. His voice was very professional. Very calm. Very reassuring. In the tradition of airline commanders everywhere.

"Ladies and gentlemen, this is Captain Riley. We have encountered some mechanical difficulty. One of our starboard engines has ceased to function. But I ask you all to please remain calm. The important thing is to keep your seat belts fastened, remain calm, and follow the instructions of your stewardesses. There is no cause for alarm . . ."

"Captain Riley," said Allan Fischer, under his breath. "You are a fucking liar."

There was a pause, the sound of crackling static over the loudspeaker, and then the captain's voice came on, tinnily:

"We are over Switzerland at the moment. Unfortunately, Geneva and the other Swiss airports are all under thick

54

cloud cover, approaching ceiling zero. Milan is fogged out, but Venice reports sufficient, although minimum, visibility. We will therefore be landing at Marco Polo airport in Venice. Please keep your seat belts fastened and observe that the no-smoking sign is now on. And I repeat again: stay calm. There is nothing to fear."

David agreed with Allan. The hell there isn't, he thought. Then, he said:

"You know what?"

"What?"

"Captain Riley. He sounds too damned calm to suit me."

"Probably scared shitless, like the rest of us."

"You think he can do it?"

"Do what?"

"Land this big bird with a dead motor."

"He could. You read about it in the papers. They do it all the time. Providing there isn't some sudden switch in the wind, just as he's putting those wheels down on the runway. Providing his hand is steady and his eye sharp. Providing he's had enough sleep the night before, after laying his favorite stewardess, or isn't too hungover or uptight after some argument with his wife or mother-in-law, or whatever."

"But if he goofs, we become a statistic."

"Exactly that. Or put it another way. You and I will become data to be programmed and stored in our own computers." He looked at David. "Frankly, my friend, I wish to hell you hadn't recommended me for this caper. For reasons you must understand . . . "

"Sorry about that."

So far, he and Allan were both putting up a bold front. Very macho. But he could feel the sweat seeping through his shirt, despite the air conditioning, and his heart was beating wildly. The stewardesses were moving up and down the aisles again. They smiled at the passengers. They reassured them that everything would be all right. The 747 flew easily on three motors. It could even fly on two, if

55

necessary. Captain Riley was a senior pilot on the airline, one of the best. He'd flown millions of air miles, thousands of hours. There was absolutely nothing to worry about. The idea was just to sit tight. Let us do the driving. And would you like a soft drink, madame? Or can I get you something, sir?

But the smiles were pasted on, very professional, like the voice of the captain. They were the kind you learned at the school for stewardesses. All you had to do was silently say the word "cheese" and your smile muscles would automatically perform. The mouths were smiling all right, lovely young-girl smiles.

But the eyes weren't.

David stared out at the wing of the plane. They were still flying through the thick, gray muck. Suddenly, he saw a line of liquid spurting out from the edge of the huge wing. It flew back from the wing, straight as a pencil, parallel to the fuselage. He saw some of the passengers on the opposite side of the cabin looking out of the windows and pointing. He knew they were watching the same thing happening at the other wingtip.

The woman in front of them was staring out of the window, her eyes wide with fright. Then she turned her head to look back at them. She seemed to think they were authorities on everything concerning a 747.

"What on earth are they doing?"

"The pilot's ejecting fuel," said David. "Getting rid of it."

"But why?"

"To reduce the risk of fire when we land."

"Oh my God," she said.

Finally, the stream of fuel pouring from the wings stopped abruptly. The motors slowed, and they could feel the big plane start to make its descent. It continued to slide down through the gray shroud. It seemed stifling, impenetrable, endless. A soft lining for your flying casket, if you wanted to think of it in a morbid way. Lovingly selected by your friendly mortician.

56

"Well," said Allan. "As they say in the movies, this is it. This is for all the marbles."

People sat up straight now, not moving, gripping the edges of their chairs. David could see sections of the wing move in their mysterious ways, as the captain prepared for landing. He tried to picture Captain Riley, sitting up there in front, on the bridge, responsible for all this machinery and all these human lives. He thought of him as ruddy-faced and blue-eyed, wearing scrambled eggs on his cap, the hash marks on his sleeve denoting the years of service and all those millions of miles flown from here to there.

He thought of the Datafax man, Lassiter, waiting for them at the air terminal in Teheran. He thought of John Boyce's irritation that he and Allan had been delayed. Just another fuckup, Boyce would say, and the shah could get terribly impatient. He thought of Cassie Knox and pictured headlines in the newspapers. He thought of something else. The title of a book. *Death in Venice*. Written by Thomas Mann. He had read it a long time ago.

Death in Venice.

It was really a fantastic title. I mean, it really grabbed you.

Then, abruptly, they slid out of the gray muck, and suddenly there was daylight, and the runway rushed up to meet them, and buildings and parked planes flashed by on both sides, and now they were very close, very close to the ground, and David thought, *Jesus, oh Jesus . . .*

Then there was a bump, and they sailed a few feet in air again, and for one terrible moment it seemed that the captain had lost control, but then there was another bump, and this time the wheels stuck to the sacred earth, they held the blessed ground, and the remaining engines roared with a banshee racket as the captain reversed them, to brake the airplane, and the passengers broke out into spontaneous applause.

The 747 went all the way to the end of the runway before it seemed able to stop. And waiting along the runway were fire trucks and ambulances and men dressed in fireproof hoods and asbestos suits.

David turned to look at his companion. Allan took off his glasses and wiped them with a piece of Kleenex. They were fogged with the steam of his own perspiration, and droplets of sweat hung between the hairs of his beard. They smiled weakly at each other.

"Well," said Allan. "*Arrivederci*, Venice."

Of course, thought David, he was wrong. "*Arrivederci*" meant "goodbye" not "hello." But he was too drained to correct his friend.

4

FINALLY, after some delay, the passengers were herded into two big buses and taken to the airport building itself.

After some time, a representative of the airline appeared. He announced that another plane would be sent on from London shortly, so that they could continue on to Teheran. Everyone was to stay in the terminal building, since the replacement plane might be arriving shortly.

To David Drew, stretching out on a seat, his long legs resting on his luggage, this air terminal looked like any other, except that it was smaller. He might as well be waiting in some airport in Buffalo or Tucson or Atlanta or anywhere else in the United States. There was the usual noise and confusion, lines of people checking in, the public-address system squawking out flight departures and arrivals. The language was Italian, of course, everybody was chattering in Italian, and the signs were in Italian, but otherwise the scene was the same.

59

Outside all he saw was a busy street, the usual traffic of cars, buses, trucks, and taxis. David was disappointed. Where, he asked Allan, was the *real* Venice?

"You're in the center of the city now. This is the mainland, on the edge of the lagoon. You have to get to the Piazzale Roma, where the Grand Canal begins. It's only a short distance from here."

"My luck."

"Yes?"

"I mean being so close and not being able to see it."

"Yeah. Too bad you have to miss it. It's a great city. Fantastic. Nothing like it in the rest of the world. I love Venice."

David had friends who had traveled to Italy. And, to a man, they all told him the same thing. "You can't go to Italy without seeing Venice." He had planned to do just that some day. Not that he was interested particularly in art or architecture or history. But they told him that Venice was unique, totally different, a tremendous spectacle. You walked out onto St. Mark's Square, his friends said, and you were in a totally different century. A different world.

They waited an hour. Then two. Then three. The passengers became impatient. Then irritated and angry. It was hot and stuffy in the building.

"Man," said Allan irritably. "If there's anything I hate, it's hanging around airports. Where *is* that damned plane anyway?"

"I wish I knew. Looks as though they'll never get this thing on the road." David noted a bar at the end of the terminal. "Come on. Buy you a drink. Might as well get loaded. We don't seem to be going anywhere anyway, and it'll make time pass faster."

He went to the exchange window and changed a few dollars into lire. They went to the bar, and each ordered Scotch and soda, which they found very expensive. David tried out his Italian on the bartender, and they chatted amiably. Allan Fischer was surprised that he knew the

60

language. He had to tell the story all over again, the same story he had told Cassie Knox.

In the middle of their second drink, the announcement came over the public-address system. It was directed to the stranded passengers of Flight 316:

"Ladies and gentlemen, we have just been informed that the plane we had been expecting from London has been delayed. It will not arrive in Venice until tomorrow."

There was an anguished groan from the passengers, and the voice continued:

"Meanwhile, all passengers on Flight 316 will be guests of the airline until the plane arrives. We will arrange to transport you into Venice for an overnight stay. We will provide you with vouchers for hotel accommodations and meals. All this will take some time, of course, and we ask you to be patient. Please have your air tickets ready for identification. In a very short time, you will each be assigned your hotel. Again, we regret this unfortunate delay, and we hope you will have a pleasant stay. You will be notified by telephone or by messenger as to the time of departure tomorrow for Teheran. Thank you."

Allan turned to David and grinned.

"Well, what do you know?" he said. "Somebody up there must have heard you."

The airline, in the interest of public relations, and embarrassed by what had happened, did well by its stranded passengers.

Both Allan and David drew vouchers for a hotel called the Donatello. Allan knew it well. It was, he explained, a fine hotel, small but first-class in every respect, located on the Riva degli Schiavoni. He remembered that it overlooked the lagoon and was just a few steps from the Danieli. At the moment, these names were meaningless to David Drew. As Allan had said, somebody up there must have heard him. He still could not believe this totally unexpected and lucky break.

Finally, they were taken in special buses to the Piazzale

61

Roma. Here the airline had arranged for a special *vaporetto* to take the passengers down the Grand Canal and to their various hotels.

This was David Drew's first sight of the Grand Canal, and he found it overwhelming. A strange excitement welled up in him as the big boat began to move down the canal. He was fascinated, enchanted by everything he saw.

The waterborne traffic on the Grand Canal was thick. David stared at the boats moving in both directions, stubby *motoscafi*, looking ready to capsize at any second, bulging at the seams with people; the big passenger boats, the *vaporetti*, lordly and arrogant, dominating the main highway, throwing out great wakes in which sleek black gondolas rolled and bobbed like corks; wide-hulled boats carrying foodstuffs and other supplies; and the *sandali*, the elegant little skiffs rowed by a single man facing forward and working with two oars crosswise. The roar and ceaseless chugging of power-driven craft, as they maneuvered and dodged each other, was a waterborne version of some parkway or freeway at going-home time.

He was a tourist here, a stranger, and this was the first time he had ever seen the Grand Canal. Yet, strangely, it all seemed familiar, he seemed at home on it. He knew this was because he had read about it and seen pictures of it in documentary films, and perhaps elsewhere. Even if you had never been to Paris, you might still have a pretty good idea of what Paris looked like before you got there, because you had seen it before in the same way. He suspected every tourist had the same reaction to a world-famous place like Venice. All of them had traveled here before, in their imagination, and now that they were here physically, they found it just as advertised. And were not at all surprised by what they saw.

"Beautiful," he heard Allan say. "Beautiful. These palazzos. There's nothing like them anywhere in the world."

He pointed out a few he knew. The Palazzo Pesaro, the Palazzo Fontana, the exquisite Ca' d'Oro, which, Allan explained, had been built in the fifteenth century and was the finest example of Venetian Gothic to survive. David studied the palaces as they slipped by on both sides of the canal, admiring their pointed and graceful arches, their elegant balconies and marble facades, their great Venetian chimneys.

They passed under the Rialto Bridge, and he saw the cafes lining the canal near the bridge, the people, Venetians and tourists alike, sitting under the gaily colored umbrellas, over coffee or aperitifs or sandwiches, and again that strange feeling caught hold of him, a kind of empathy he felt for this place and everything in it, and, more than that, an inexplicable exhilaration.

They passed the Accademia, Santa Maria del Giglio and the San Marco station. David caught a side view of the Doges' Palace, then the Bridge of Sighs, looking exactly the way they did on the picture postcards.

Finally, the *vaporetto* stopped at the station marked Riva degli Schiavoni, where crowds waited to embark. Porters in loose blue coveralls and peaked hats, probably alerted by the airline, were there to take their luggage, and in a few minutes they were checking into their hotel.

As they rode up in the elevator, Allan said:

"Meet you in an hour. Down in the lobby."

"And then what?"

"We'll walk around to the Piazza and have a drink. Naturally. That's mandatory—*numero uno* for a tourist like you. After that—we'll have dinner."

David's room was a pleasant one, overlooking the lagoon. From his window, he could see the island of San Giorgio Maggiore, with its cluster of red brick and white marble buildings, anchored by an immense detached campanile, tipped with a tall golden angel. Off to one side, at the point where the Grand Canal met the lagoon itself, he could see the huge dome of the Church of Santa Maria della Salute, looking like some great balloon, its baroque scrolls and statues of the Apostles standing on a lower level of the church, tinted rose-color in the luminous light of the late-afternoon sun reflected from the lagoon.

He had seen the same scene in a painting somewhere, or perhaps in a magazine illustration, and it was beautiful, beautiful, it took his breath away.

He unpacked, shaved, and showered, and then sat down for his twenty-minute meditation.

He began the mantra.

Shoom, shoom, shoom.

After a while, the sound of it became fainter and fainter. His breathing became shallow, his blood pressure fell. The mantra became a faint echo in his head now, distant and receding. Finally, it vanished completely, and his mind was an empty vessel, drifting and totally thoughtless.

By this time the stone images had vanished completely.

He drifted luxuriously for a time, his PA stage empty and totally clear.

Then the mantra came back, and after a while, he came out of his meditation. Just as he did, the phone rang. It was someone from the airline.

"Your plane will leave for Teheran tomorrow evening at eight o'clock, *signore.* Please be at the airport an hour ahead of time. Again, our apologies for causing you this inconvenience, and we hope you have a pleasant evening in Venice."

He hung up, his mind still occupied with the stone heads and faces. Now you see them, now you don't. It was weird. The whole thing was pretty damned weird. He didn't know what to make of it. He was disturbed, but in a way he was also relieved. Out of sight, out of mind. His meditation this time had been entirely normal. From here in, he could write off Fat Face and his friends as just one of those things. Something you couldn't really explain, some queer quirk of the mind or memory.

The Mystery of the Vanishing Heads. It was a hell of a title, he thought, for some mystery story. It was the kind of title Conan Doyle might have thought up for Sherlock Holmes.

5

H<small>E</small> was stunned by his first look at St. Mark's Square, or, as the Italians called it, Piazza San Marco.

Like any tourist who comes to Venice for the first time, he found it an enchanting fantasy, this vast enclosed piazza with the arcaded buildings enclosing it on three sides, its golden mosaics glittering wherever you looked, its pillars and white domes and vaulting arches clustering into a long pyramid of changing light, gold and opal, coral and amethyst. His eye instantly picked up the familiar and world-known fixtures of St. Mark's. The Palace of the Doges, which Allan and he had passed just before they entered the square; the thick, red campanile, the great cathedral, the famous golden horses, the clock tower on the north side, astride the entrance to the Mercerie, with its two bronze Moors who hammered each hour on the bell.

The whole place had an ethereal quality. You had to

blink to make sure it was not some optical illusion. Somehow, David expected it to stay there for just a moment or two. Then it would float away or vanish instantly, like a mirage.

"Well," said Allan. "What do you think of it?"

"Fantastic," said David. "I see it. But I don't believe it."

"Tell you something. In my opinion, it's one of the most exciting experiences in a lifetime. I mean, this first look at St. Mark's. It's really a grabber. Every time I come back here, I get the same reaction. Incredible. You know?"

It was early evening, and the huge square was animated, buzzing with tourists and natives alike strolling under the arcades or feeding the pigeons, having their pictures taken or buying souvenirs from the vendors. At Florian's and Quadri's, facing each other on opposite sides of the square, the cafe sitters drank their aperitifs, spooned their ice cream, ate their cake and sipped their coffee, and thus, royally ensconced, stared regally at the passing parade.

Allan explained that if you liked the sun, you sat at Quadri's in the morning and at Florian's in the afternoon. If you liked the shade, it was vice versa. After the sun went down, take your pick. They sat down at a table at Florian's. David ordered a beer. Allan ordered something called Aurum, which was an orange-flavored drink. Then they leaned back, surveying the huge square.

David had been on St. Mark's only a few minutes, and his first glimpse had taken his breath away, but now he had a totally different reaction. Sitting here at Florian's, listening to the chatter of the crowd, studying the animated show before him, watching the colors of the buildings, domes, and mosaics change as twilight changed to darkness, he felt an almost eerie sense of being completely at home. He experienced a warmth for this strange place he could not fathom. It was remarkable. He tried to convey this feeling to Allan, who said:

"Nothing new in that. Most foreigners who come to Venice fall in love with it. If they stay here any time at all,

66

they consider themselves citizens. This square is full of the ghosts of the great ones who felt as much at home here as the Venetians themselves. For example, take Wagner. You might be sitting in the same spot he used to like, years ago."

"Wagner?"

"You know. The music man. He liked to sit here at Florian's and complain that no one appreciated his works. And Proust dreamed some of his dreams here as well. And these two are just for openers."

"Yes?"

"And Nietzsche. Your friendly neighborhood philosopher. He'd sit here, or at Quadri's, for hours and days. Just staring at the pigeons. They seemed to mesmerize him."

"Does anyone know why?"

"No. Probably trying to find some meaning in life by watching them. Although as I see it, all they do is eat and crap all over the place. But they did become the subject of one of his most beautiful poems."

David continued to marvel at his friend's apparently limitless store of information.

"Allan, I have to tell you I'm impressed."

"Yes?"

"I still don't understand how you manage to remember all this stuff."

Allan shrugged. "I think I told you. I have this ability to read and retain. And you already know I'm a fact collector. Anyway, take Ruskin. He was a great fan of this place. Goethe liked to look at the sea from the top of the campanile, and Galileo demonstrated his telescope from there. Am I boring you?"

"Not yet."

"Well, of course, there was Henry James and Robert Browning and Thomas Mann, and, hell, I could go on and on. They all loved the place. But some hated it. And I mean violently."

"I find that pretty hard to believe."

"Would you believe Mark Twain?" David shook his head

and Allan continued: "It's on the record. Twain thought St. Mark's here looked like some big and warty bug taking a walk. Horace Walpole thought Venice was a place of stinking ditches. James Boswell hated it, Montaigne, Gibbon, James Adams couldn't stand it. They considered it decadent, pestilent, a slimy swamp, damp, dank, a melancholy city that smelled of death." He paused and looked over David's shoulder. "Here comes my drink. So—end of lecture!"

Across the Piazza, the band at Quadri's began an overture by Rossini. The conductor was giving a histrionic performance. He waved his arms wildly, his hair flopped over his forehead. He wiggled his fingertips toward the woodwinds, begging them, cajoling them to play gently, gently. He waved his hands regally, swung his arms violently at the percussion players, and swished his baton through the air at the brass. He suffered through varying moods: passionate despair, ecstasy, remorse. He was an accomplished actor, but the players under his command were indifferent. They had seen this performance many times before, and they all looked as though they would rather be elsewhere.

David sipped his beer for a while, watching the show. Then he told Allan what had happened during his last meditation.

"All the faces disappeared? Just like that?"

"Yes."

Allan thought for a moment. "That's funny."

"Any ideas? Theories?"

"No. I don't get it. I don't get it at all. Not yet. But there has to be a reason. Both ways. Why those images crossed your PA level—and why they suddenly got lost."

"The whole thing's a little sick," said David. "I'm beginning to feel like some kind of psychopath. I mean, who is Fat Face? And the rest? What do they want with me? How did they get into my meditation, and where did they go?"

"I said it before, and I'll say it again. There's nothing mysterious about it. Those fucking stone heads and faces you've been seeing are part of your conscious memory. There's a handle to this whole thing somewhere."

That was Allan Fischer. He had no belief whatever in anything mystic. If you couldn't see it, feel it, hear it, taste it, and so on, it simply did not exist. He was a disciple of his computers. David had heard him argue once with someone at the office who thought transcendental meditation was some kind of mystic hoodoo voodoo, mumbo jumbo because it originated with Maharishi and came from the East. Allan had become really uptight about it.

"TM is a science," he had said. "It's a goddamn science. Yeah, I know Maharishi's a Hindu monk, but he's a scientist, too, and that's where he made his contribution. There's no Hinduism, or any other kind of ism, or an ounce of religion in TM. It's logical, man, totally logical, and if you observe the procedure, it *works!*"

The orchestra at Quadri's completed its number and took a break. David finished his beer and said:

"Allan, about tomorrow. Our plane doesn't leave until eight in the evening. That gives us a whole day. What do you plan on doing?"

"Nothing in particular. Why?"

"I thought I'd book a tour. You know, just to get some idea of what this place is all about. Maybe you'd like to come along . . ."

"No, thanks. I've been there already. I've seen the cathedral and the Palace of the Doges and the paintings by Tintoretto, Titian, and Guardi, and I've heard all the history. It's a lot of walking and talking, and I'd rather sit on my ass and drink coffee and read the paper and watch the girls. But I recommend it to you." Allan drained the last of his drink and looked at his watch.

"How about dinner?"

"Good thinking."

They stopped first at CIT, the big Italian tourist agency. David booked a half-day tour. He paid for it, and the clerk gave him a ticket. He told David the tour would begin at nine-fifteen in the morning. The guide would be waiting for his group in front of the office, and please, *signore,* it was important that he be there on time.

They had dinner at a restaurant Allan knew called Ludovico's. It was near the Rialto Bridge, on the Frari side, and Allan pointed out that its food was truly Venetian, that it was, in fact, a great favorite of Venetian businessmen and other locals. It was a noisy, busy place. The decor was simple and functional, and it was plain that here it was only the food that counted.

They were led to a table in the rear, and a waiter, who spoke some English, handed them a menu. Allan ordered a spaghetti dish, and then a bouillabaisse. David began with a *zuppa di verdura*, or vegetable soup. He ran his eye down the menu, then suddenly he looked up at the waiter and said:

"Do you have *canocce?*"

"Ah," said the waiter. He smiled in appreciation. "You are a man who knows a good dish, *signore*. It is not on the menu, but we serve it to those who ask for it. I see you are a true Venetian. Or else, you have lived here for a long time."

"No," said David. "This is my first trip. I just got here today."

The waiter stared at him. "But that is impossible, *signore*."

"Why?" said Allan. He was watching the waiter curiously. "Why is it impossible?"

"Because your friend here speaks of it in the Venetian dialect, *canocce*. In other parts of Italy, it is called *canocchie*, or *pannocchie* and even *spannocchie*. But only a real Venetian would speak of it as *canocce*. No tourist would know of it, or speak of it in this way. It is a very special kind of Venetian dish, and the people here have been eating it since the time of the doges." He shrugged. "And, naturally, when I heard the *signore* order it, I was surprised . . ."

Allan turned to David, interested.

"Where *did* you hear of it?"

"I don't know. I don't remember."

"Well, what's in it? What's it made of?"

"I can't tell you."

70

"You can't tell me?"

"I just don't know."

"But you *ordered* it, for God's sake!"

"I know. But I swear, I never heard the word before. It just, well—popped out of my mouth."

Allan Fischer was looking at him rather queerly now.

"David, you're being a little weird. I mean, think about it. You sit here, like an old Venetian, and you order this *canocce* dish as though you've been eating it all your life, and you claim you never heard of it before and don't even know what's in it. You know, you're beginning to worry me."

"I'm beginning to worry myself."

"You heard the word somewhere, of course. You've just had a memory lapse. Like those stone faces you saw in your TM. It's the only possible explanation. Do you buy it?"

"I guess I'll have to."

"Okay." Allan turned to the waiter. "What is this *canocce* anyway?"

The waiter explained that it was an insectlike shellfish. Extracting the meat was difficult, and for this reason it was not eaten in most parts of Italy and was unprofitable for fishermen to catch. But in Venice, those small shellfish were relished as the most succulent of the *frutti di mare* in Adriatic waters.

David tossed and turned half the night, saying the word *canocce* over and over in his mind, trying to remember where he had heard it.

The name tormented him. Somehow, it had a familiar ring when he spoke it aloud. But, try as he might, he could not place it in his memory.

But, of course, Allan Fischer was right.

He couldn't have simply invented the word. Somewhere, he must have heard it.

6

Aᴛ ten minutes after nine the next morning, David Drew walked through the Piazzetta and entered St. Mark's Square.

There was a mist, which the morning sun would burn off later. But now it was a curtain of gauze, filtering the light, tinging the arcades and pillars and domes with silver, enfolding the buildings, touching them with a mystic brush, heightening their grandeur.

He headed directly for the CIT office.

A group of about thirty people waited in front of the travel agency Obviously, it was the tour group he was supposed to join. Most of them were Americans, with a few scattered English and Canadians. They were all either senior citizens or in late middle age. Most of the women had blue hair, were dressed in slacks and print blouses, and wore sensible walking shoes. The men wore slacks and short-sleeved sports shirts and carried cameras. It was the same kind of tour group you would see anywhere in the world, from Kyoto to Dubrovnik to Mexico City.

David felt a little out of place among all these older people. He stood a little to one side, while they chattered about their hotel accommodations and other tours they had scheduled, the gondola rides they had taken, and the shopping they had done. Finally, their guide appeared.

It was a girl. And she was young, about his age.

David was a little surprised. And pleased. All of the tour groups he had seen on the plaza, as far as he could recall, had been led by male guides.

She stood before the group, addressing it in a rather formal way.

"I am Adriana Manzoni," she said. "And I will be your guide for this morning's tour. Since our time is limited, we will confine ourselves to the area of Piazza San Marco, in which we are now standing, the Basilica, and the Palace of the Doges." Her English was studied, precise. "As we proceed to examine the many points of interest, please do not hesitate to ask questions. I will answer them to the best of my ability."

She was an attractive girl, rather tall, firm of body and well-bosomed. She had blue eyes, and she wore her blond hair carelessly. David was a little surprised at her fair skin and light complexion, until he remembered that not all Italians were necessarily dark, that many from the north were blue-eyed and blond, like Signorina (or perhaps Signora) Manzoni here. She wore a brief blue skirt with a large brass buckle, a sleeveless blue blouse of a paler hue, and low-heeled walking shoes. Her face was set in a professional way as she addressed the group. She couldn't help looking a little bored; she had seen this kind of group a hundred times before. But then her eyes caught his, and he detected a flicker of interest in them, and he smiled. She did not return his smile but turned away, looking a little more

73

severe than normally. He grinned, realizing there had already been some contact between them. Even if it was very small, she was personally aware of his presence, there was some unspoken community of interest between them—almost by definition, since they were the only two there wh⁼ were under thirty.

"Now," she continued. "There will be many people, many tour groups, in both the palace and the Basilica. It is very important that we stay close together. When we are ready to move from one place to another, I will raise this umbrella. So." She took a telescoped umbrella from the large shoulder bag she carried, stretched it out, and raised it above her head. It was very colorful. It had a candy-striped pole, and the umbrella itself was a vivid red, white, and blue. "If you get separated in the crowd, ladies and gentlemen, always look for this umbrella. It will identify our group." She folded the umbrella. "Now, are there any questions?" There were none, and she continued: "Very well. I will now collect your tour tickets, and then we shall begin."

They came forward to give her the vouchers for the tour. She took them and stuffed them into her shoulder bag. When David gave her his voucher, their eyes caught again, and he smiled. This time he caught a small smile in return. It was reluctant, as though she couldn't help herself.

She took them first to the Basilica, lectured on the facade, then took them inside. They crossed the interior, went into the baptistery, and then through a door in the right wall into the Zen Chapel. Someone remarked that it was odd that they practiced Zen in the cathedral, making a little joke of it. It was clear that Adriana Manzoni had heard this a hundred times before, and she explained it was named after the tomb of a Cardinal G. B. Zen and that it was built in 1521, together with the altar and the statue of the Madonna of the Shoe.

It was warm in the Basilica and jammed with individual tourists and tour groups; the chatter of many languages coming from these groups and intermingling made hearing

74

difficult. They followed the red, white, and blue umbrella, saw the treasury, the crypt, and the presbytery and oohed and aahed at the golden altarpiece.

Again, David experienced the same rush of emotion, the same awe, the same empathy, he had felt for everything Venetian. Somehow, the Basilica seemed a sacred place to him, not for religious reasons and not for historical reasons.

He had the strange feeling that all this was very familiar. That he had been here before.

But, of course, that was absurd.

Yet, when the group started its tour of the Doges' Palace, he felt the same way. Removed from the tour group itself. Caught by some personal and intimate relationship with these rooms, wherever they went, up the Staircase of the Giants, into the Shield Room, the Collegium and the Great Council Room, the Notaries' Rooms and the Lawyers' Rooms, and across the Bridge of Sighs into the prisons themselves.

He tried to listen to what Adriana Manzoni was saying, but somehow he couldn't concentrate. He had the feeling that he already knew what she was going to say about this room or that, this altar or that. But he knew that was ridiculous, too. There was no way he could possibly know.

Again, he felt hypnotized by his surroundings, these stones, these walls, these monuments. He moved in a kind of trance, he seemed to walk alone through these halls and rooms, oblivious to the crowds milling about all around him, unhearing of the din and chatter and the confusion of the many languages, walking dreamlike through a silence of his own.

The moment they stepped out into the Piazza again, his strange mood ended abruptly. It was the finish of the tour. The morning mist had dissipated, and now they stood in bright, hot sunlight.

His attention focused on Adriana Manzoni again.

He hadn't paid too much attention to her inside the Basilica and the palace. He had been too preoccupied. Now, she looked even more attractive than before. She had dropped the cool, professional attitude she had shown when she first met the group. The members of the tour were saying good-bye, shaking hands, and telling her how much they enjoyed it. She smiled warmly and thanked them graciously.

And he thought, why not? Allan Fischer was off some-where, and they had no set appointment to meet until they were ready to leave for the airport. It would be interesting to meet and talk to a real Venetian lady like Adriana Manzoni.

He delayed his own approach until everyone else was gone. Then he said to her, in Italian:

"*Mille grazie. La gita é stata veramente interessante.*"

She looked at him, startled.

"Oh. You speak Italian."

"Does it surprise you?"

"I—yes. I mean, I didn't expect—you don't look like an Italian."

He grinned. "No? What do I look like?"

"I—well, you look very American." She laughed. "Really, you *did* surprise me."

"Look, how about lunch?"

She studied him a moment. "Oh, I'm sorry. Thank you very much, but I think not . . ."

"You don't have a date for lunch, do you?"

"Well, no. But—"

"Okay," he said. "My name is Drew. David Drew. This is my first time in Venice. I'll only be here for a few hours, I'm leaving tonight. I hate to eat alone, and I'm sure you do. I promise not to talk shop, I mean ask you a lot of questions about Venice, and this'll give me a chance to practice my Italian. Besides, I find you very attractive and very charming, and I'd love to talk to you. How about it?"

"You're very persistent, Signore Drew."

"I'm sorry. I didn't mean to come on so strong."

The corners of her mouth crinkled. The blue eyes sparkled. "Persistent," she repeated. "And very persuasive."

76

"Then it's a deal?"

"Okay," she said, laughing. "It's a deal."

"*Meraviglioso*," he said. "Where shall we go?"

She told him she knew of a little restaurant he might like. A neighborhood kind of place, patronized only by the local people. It was near the Campo Santa Maria Formosa, about a ten minute walk from San Marco. She would have to be back at the Piazza by three, to lead an afternoon tour.

They walked for a minute or two down a busy *calle*, or narrow street. It was hemmed in by buildings, and lined with small shops and restaurants.

The *calle* was crowded with people, shoppers looking for bargains, others just strolling. It twisted and turned, and now and then there was an entry to another street, or to a bridge leading across a canal.

"Better stay close to me," she said. "Or you'll get lost."

He grinned. "Try and lose me."

But a few minutes later, it almost happened.

Adriana had stopped to admire something in a shop window. He had gone on a few steps alone. The street itself came to a dead end, but there was a wide and busy entry to the left, and a narrow alley to the right. Without thinking, almost automatically, he ignored the crowd to the left and, instead, turned right up the alley. It was dark and dank, and he was the only pedestrian who had ventured into it.

"Signore Drew."

He stopped and turned. Adriana Manzoni was at the entrance to the alley, staring at him. Then she came toward him.

"I thought you said you'd never been to Venice before."

"I haven't."

"Then how did you know this was a shortcut to the Campo Santa Maria Formosa?"

He looked at her, confused. "I didn't. I must have been daydreaming."

"Daydreaming. Yes. It couldn't have been anything else,

could it? Otherwise, you would have followed the crowd up the main *calle* here."

She took his arm, and they continued down the alley. He was a little upset. He hadn't been daydreaming at all.

It had just seemed the way to go.

7

THE restaurant was located on a small canal and was called Da Giuseppe. She ordered a *fritto misto,* or mixed fry of shrimp, scampi, octopus, soft-shelled crabs, and sardines. She suggested that he try the same. He found it delicious, along with a dry white wine, which she identified as a Soave from the district around Verona.

David noted that here *canocce* was on the menu. He was still blank as to where he had heard of it. The name continued to torment him, it bounced around elusively . . .

"I see you are still daydreaming."

"What?"

He was startled by the interruption. Adriana Manzoni was smiling.

"You seem very far away, *signore.* So lost in space just now. What is it they say in English? Oh, yes. A penny for your thoughts."

"I'm sorry," he said.

"You must miss her."

"Who?"

"This girl you left back in America."

"There isn't any girl. I mean, not seriously."

"You are a very attractive man, *signore*," she said. "I find that hard to believe."

Finally he said, yes, there was a girl, in a manner of speaking, but she was what you might call maybe, perhaps, or possibly. Nothing definite, no commitment, just a kind of interesting relationship, you understand. She laughed and confessed that she too had the same kind of maybe and possibly relationship with a boy named Giorgio, who was a civil engineer, currently on a road-building project in Libya. In fact, it was even less than that. He was a friend, nothing more, really.

They seemed to hit it off and knew they liked each other. Adriana told him she had been born and brought up in Venice and that the Manzonis had lived here for several generations. She was twenty-four. She had learned to speak English in school, had spent two years in the United States, with an uncle in San Francisco, and increased her knowledge even further there. Like most of the Venetian guides, she was proficient in other languages; she was also booked for French and German-speaking tour groups. But when you spoke some other language all day, it became very tiring after a while, and you really had to concentrate; it was very pleasant to sit here, with a very attractive young American close to her own age, and still talk her own language. His Italian was good, very good, although he spoke it with a kind of American accent, but she loved to listen to it, and he could get by with it anywhere in Italy.

She was very curious about him, and he told her that really he had led a very unremarkable life. He was born and raised in a city called Canton, Ohio. It was a city that had some kind of national reputation because it housed the Football Hall of Fame. He had some difficulty explaining to her what this meant and why it was important.

He was an Episcopalian and the only son of a dealer in

the wholesale hardware business. He had decided that he was not interested in hammers and screwdrivers and ten-penny nails, but in a different kind of hardware, much more sophisticated, called computers. He had gone to Ohio State University, studied mathematics and engineering, special-izing in the computer sciences. He had also played tight end on the varsity football team, which was something else he found difficult to explain to Adriana Manzoni. He told her how he had come to learn Italian, the same story he had told Cassie Knox back in New York, and she laughed and thought that was funny, very funny indeed.

Finally, upon graduation, he had this offer to come to New York, and he tried to tell her what he did in computers but found that very difficult to explain, and finally he gave up. Anyway, he had been on his way to Iran on an assignment, when this plane thing occurred, and that's how he happened to be in Venice.

He told her of the strange fascination Venice had for him, that somehow he felt *different* in it, not quite himself, that he seemed to overreact to it, for want of a better word. Adriana Manzoni told him this wasn't unusual.

"I've heard many people speak this way before. Of course, I've lived here all my life, this is my city, I'm used to it. I appreciate the monuments we have here, I really do, but, after all, they're my business as well. But to strangers, Venice must appear to be some kind of fantasy. I've heard people say that when they walked into the Piazza San Marco, they really feel for a while that they've actually walked back into the Middle Ages. I've heard others say that they found Venice terribly—what's the word they used?—unsettling, in the few days they stayed here. And of course, all you have to do is read the writers and poets. Read Ruskin, read Browning." She laughed. "But I sound like a lecture. And I don't want to. I have enough of that all day."

"Damn it," he said, suddenly. "I wish I didn't have to leave tonight."

"I'm sorry you do," she said. She looked and sounded as

81

though she really meant it. There's really so much to see and experience here." He looked at her intently and then grinned, and she colored a little. "I'm sure you'll be back."

"I *know* I will. I have some vacation time coming up in a few months. I'm going to make it my first order of business." He smiled. "Maybe this time, I'll take the afternoon tour with you."

"That," she said, "is basically an art tour. We view the paintings of Bellini and Tiepolo and Guardi, Titian and Tintoretto. . . ."

"I love Titian and Tintoretto," he said.

They laughed a lot together, and by the time they left the restaurant she was Adriana and he was David.

They walked out into the Campo Santa Maria Formosa. It was a big and handsome square, colorful with stalls of fruits and vegetables, and bustling with people. David saw no tourists about, although the *campo* was only a few minutes from St. Mark's. He was about to remark on this to Adriana, when suddenly he saw it. Something he had missed when he had walked through the area before.

Fat Face.

The huge stone face was embedded at the base of the campanile.

It was the same face he had seen in his meditation. Exactly the same. Right down to the smallest detail.

It was bestial and degraded. It leered at him with such an inhuman expression, so foul and evil, that he wanted to turn his eyes away. But he couldn't. He could only stand there, riveted to the spot, and look at it. It was a horror that degraded the beauty around it. To David Drew, at this moment, it seemed almost alive, the stone transformed into living muscle, the lewd mouth exhaling a stinking breath.

"Horrible, isn't it?" said Adriana.

"Yes," he heard himself say. "Yes."

He felt a chill run up his spine. His skin prickled. This was insane, he thought.

How could he have seen Fat Face in his meditation, before he had ever come to Venice?

"This particular piece is really monstrous," he heard Adriana say. "Probably carved in the seventeenth century, an expression of revolt against the classical canons." She smiled at him. "Really, I'm almost ashamed of my ancestors for creating something like this. They loved beauty, yes, but they also loved the bizarre and baroque. They loved to shock the spectator, to shake him up, as you Americans say. And they did it in street sculpture like this. Venice is just full of bizarre heads and faces. Surely, you've noticed."

The funny thing was, he *hadn't* noticed. Somehow he had blocked them out in his mind. Or he had seen them but made no connection with the images he had seen in his meditation. He continued to stare at Fat Face, dazed, fascinated. If the old Venetians wanted to shock the spectator, he thought, then they had certainly succeeded.

They had certainly shocked the hell out of *him*.

"It's getting late," said Adriana. "We'd better be getting back to the Piazza."

She took him back to St. Mark's by a slightly different route. They walked down a *calle* dominated by a big church. Adriana identified it as the Ospedaletto Church. Its great facade bulged with muscular telamones, baroque heads and faces, huge giants, lion heads wearing fierce masks. On the way back he saw stone faces and heads everywhere now, those he had completely missed before. Some were life-size, some small, but they were everywhere—on the eaves of roofs, in niches on the palace walls, on the doors and sides of the churches, and on the little arched bridges crossing the canals. Most of them were human, but some were animal. Notably lions. There were lions, lions, all over the place.

The figures were stained by long exposure to the elements and the droppings of pigeons. Some of them were partly eroded or were missing an ear, a nose. There were heads whose bearded faces looked like those of Moses and Jeremiah and Noah and Christ and others who peopled the Bible. There were stone heads with elfin faces, grotesque and leering heads who stuck out their tongues at the passerby, angelic faces of classic beauty who smiled down serenely at the same passerby, other female faces smiling secret smiles of lust, male faces and female faces, nymphs and satyrs.

To David Drew, they all looked familiar.

Because he had seen many of them before.

The afternoon tour group was waiting for Adriana when they came to the square.

She shook hands with him gravely.

"Thank you, David," she said. "You have been very nice. Please come back to Venice."

"I will," he said. "I will."

"*Addío*. And good trip."

Their goodbye was very short. She had wanted to say more, but she saw that he was preoccupied. She knew that he was hardly aware of what she said. For some reason he had become withdrawn; he had hardly spoken to her on the way back. She had sensed his change in mood the moment he saw that carving in the campanile. It had really seemed to upset him. And she was puzzled as to why this should be so. It was very strange, really. Of course, the face was ugly, but, after all, it was only a carving, made of stone . . . .

She turned and walked toward the tour group, which was waiting for her.

David watched her go. He felt light-headed, faint. All these buildings, the crowds flowing and swirling about him, all seemed unreal. He stood there for a while, indecisively. He had no desire to seek out Allan Fischer and tell him about this. Allan would think him completely mad.

He had this monstrous suspicion growing in him, and he wanted to disprove it. To put it to rest. Simply because what he was thinking of was pure fantasy. He knew it was impossible. He was shaken, true. But he still had his head on straight. He knew that what he had encountered was a series of coincidences, bits of fantasy, fragments of imagination.

Allan Fischer was right, of course. There was a reason for everything.

A reason for everything, David told himself. *A reason for everything, a reason for everything* ...

He began to walk.

He picked an exit from the square at random, passed under an arcade, and walked down a wide and busy street lined with shops and travel agencies. He passed a big church called San Moisè, then the Bauer-Gruenwald Hotel, and crossed the bridge over the canal running alongside it. A group of gondoliers waited for clients at the base of the arched bridge. David noted the water level of the canal. He could see that it had dropped about a foot from high tide.

And along the side of the canals, their manes and faces half-emerging from the water, was a series of stone lion heads. It was clear that the heads were completely hidden at high tide and exposed at low tide.

He shivered, remembering this too ...

He watched from the top of the bridge for a while. Then he proceeded down a wide street. A sign said it was the Calle Larga XXII Marzo. It was lined with banks, travel agencies, antique shops, and cafes. Several narrow alleys led down to the hotels on the Grand Canal.

David came to a street leading off to the right, and he stopped suddenly.

The name of the street was the Calle della Veste.

He could not see what was at the end of the narrow street, since it curved away. But a picture flashed in his mind as to what was there. It was very clear. He saw another canal and a small bridge crossing it. Then, just beyond, there was a courtyard. Enclosing the courtyard were three buildings.

One building was a small and elegant church, built in the classic Renaissance style; the second building was an exquisite little theater, built in a much later period. He visualized it now; its door was open, and inside he could see the auditorium, pink plush and gilt everywhere, with round-cheeked cherubs flying about on the ceiling. He was unable to identify the third building distinctly, except that it seemed to be a kind of school, and there were curious curled ornamental gables over the windows. In the courtyard itself, there was an open-air cafe.

He wanted to walk down the *calle* and see for himself exactly what was at the end of the street. But somehow he could not. He did not dare.

He saw a priest walking toward him. The priest wore a brown habit and carried a large leather sack over his shoulder.

"Father, if I may trouble you for a moment."

"Yes?"

"Can you tell me what is down that street?"

"Why, yes. The Campo San Fantin."

"Is it worth seeing? Could you tell me what's in the *campo?*"

The priest, noting that he was a tourist, smiled benevolently.

"Of course. On the *campo* you will see the Teatro La Fenice. It is the oldest and most famous theater in Venice. Then there is the Church of San Fantin. If it is open, you would be well-rewarded to see its chancel. It is beautiful—no, that is not the correct word—it is noble. And then there is a *scuola* there."

"A *scuola?*"

"The Scuola di San Girolamo. I do not think you will find it of particular interest. It is occupied by the Ateneo Veneto Society of Arts and Letters at present."

"And—" David hesitated a moment. Then he blurted out: "Is there an outdoor cafe there?"

The priest looked at him, puzzled.

"Why, yes. There is. But how would you know that?"

David shrugged, confused. "I didn't," he mumbled. "I just thought that perhaps . . . "

"You'll find the cafe right on the *campo* itself. I recommend it highly. It is very charming, and the food is excellent. It is a favorite not only of tourists but of Venetians as well."

"Thank you, Father."

"Not at all, my boy. Not at all."

The priest waved, threw him another benevolent smile, and then left.

He was sitting on a stone bench in some small courtyard. The sign said it was the Campiello Aretino.

He dimly remembered that he had been walking. Aimlessly. Through alleys, streets, across bridges. He seemed to be in some kind of dream. He had no idea how he had come to be here, or where it was, or how long he had been sitting here.

In the center of the courtyard, three small satyrs held hands and danced around a tiny fountain. Their heads were thrust back, and they were laughing in delight as the cool spray washed their faces and sprayed their bodies. A group of matronly women sat in a semicircle of chairs, sewing and knitting, gossiping and smoking cigarettes. Their eyes constantly flashed to their shouting youngsters, who were riding around the fountain on tricycles. Occasionally, they glanced at David curiously.

Two cats nibbled at a plate of fish leavings. They emptied the plate. One of them licked its paws, then walked gracefully to the fountain. It leaped up on the edge, drank a little, then jumped down again. One of the children raced directly at it with his tricycle. The cat leaped out of the way and ran down a narrow alley. Its companion followed it. The boy on the tricycle lost his balance and fell. He lay on the pavement, crying. One of the mothers put down her knitting, rose, went to him, and picked him up. She was very calm about everything. She cuddled him to her ample bosom, crooned a little to him, wiped his eyes with a handkerchief. He stopped crying. She picked up the tricycle, and he joined the others again. She returned to the group, lit a cigarette, and resumed her knitting.

He knew it now. There was no longer any doubt in his mind.

87

He had lived in Venice before, as someone else, in some other life, at some other time.

Reincarnation.

Some of his friends were into it, but he had never believed it. If your heart stopped and your body ceased to function, you were dead, man, dead. Every part of you, including what they called your soul, went into the grave or cremation furnace with you. You became a memory, but you did not become someone else. You simply became dust, food for the worms. He, David Drew, could never buy reincarnation because he believed in fact, he was a pragmatist and a realist; if you couldn't see it, feel it, hear it, touch it, taste it, or measure it, then it did not exist. Reincarnation was only a superstition, a belief, a faith, a kind of religion; if you were really into it, it could be comforting, because maybe you could face death a little better, believing that you'd have another shot at life later on. That was fine for people who wanted to believe it; everybody had a right to indulge in his own thing. But he, personally, had never been able to take it seriously. It was fun to discuss; reincarnation was a great conversation topic with the right people, but as yet no one had ever proved it out.

Until now.

He, David Tavish Drew, was his own proof.

It was incredible, it staggered all reason, that he, an American, born of John and Amelia Drew, in Canton, Ohio, of Scotch-Irish descent, was in fact the incarnation of some Venetian who, a long time ago, might actually have sat on this same stone bench, alongside the wall of this old palazzo, and watched this same kind of scene. Of course, if he had lived a long time ago, the women wouldn't have been smoking cigarettes and the children wouldn't have been riding tricycles, but otherwise, it would have been the same. There would be women sitting and sewing and gossiping, as they always had, and children would be playing around the fountain and, of course, there would be the cats. Venice had always loved cats . . .

He began to question his sanity. He began to wonder what he was doing in this particular place, in this particular moment in time, sitting on a stone bench in the Campiello Aretino, in the city of Venice, Italy, which was a hell of a long way from anyplace he called home.

He had the feeling, the definite feeling, that all this had been *arranged,* that all this was not an accident, not a series of coincidences, but that it had been planned. More and more he felt he had been *manipulated* by some mysterious Hand, moved around like a pawn for reasons he couldn't even begin to understand, that the entire sequence of events had been programmed to bring him to this point.

It made a fantastic scenario. He played it out now, step by step.

Long ago, presumably by accident, he learns Italian. Later, he gets into TM and sees the stone images. He is assigned to go abroad on a job. The plane develops engine trouble. And where does it make its forced landing?

Venice.

Continue this scenario, or sequence of events. Put it in the computer and see what tapes out. A replacement plane is supposed to pick them up. It is delayed. Coincidence? Or design? And so he has an overnight stay in Venice. After that, the series of revelations. From Fat Face on . . .

Program it into any computer.

And what do you get?

A reading of No Answer. No Answer whatever.

He felt feverish, giddy. He began to tremble uncontrollably. And he asked himself, why me? *Why me?* He knew it, he felt it in his bones, that the scenario was just beginning, that there would be more, much more, unless he acted swiftly.

And his gut reaction was immediate. He didn't want to know any more. Unless he acted, and acted now, he would be pushed further and further through a door he did not want to enter, with God knew what on the other side.

Turn it all off, and get out.

He looked at his watch. Twenty minutes to six. It was later than he had thought. He had to get back to the hotel and pack. He had a plane to catch.

He rose and hurried away from the *campiello*. He asked directions to St. Mark's. He found he wasn't too far away. A walk of about twenty minutes. Once there, it was only a short walk to his hotel. He decided not to tell Allan Fischer of what had happened. There was no point to it. Allan would never believe him anyway.

Reincarnation? he would say. *Come on, David, you're putting me on. This is total bullshit.*

On the way back to the square, something strange happened. His whole reaction to the city reversed itself. His mood toward it changed abruptly.

Now, he saw only ugliness. The canals looked dirty, their stink offended his nostrils. The palazzos and buildings looked decayed, they seemed ready to crumble, the paint was peeling, as was the gilt on their ornaments. The sound of the motorboats seemed too loud, the clothing on the lines between the windows looked dirty, the flowers in the pots seemed too garish, like overblown hussies. The men who passed him looked furtive and treacherous, the women seemed blowsy and unattractive, too shrill and raucous in their conversation. The cats in the courtyards and alleys seemed mangy, half-starved; they stared at him with glassy, hostile eyes and then turned to slink away.

He felt repelled by everything he saw. The whole place now seemed to reek of decadence, of melancholy, of death. Its art and architecture, for the most part, were too baroque, too overdone, too much overkill. He wanted only to abandon this place, to leave, and in a hurry, flee it like a plague.

Fortunately, at eight this evening, he would be aboard a plane for Teheran, and he would leave this whole weird, sick thing behind. In time, it would simply become a bad dream, some kind of nightmare. And finally, he hoped, he would forget it. Finally, he would be able to persuade himself that it had never really happened, it had never happened at all.

He had just started to pack when the phone rang. It was Allan Fischer.

"Man, where have you been?"

"Oh, just walking around."

"Well, Jesus, you had me worried. We're due to leave for the airport in a half-hour. I've arranged for a private boat to get us there. And for porters to take our luggage to the dock. You all packed?"

"Just about."

"Meet me in the lobby in fifteen minutes. Okay?"

"Okay," said David.

He hung up. There was very little packing he had to do. It took him only a couple of minutes. He did it all mechanically. He was still in shock.

He zipped his suitcase shut. He still had some time before he went down to meet Allan. He sat in a chair by the window and looked out across the lagoon.

The lagoon had a curious sheen on its surface, the effect of the Venetian light, which seemed to change in quality and intensity every hour. The clouds over the island of San Giorgio Maggiore were clustered in a strange effect, those in the foreground bright white, reflecting the sun, and those in the distance darkened, the color of lead and streaked with subtle shades of blue and green. The buildings on the island seemed to shimmer in this light, they all seemed transient and barely anchored, so that at the slightest shaking of the earth they would fly off into the sky. The light bathing the Church of Santa Maria della Salute was of a different kind. It was luminous, yet flat, the color of pink marble. The great balloonlike dome, the scrolls, and the statues looked as though they were painted against the sky, a great theatrical canvas.

Once before, he, David Drew, had been part of all this. Once before, as someone else, he had walked along the Riva degli Schiavoni, filled with strollers then, as it was now, and gazed upon the lagoon and the buildings opposite, just as he did now. This had been his home. He had had an identity, a name.

But who was he?

He might have been anybody. A noble, merchant, sailor, priest, painter, or sculptor. He might have been a gondolier, a musician, a tailor, a goldsmith, a glassmaker, a street vendor, a beggar. Or, who knows, even a doge. He could have been anybody.

He could have lived very early in the eleventh century. Or in the sixteenth century, at the height of Venice's glory. But it could have been anytime; it was useless to speculate.

He wondered who his parents had been, and how long he had lived, and how he had died, and when. He wondered whether he had been rich or he had been poor, whether he had worn silks and damasks, the rich costumes of the dignitaries of state he had learned about on the tour, or whether he had worn the simple homespun of the canal digger. He wondered whether he had been handsome or ugly, fat or thin, a decent man or a bastard, healthy or handicapped, intelligent or stupid, whether he had enjoyed the life he had had or found it miserable. And now that he had found out that death was not permanent, that one did indeed live over and over, he wondered who he had been before he had been this unknown Venetian, and who he would become in some distant day or year or century, when he had long since ceased to be David Drew ...

The phone rang. It was Allan.

"David, I'm in the lobby. What the hell is holding you up?"

He had meant to tell Allan that he would be right down. But instead, and to his own astonishment, he heard himself say:

"Allan, I'm not going."

"*What?*"

"I'm going to stay here for a little while."

There was an incredulous pause. Then:

"Man, you've got to be joking. I mean, you're not making any sense. We've got a job to do in Teheran, remember? And we've already been delayed ..."

"Look, tell everybody I got hung up for a couple of days. Tell them I'm sick, tell them anything. But I can't leave Venice yet."

"Why not? Christ, what's so important?"

"I can't tell you. I can't even discuss it."

"David, this is me. Remember? Allan Fischer. Your old friend and father confessor."

"I *told* you. I can't talk about it."

"Okay, okay. But I think you've lost your mind."

"I don't know. Maybe you're right. Maybe I have."

"John Boyce is going to be very upset when you don't show. He'll have your ass for this."

"I'll have to take my chances."

"All right." Allan sighed. "Then I'll see you in Teheran. In a day or two. I hope. Take it easy, and *ciao*, baby."

David said goodbye and hung up. He couldn't believe what he had just done. He hadn't really meant to stay. He hadn't meant to stay at all.

He sat in the chair by the window for a long time.

Finally, he became aware that it had grown dark. A full moon was out. It tipped the lagoon with gold, glinted the buildings with flecks of yellow. Beads of lights sparkled like strings of jewels along the waterway.

He felt the small pangs of hunger. It was time for his usual twenty-minute meditation and then dinner.

His mantra came up loud and strong; vagrant thoughts flitted and paraded across his mind. The sound of his mantra, *shoom, shoom*, became fainter and fainter, and then, at last, it vanished.

Finally, deep in the PA stage, his mind drifted, entirely empty of thought.

Then he saw faces again.

But this time, the faces were not carved out of stone.

This time they were human. They were flesh and blood, and alive.

He could see the eyes move, the facial muscles twitch.

Some were smiling, some were stern, some looked quizzical, some looked sad. On some, the mouths moved wordlessly, as though trying to tell him something. The faces were blurred, they moved swiftly across his screen, one following the other in very quick succession, like a montage on speeded-up film. They flipped by so quickly that he could identify none of them.

He came out of his meditation, perspiring and unrefreshed.

PART
TWO

8

AFTER a while, he was able to pull himself together and think clearly again.

He left his hotel and walked along the *riva,* headed for St. Mark's. Some of the vendors' booths in the Piazzetta, along the wall of the Palace of the Doges, were still open. He found a bookstall. There he picked up a guidebook and a history of Venice, both in English.

After that, he went to the CIT travel agency. A lone clerk was just closing the place. He left a message for Adriana Manzoni, asking her please to call him at his hotel the next morning.

He walked up the nearest *calle* and picked a restaurant at random. He did not notice its name, and he did not care. He ate a solitary meal and returned to his hotel. He felt very tired, emotionally drained. He told himself he should never have stayed in Venice, it was madness, he should have left well enough alone. He'd give it just a day or two and then take off for Iran.

Back at the hotel, he tried to sleep. But he could not. The faces he had seen in his TM meditation, the living faces, flipped across his memory again. They were blurred and indistinct now, but if experience meant anything, they would gradually become clearer and clearer.

The prospect of this sent a chill through him. He was not sure he wanted to know to whom they belonged. He was sure they had been part of his previous life. He told himself that, if he wanted to shut them off, it was within his power to do so. It was simple enough. All he had to do was stop meditating.

But he knew he could not.

Now he knew he was in too deep. He didn't have the power to stop, even if he wanted to. His curiosity no longer merely nagged him. It was painful, compelling. He could not blunt its charge, he was helpless.

The question was, where did he start?

Venice was a big place. He knew that from a cursory look at a map in the guidebook, while he was having dinner. It wasn't just St. Mark's and the immediate area around it. There were huge, congested districts and neighborhoods far beyond—*campo* after *campo, campiello* after *campiello,* streets and alleys without number. Stick a pin anywhere, and go on from there.

And what was he looking for?

Someone he used to be. Someone long dead, name unknown, food for the worms, ashes.

It sounded absurd. It *was* absurd

Still, sleep would not come.

Finally, he turned on the light and began to read. He stayed up all night, reading. First, he scanned the history book he had bought.

He found it fascinating. It was filled with all kinds of curious information. The Venetians had concocted a scheme for poisoning the entire population of Turkey. A wedding festival at a palazzo was interrupted by a brawl, and the bridegroom thrown into a canal by an unsuccessful suitor. A band of heretics had kidnapped a nun. A great gondola funeral was held for a famous courtesan. A priest was condemned to die and sentenced to hang, head down, in a cage suspended from the campanile. At the Palazzo Cornaro, cardinals danced, the crosses around their necks and their habits twirling wildly as they pirouetted and spun.

But it was in the guidebook that he found something interesting, a small scrap of information.

It referred to the Teatro La Fenice. The same theater he had seen, in memory, without ever walking down the street leading to it. According to the guidebook, it was designed by one Giovanni Antonio Selva in 1790, was burned down in 1836, and then rebuilt with only slight alterations.

His previous self had obviously lived at the time the theater existed. Otherwise, it would not have been included in David's memory. Which meant that the Venetian he once had been lived sometime *after* 1790, and not before.

Well, thought David cynically, big deal. Now I know I lived and died sometime within the past two hundred years, before I came into life again as David Drew. That really narrows it down. Still, it was something. A small start.

And tomorrow was another day.

Finally, shortly after four in the morning, he fell asleep.

He woke abruptly, to hear the phone jangling.

He lay there for a moment, bone-weary, still drugged with sleep. The phone rang again. He checked his watch. It was eight-fifteen. The phone rang still again and this time he answered. It was Adriana Manzoni.

"Oh, David. I am so sorry. I forgot—it's still so early. I seem to have awakened you."

"No. It's all right."

"I'll call back later. You sound so sleepy."

"No, please. It's all right. Time I got up anyway."

"I just picked up your message. I am so surprised. I thought you were leaving Venice . . ."

"I changed my mind."

"Oh? Any special reason?"

"I didn't want to miss your afternoon tour."

He heard her laugh. "You are a very charming man, Signore David Drew. You are also a very charming liar. Really, David, be serious. Why have you decided to stay over?"

"It seemed a waste to come to Venice and spend just one night. A place like this deserves a little more time."

"But your job . . . "

"It can wait. How about dinner tonight?"

"Oh, I'm sorry. I can't. I'm having dinner at my mother's house."

"Maybe she'll give you a raincheck."

"A what?"

He took some pains to explain what a raincheck was. She laughed and said it was a marvelous word, she must remember it. Still, she could not possibly ask for a raincheck in this case. It was her mother's birthday, and it would be a big family dinner, with all the relatives there. Then she said: "You *could* ask me for lunch."

"Okay. Then it's lunch."

"I'll look forward to it, David. Today, all I have is the morning tour, and I'm free in the afternoon. So we won't have to hurry."

They arranged to meet at a second-floor restaurant on St. Mark's, where they would have a fine view of the Piazza.

He shaved, showered, and then sat down for his usual prebreakfast meditation.

The living faces appeared again, as before.

This time they had lost some of their fuzziness. They still flipped by rapidly, but they had slowed just enough for David to get a reasonable look at them.

He saw the face of a young woman. It had a rare, haunting beauty. Dark, liquid eyes, an aristocratic nose, soft red mouth against flawless olive skin.

Next, the face of a dark-haired young man. It was a peasant face. Hooked nose, a large wart on the right side of his chin . . .

100

Next, the face of a young man, about his own age. Dark hair, blue eyes, small mustache, a noble and handsome face, which smiled at him warmly.

After this, the face of an infant—

There were other faces in the parade of images, but none that he had ever seen before.

Not in his own memory. Not as David Drew.

He spent the morning walking through Venice.

He prowled up and down the narrow streets, studied the various churches, the palaces, and the other buildings. He explored a number of the *campi* in the vicinity of St. Mark's —Campo San Zaccaria, Campo San Maria del Giglio, Campo dei Miracoli, Campo San Bartolomeo. He walked till his legs ached.

He could identify nothing for sure. But everything seemed familiar, everything seemed to evoke some deep stirring of memory. More and more, he seemed to know where he was going. He seemed to know where a street would turn, and the kind of area it would lead into, and whether there would be a canal up ahead, and so on. He seemed to know that this church would be there, or that palazzo. He did not know them by name, but they appeared in his mind as mysterious shadows; he saw them before he came upon them.

About noon, he came upon a *campo* that seemed much more familiar than any of the rest. It was the Campo Francesco Morosini.

In its center stood a statue of a man. The face of the statue was very familiar. David was sure he had seen it in his meditation. The man had a noble look and posture; he must have been prominent somewhere in the history of Venice. Otherwise, he would not be given a place of honor here. But the noble cast of the face looked a little ridiculous at the moment, because a pigeon was standing on the man's head, cooing a little and flexing its wings.

There was a cafe in the *campo*. Inside the cafe, a radio blared out rock music. David sat at a table, and ordered an espresso. He asked the waiter whom the statue represented. The waiter told him it was Niccolo Tommasseo. Some kind

101

of patriot during the Risorgimento, he believed. That was the extent of his knowledge.

David drank his espresso and studied the large Gothic church at one end of the square and the palazzo on the other side. It seemed to be some kind of music school. He heard a piano being played from somewhere within, a violin. Clearly, the performers were amateurs. Children were playing games all over the *campo*. But they did so in every open area of this sort.

Strangely, he felt completely at home here. Far more so than anywhere else in Venice. A nerve tingled. He couldn't help thinking that possibly this could be a lead. Maybe this was actually the neighborhood in which he had once lived. This or somewhere close by.

He looked at his watch. It was time to get back to the square and meet Adriana. It seemed a long way back to St. Mark's. He was bone-weary from all that walking.

But tomorrow, he decided, he'd do more of the same. He'd come back here, back to this *campo,* walk in widening circles around it, and see what he could see.

He arrived at the restaurant to find Adriana already there, waiting for him.

As they lingered over their coffee, shortly before two o'clock, St. Mark's Piazza became a strange sight. Every pigeon in Venice seemed to have converged on it. The vast expanse was covered with a living carpet, vibrating with fluttering wings, shimmering and iridescent with color. Thousands upon thousands of pigeons crowded together, pushing each other a little for enough space to stand, their glittering wings throwing off glints of green and slate and purple.

"What's all this?" he wanted to know.

"They're waiting to be fed," said Adriana.

"How often does that happen?"

"Twice a day. At nine in the morning and two in the afternoon."

102

Those who were walking in the Piazza did not venture to cross through this solid birdswarm, but instead kept to the arcades. David heard a distant chime from a church somewhere. He checked his watch. The church bell was a little early. It was three minutes to two.

Then, some deep memory stirred in David Drew. An old picture, projected from some other time. He knew exactly what was going to happen next. His eye was fixed on one of the arcades to the left of the Correr Museum.

He knew that a man would appear now, at any second. From under that particular arcade. He would be carrying two heavy pails, each of them covered . . .

The man appeared. He was carrying a covered red pail in each hand. He started to walk slowly through the living feathery carpet. The pigeons in front of him parted briefly. They let him through reluctantly and then quickly came together to box him in again. As he moved, the small puddle of space on which he walked moved with him, like his own shadow. The pigeons showed no signs of any excitement. They were passive, placid. They did not flutter their wings. They stopped competing for space. They were very patient, knowing what was coming, observing protocol.

"Watch what happens now," said Adriana. "I think you'll find it interesting."

David watched the ritual, fascinated. He already knew what would happen. He had seen it a long time ago. In a moment, the man would put down the pails. Then . . .

The pigeon man set down one of the pails. Then he shuffled on toward the center of the Piazza, and there he set down the other pail. Then he straightened and stood there waiting.

The pigeons watched with him.

It gave David an eerie feeling to sit there, knowing what would happen next. Even though he had never seen it before—that is, not in this life. It gave him a feeling of omnipotence, of a power nobody else had. For this moment, at least, he did not find it frightening. He found it exhilarating.

103

Now, the man and the pigeons would wait for the bells . . .

Almost on the heel of his thought, the clock on the Torre dell' Orologio began to strike. It struck two. But neither the man nor the pigeons moved. Five seconds passed. There was absolute silence. David was puzzled. Why did they wait? He had been sure that when the bells struck, they would . . .

Suddenly, there was a sharp report, almost like the boom of thunder, as thousands of pigeons lifted themselves up in unison, their wings beating. A fraction of a second later, the bells of the campanile began to erupt. Their deep-bellied, resonant tones deafened the Piazza.

"You see?" said Adriana. "The pigeons really know when lunch is ready. They even anticipate the bells a little, because they react to the sound of the clapper, as it starts to move."

Now the green and gray and purple horde, the entire winged army, hovered vulturelike a few feet in midair, waiting to dine. The pigeon man had vanished in their midst, as though smothered in a shroud of wings and feathers.

Finally, like those of a swimmer coming up for air, his head and arms and shoulders appeared through the fluttering sea. The flying horde thinned out quickly, and the Piazza again became covered with the living carpet. The pigeon man had emptied the pails of their corn, and now, his entire torso exposed at last, he headed for the sanctuary of the arcade from which he had first appeared. The entire square was a great sea of bobbing birds, crowding each other, raising and dipping their heads, pecking away for dear life at the kernels of corn spread on the pavement, knowing the supply was limited.

"A lot of people here hate the pigeons," said Adriana. "They foul up the monuments, they're nuisances in every other way. But, of course, they're a tourist attraction; Venice wouldn't be the same without them."

"Who arranges this feeding?"

"One of the insurance companies here. It's hired a man to feed the pigeons in this way for the last forty years."

"Funny," said David. "They didn't react to the other bells. Just to the campanile."

"Well," said Adriana. "You might call them Pavlov's pigeons. All they know is the ringing of the *campane* in the campanile, at nine in the morning and two in the afternoon. Those are the ones which represent feeding time. But in the spring of 1966, the entire pigeon population around San Marco here went crazy."

"Yes? Why?"

"Because it was then that Italy first went on daylight saving time. It was an awful day for them. When nine o'clock came—or what *they* thought was nine o'clock—they were all set to feed. But nothing happened. Nobody came with the corn. The Orologio bells struck only eight. And the campanile bells were an hour late, as far as the pigeon clocks were concerned."

"What did they do? Just wait around?"

"No. Most of them stayed a little while, then just gave up and flew away. When the man came to feed them an hour later, there were only a few around."

"How long did it take them to go on daylight saving time?"

"It took them days. A couple of weeks, I think. Then, they became even more confused when the country went back on standard time. Then they all came to the Piazza an *hour after* feeding time. The poor things had to unlearn what they had just learned."

He grinned. "You know, I'm lucky."

"Yes? Why?"

"It isn't every tourist who can have the advantage of a private guide. At absolutely no cost."

Adriana laughed. "Be careful what you say. I *may* send you a bill."

By this time, every bit of corn on the square had disappeared. Almost all of the pigeons had gone, except for a small flock in front of the Basilica. They were hungrily beaking up the kernels of corn thrown to them by tourists who had bought little paper bags of the grain for a hundred lire each.

He watched idly for a moment or two. Then his relaxed mood began to change. A nerve started to tingle somewhere. He had the distinct impression that somewhere, buried in Adriana's explanation of the pigeons, she had inadvertently revealed some fragment of information that was important to him. He had missed it cold, it had gone right by him, and yet he sensed it had been there. He couldn't put his finger on it. It was simply a *feeling* he had.

In his mind, he reviewed what she had just told him. But he came up with nothing. He became irritated with himself. Then he began to doubt that there had been anything else. It was, he decided, just some wishful thinking on his part. What could there possibly be in a flock of pigeons that could . . .

"Remember me, David?"

He came out of his reverie to see Adriana smiling at him.

"Oh." He was confused, apologetic. "I'm sorry."

"David, you're a very strange boy. One moment, you're very much here—and the next, you seem to be in some other world. Really, it's not very flattering. I began to think —well, that I was boring you."

He reached out and took her hand.

"Believe me, Adriana, you weren't."

"All that talk about the pigeons. I can't seem to forget that I'm a guide."

"I enjoyed it. I really did." He continued to hold her hand. He knew she was joking. Or half-joking. At least, he hoped so. He liked her. He wanted desperately not to offend her. He wanted to see her again. "Adriana, look. I've had something on my mind."

"I've noticed that before. It must be something important."

"It is."

"If you'd like to talk about it—well, I'm told I have a sympathetic ear."

106

For a moment, he was tempted. For a moment, he thought, why not? Then he decided against it. It was just too much to ask anyone to swallow. She would never believe him. She would think he was crazy. So would anybody else.

"I'm sure you have a sympathetic ear. It is also a very lovely ear. But it's something I can't talk about."

"Something personal."

"Put it that way." He looked at her anxiously. "I hope you don't mind . . ."

She laughed. "No, why should I? Sometimes, as they say, it helps to talk about it. But there are some things I would never discuss even with a friend—let alone a stranger." She rummaged in her purse for another cigarette. "But now, I must go. I have things to do this afternoon."

"Important things?"

"Very. I must do some marketing for my mother's birthday dinner. Of course, almost all the food has been bought, but there are always the last-minute things. And so, *signore,* I thank you for a lovely lunch."

"I wish you were free for dinner."

She looked at him gravely. The blue eyes suddenly made a decision.

"I wish I were, too."

"How about tomorrow night?"

She hesitated. "You're sure you want to?"

"I am very, very sure."

"All right, then." She laughed. "I should tell you I have an appointment with another man. Just to let you know I'm in demand. And I do get many telephone calls. Many offers. I honestly do. Do you believe that?"

"I do."

"But there's Giorgio. The boy I told you about."

"Oh, yes. The engineer. The one who's maybe, perhaps, and possibly."

She laughed. "Yes. He'll be back from Libya in a month. We're not engaged, but, well—I guess I feel attached. I've said no to a number of Venetian boys I know. For that reason. But of course, you're a—well, just a tourist. A very

107

nice one, and I enjoy your company, and besides you're—"

"Completely harmless?"

"Yes. Exactly that."

He grinned. "Maybe I'd better warn you. Don't count on it."

She laughed, and he called for the check. And as she rose to go, he said:

"Wish your mother a happy birthday for me."

"She'll appreciate that. Especially since she's never heard of you."

"Maybe you'll introduce me sometime."

"I might," she said. "But I don't think it would be a very good idea."

"No? Why not?"

"She's very old-fashioned. If I bring a man home, it's serious. She's got her heart set on Giorgio."

"That's nice. But have *you*?"

She made a face at him.

"It's none of your business."

He grinned. "No. I guess it isn't. See you tomorrow night, then."

Her smile was dazzling. "I'll look forward to it, *caro*."

The word of endearment fell naturally from her lips. She did not seem conscious that she had used it at all.

9

Late that afternoon, when he entered the lobby of his hotel, he noticed a small sign standing on the desk clerk's counter. It advertised the fact that Verdi's *La Traviata* was being performed at the Teatro La Fenice the following evening.

He was a long way from being an opera buff—he had been to only two or three operas in his life—but it struck him that it might be interesting to go. His guidebook said that an opera at La Fenice was something not to be missed, and he was sure that Adriana would enjoy it. He went to the concierge and asked him to book two tickets.

"It will be difficult," said the concierge. "It is an opening, very gala. But if you will wait a moment, I will try."

The concierge picked up the phone. After a short conversation, he made a few notes and hung up, smiling.

"You are very fortunate, Signore Drew. There has been a cancellation. Two seats. They will hold them for you at the box office."

David thanked him. Then he asked the concierge to phone in a message for Adriana Manzoni at CIT, about the new arrangements. There would be the theater first and, after that, supper.

He went up to his room, and just as he entered, his phone rang.

It was the hotel operator. "I have an overseas call for you, *signore*. From New York City. Please hold on."

There was a buzzing sound, then some crackling, then a distant, echoing exchange between the two operators. Finally, a voice came on, loud and clear. It belonged to John Boyce.

"That you, David?"

"Yes, sir."

"What are you doing in Venice, for Christ's sake? You're supposed to be in Iran."

"I know. But I just thought I'd stay over for a day or two." There was a hostile silence, and he added, lamely: "You know, just to see the place . . . "

"Look, Mister Drew. You're not on vacation. This is a business trip, and you're on company time. Now get your ass on a plane for Teheran right away. You can make connections at Rome or Milan."

"Mr. Boyce, I need a couple more days here."

"No way."

"It's important," David said desperately.

"Why?"

"For personal reasons."

"*What* personal reasons?"

"I—It's something I can't explain."

"What's with you, boy? I know it isn't the art and architecture of old Venice. You run into some broad you want to sack or something?"

"No. No, it isn't that. I just can't explain."

"Okay. Don't try. Let *me* explain something to *you.* I don't know what your problem is, and I couldn't care less. Now, I've told you what you have to do. Don't argue with me, just *do* it. Get your ass on that damned plane, Drew. I expect you to be in Teheran by tomorrow, the latest."

Before David could say anything else, Boyce hung up.

He sat there awhile, thinking about it. It was a good job, and now it was in jeopardy. But there were others.

And he knew he couldn't possibly leave Venice. Not now. Not yet.

Later, in the pure-awareness stage of his meditation, he saw the same human faces.

Nothing had changed. Nothing new had been added, nothing subtracted. Again, they smiled at him or looked sad, or tense, all trying to tell him something.

The mantra drifted in again and began its regular beat, obliterating the PA level.

Finally, the mantra ended. He sat quietly for a while, eyes closed, almost asleep, very relaxed. His blood pressure came back to normal, as did his heartbeat.

Then he opened his eyes.

The first thing he saw was a pigeon on his windowsill. It stood there, preening itself, flapping its wings just a little, balancing itself on the sill.

It was unaware of his presence, or it did not care. He watched the pigeon for a while. He thought of the mass of pigeons being fed on the square, and again the feeling came back to haunt him. It was something Adriana had said. Something about those damned pigeons or the pigeon man that had caught his attention for a fraction of a second and then slipped by him. Something he knew was important. But no matter how hard he tried to reach back, he couldn't find it. Try as he might, it continued to elude him.

But he knew that something had been there, *something.*

Adriana had told him that the pigeons were fed twice a day. At nine in the morning and at two in the afternoon.

111

He decided to be on St. Mark's bright and early tomorrow morning and watch the whole pigeon-feeding ritual again.

Maybe it would jar him into remembering.

At eight-thirty, David Drew sat at Quadri's and ordered a roll and coffee for breakfast.

The square was already alive with people. Tourists were taking pictures of the cathedral and the Doges' Palace. Sightseers were already perched on the balcony of the church, lined up at the rail, looking like birds. A group of nuns in white habits and white stockings with black hoods and black shoes, passed in front of David. They carried black coats, and they were in high spirits, giggling and laughing about something, having a marvelous time. He heard snatches of their conversation. They had been given the day off, and they were going on a tour to Murano and Torcello. The vendors of *gelati*, postcards, guidebooks, and jeweled gondolas, as well as other souvenirs, were setting up their mobile sales booths under the arcades. The usual blue-smocked porters rolled the luggage of the usual newcomers across the square, heading for the various hotels.

Gradually, the square itself emptied as the pigeons took over.

Finally, the living carpet again covered the entire square. Cooing and fluttering their wings just a little, waiting for dinner, as before.

David watched for the pigeon man.

He appeared from the usual arcade, carrying the two pails. The pigeons in front of him parted to let him through. He set down one pail and then the other. Then he stood quietly, along with the pigeons, waiting for the *campane* in the campanile to ring . . .

The moment the bells boomed, it came to David, it hit him suddenly.

Something Adriana had said.

Jesus, it had been right there, in front of his nose. How could he have missed it?

112

She had said a man had been feeding pigeons in this way for forty years. And David had known about the pigeon man even before he had seen him. He had known the man would appear from a certain arcade, and that he would be carrying two pails . . .

But he, David, couldn't have known of the existence of this man, unless it was within the experience of his former self. In other words, the man he used to be in his previous life had been around to *see* this ritual. Otherwise, he, David Drew, the successor to this unknown Venetian, would have no memory of the pigeon man.

In short, whoever he had been in his former life had to have been alive sometime in the last forty years.

The thought staggered David. It was possible that his old self had sat in this very chair at Quadri's, at this very table, and watched this same ritual. People were still alive, very much alive, who had known him in his previous life. That gray-haired, well-dressed Venetian businessman threading his way among the tables, carrying a briefcase. The elderly tour guide, leading a group along under the arcades. The shopkeeper, lowering the bars of his shop across the way, ready to open for the day. The grizzled porter, carrying two heavy bags, trying to decide whether to plow his way across the square through the feeding pigeons, then deciding against it. The priest, with snow-white hair, wearing black habit and white collar, walking purposefully on some sacred business.

"Can I bring you something else, *signore?*"

David came out of his trance to look up and see the face of the waiter above him. The man was about sixty, with a patient and weary look, a little sad in the eyes. David wondered whether they had met before, a long time ago. He wanted to ask the waiter, *Did you know me once, did you know who I was, did I come to this cafe a long time ago and order breakfast and watch the pigeons, just as I am doing now?*

But, of course, he said nothing. He answered the waiter's

question by shaking his head, and the man shuffled off. Shivers ran up and down his spine. It was weird, frightening just to think of it. This man has probably seen me before. In some other life.

He sat there for a long time.

When he finally focused his attention on the square again, everything was normal. The mass of pigeons had finished their meal and gone. The square was again filled with pedestrians, peddlers, poodles, photographers, and tourists who stared at the monuments and at each other.

Directly in front of him, a blind woman stood, her hand outstretched. She was white-haired, elderly, a Venetian woman. A friend stood next to her, putting corn in her hand. A few pigeons, still unsatisfied, loitered on the square. They flew up and took the corn from the blind woman's hand. The look on her face was blissful, ecstatic . . .

David wondered whether she had been able to see a long time ago and whether *she* had known his predecessor . . .

He decided that it was foolish to speculate. You could only drive yourself crazy doing that. He called for his check, paid it, and left.

The performance of *La Traviata* at the Teatro La Fenice was indeed an occasion, and, as the concierge had pointed out, a gala.

This season, the Teatro was honoring Giuseppe Verdi by presenting his operas. It was Verdi who had been commissioned by the Teatro La Fenice to write *Rigoletto,* and the opera had opened at the theater in March of 1851. The next opera Verdi had written for the Teatro was *La Traviata,* and Verdi had come to Venice to cast the opera himself and supervise the production.

When David and Adriana came up the Calle della Veste and into the *campo,* they saw some of the prominent citizens of Venice, dressed in evening clothes, arriving by gondola; ushers wearing wigs and uniforms in gold waited to escort them inside. The Campo San Fantin itself was crowded with people, formally dressed for the occasion, smoking and chatting.

"I *am* impressed," said David. He looked at the crowd and grinned. "If I'd known, I would have brought my tuxedo."

"You look fine, just the way you are."

"I didn't expect it to be so formal."

"Well, this is what you call a true gala. In a way, the Venetians are apologizing to Verdi tonight."

"Yes? For what?"

"Well, the opening night of *La Traviata* here at the Teatro was a total disaster. Maybe the worst that ever happened in the history of opera. Verdi had miscast it dreadfully. You remember what happens in the third act?"

"Frankly, no. I'm pretty stupid when it comes to opera. And I've never seen this one."

"Well, in the third act of *La Traviata*, the doctor tells Violetta that she is about to die of consumption and has only a few hours to live. The prima donna, a lady named Fanny Salvini-Donatelli, was very large and very bosomy— the kind of lady we here in Italy call *troppo prosperosa*. Anyway, the whole idea of this huge woman withering away to skin and bones in just a few hours just destroyed the Venetians. They started to laugh and couldn't stop laughing. Verdi, of course, was humiliated. Later, the Venetians felt a great deal of remorse for being so rude to the genius. The production was changed, came back to Venice, and was shown, not here, but at the Teatro San Benedetto. It was a huge success. In this way, they apologized to Verdi and are still, I think, doing it."

They entered the Teatro. David saw that it was a jewel-box of a theater. And everything in it seemed familiar, everything rang a distant bell. The gilt-and-pink plush of the decor, cherubs flying about on the ceiling, the many reception rooms, the boxes, each decorated with red carnations. David reflected on his previous Self, the man he now had begun to think of as the Venetian. He had attended the

115

Teatro in his time, or it would not have seemed familiar to David. It was a guess, but only a guess, that he had probably been a man of some means. He assumed that gondoliers and porters did not normally attend openings like this at the Teatro, but he couldn't be sure, because of the Italian love of opera. Perhaps they did come.

David had just settled in his velvet armchair when he saw them.

The couple sitting in a box across the auditorium and to the right.

Their faces were familiar to him, because he had seen them before, in his meditation.

The lady with the clear olive skin and the dark eyes. The straight, aristocratic nose, the soft red mouth. She was older now. Older than the image he had seen in his meditation. But he recognized her immediately. There was a streak of gray running through her black hair, and she seemed fuller in body, more rounded out. Her evening gown was cut low, revealing the rounded curves of her full breasts. She glittered with diamonds. She was still a beauty, a rare beauty, and many heads in the theater turned to stare at her in appreciation.

The man with her was the older man whose image he had seen. The powerful-looking, thickset man with the beetling eyebrows and hard eyes. He, too, was older now; his black hair had turned iron gray. David guessed that he was somewhere in his late fifties.

He sat frozen, in shock, watching the couple.

They seemed to be arguing about something. It was all in pantomime; he could not, of course, hear what they were saying. But the man was speaking to her about something, angrily. She simply sat there, staring out at the audience and shaking her head stubbornly to whatever it was he was saying or wanted. He continued to speak, leaning his head close to her. She tilted her head away from him.

Finally, David heard himself say to Adriana:

"Who are they?" He pointed to the box. "That couple .."

116

"Oh. That's the Contessa Favretto. Bianca Favretto. And the man with her is Teodoro Borsato, her second husband." Adriana paused for a moment, noting the rapt expression on David's face. "Beautiful, isn't she?"

"Yes," he said. "Yes."

"Interesting that she's here tonight. She's rarely seen in public anymore."

"No?" he said. "Why not?"

At this moment, the lights went down, and the chatter died to silence, and when David tried to press his question again, Adriana hissed "Shhhh," and then the curtain went up.

David wasn't interested in what was happening on the stage. He strained his eyes, trying to make out the two in the box. But it was dark in the theater; another couple had come in at the last moment, in the box just in front of the one in which *his* couple was sitting, and cut off his line of vision completely.

He could hardly sit still. He squirmed impatiently, waiting for intermission. He wanted to get out, get a close look at the *contessa*, in the foyer or one of the reception rooms. He was much more interested in her than in the man with her. What was his name? Teodoro Borsato.

Her face haunted him. It filled him with some deep emotion. It wasn't just her beauty, her elegance. It was something more than that.

The gooseflesh popped out all over his skin. He felt hot, as though running a fever. And then, just as quickly, chilled.

And he thought exultantly: *This is a breakthrough. Now, we're getting somewhere.*

The first act of the opera seemed interminable. It seemed to David Drew that it ran for hours and hours. He wanted to shout to the colorfully costumed singers on the stage to get on with it, rush it, get it over with.

Finally, the act was over, and the lights went on.

David craned his neck to look at the box. But it was empty.

He hurried out into the foyer with Adriana. He looked

117

everywhere for the *contessa* and her escort. But he could not find them.

Apparently, they had left the theater, even before the end of the first act.

Later, Adriana and he had supper at a restaurant near the Ponte delle Ostreghe, the Bridge of the Oysters.

He was curious why Adriana referred to the *contessa* as Favretto, when her married name now was Borsato.

"Oh," she said. "Her first husband, now dead, was Count Vittorio Favretto. And everybody in Venice still calls her Contessa Favretto. They're simply used to thinking of her in that way, rather than as plain Signora Borsato. You see, she is what you call a personality, a celebrity, here in Venice, and of course, as the *contessa*, she was very much in the news. It is like your Elizabeth Taylor. She had been married to many husbands, yes?"

"Yes."

"But nobody ever called her by her married name. They still know her as Elizabeth Taylor. It is the same with Contessa Favretto. You see?"

He nodded. He asked Adriana to tell him more about the *contessa*.

"Why are you so interested, *caro?*"

"You said she had been in the news . . . "

"Ah," said Adriana, smiling. "But this is not the only reason you are curious. It is more than that, eh?"

"Well," he said, lamely. "It's just that she's so . . . "

"Beautiful?"

"Yes."

"So. You've already fallen in love with her." He started to say something, and she laughed. "It's nothing to be embarrassed about, *caro*. Join the crowd. A lot of men in Venice are in love with Bianca Favretto. Without ever really meeting her." Then, with a touch of small malice. "Oh, she is a real heartbreaker, all right. A lot of women here would like to scratch her eyes out."

118

"Seriously, I'd like to know more about her."

"Well, then, I'll have to play guide for a little while. The Favrettos are old Venetian nobility. The family goes all the way back to the thirteenth century. A Favretto was a member of the Grand Council and a *procurator* to the doge, Enrico Dandolo. The doges were mostly rather boring as fas as charisma goes, but Dandolo had a certain amount. He was blind, but he led the Venetian forces to the sack of Constantinople, and this same Favretto—Antonio, I think his name was—was also one of the doge's generals. As for the *contessa*, she comes from a noble family herself—the Gattis."

"When did Count Favretto die?"

"About twenty-five years ago. He was only in his middle twenties. Actually, he was declared legally dead. The circumstances were very strange."

"Yes?"

"It was quite a story here in Venice. Of course, it was before my time. But people still talk about it, and every once in a while, the newspapers in Milan or *Il Gazzettino*, here, will run a rehash of it. It had certain sensational aspects, I suppose."

"In what way?"

"The fact is, nobody really knows whether Count Favretto actually died or not."

He stared at her. "I don't understand."

"They never discovered the body. One evening the count said goodnight to his wife and walked out of the palazzo. He had a date to meet his lawyer and old friend, Teodoro Borsato, on the Piazza, to talk some business. The man she's married to now. Anyway, the count dismissed the family gondolier—the Favrettos were one of the few families who still employed one at the time—and said he would walk. Anyway, he simply walked out of the palazzo that evening and disappeared. So, in fact, nobody is absolutely sure whether or not he actually died. He might still be alive, elsewhere in the world, for all anybody knows. That's why

119

the newspapers are still intrigued by the case. It's something like the one in the United States I used to read about—who was it? That judge . . . "

"Judge Crater."

"Ah, yes. That's the one. Anyway, after a time, of course, Count Favretto was declared legally dead. And his widow, after a time of mourning, finally married Borsato." She hesitated. "But there are rumors."

"What kind of rumors?"

"Well, it's just gossip, really. But there's talk that there's trouble in the Palazzo Favretto. They're not getting along— their marriage is more or less on a formal basis. They say that Borsato is a womanizer and has had a series of mistresses. The *contessa* hardly ever goes out in public, and they say she has had many lovers." Adriana laughed. "But again, all this is just talk. You must understand that gossip is the staff of life for upper-class Venetians; they'd be terribly bored without it. You can believe all of it or not a word of it, just as you choose." She looked at him and then said tartly:

"There. That's about all I know. Would you say I sang for my supper?"

"You did indeed."

"And I sang very well?"

"Very well indeed."

"Then, *caro*, would you be good enough to order some more wine?"

After that, he took Adriana home.

She had a small, neat apartment just off the Campo San Polo, not far from the Rialto Bridge. She invited him in for a drink.

Finally, he took her in his arms, and she pressed her body against his, and her hands caressed the back of his neck, and her kiss was warm and full and asked for more.

He tried to respond, he wanted to respond, but somehow he could not. He was limp against the demanding pressure of her soft body. She had failed to arouse him. She knew it, she knew his heart wasn't in it, and she drew back and said:

"*Buona sera,* David."

"Look," he said. "Adriana, I . . . "

"It's all right. You have other things on your mind. It doesn't matter, it's not important. We've both had a long day, and we're tired. *Buona sera, caro.*"

10

THE next morning, when David reached the PA level in his morning meditation, two faces were missing. That of the Contessa Favretto and her husband, Teodoro Borsato.

The faces had been young, the images reflecting the way they had looked at perhaps half their present age. It was clear to David now that once he saw the actual images in real life, they would disappear in his TM. As though he had no need of them anymore. The other faces remained as they were.

But something new had been added.

David could not quite identify it. It seemed to be some kind of object, rather than a face. It was blurred, indistinct. He had the vague impression that it was curved in shape, small in size, and was some kind of sculpture. But he could not be sure.

After his meditation, he went downstairs and had breakfast at one of the cafes facing the lagoon.

Again, he thought of the sequence of events that had brought him here. The scenario. The coincidences that were more than coincidences. He sees a sign in the hotel lobby. It advertises an opera at the Teatro La Fenice. He goes there. He sees the shadow images turn into real people, people of flesh and blood, living now. Point counterpoint. Run that through the biggest computer they make at Data-fax and punch it out. What kind of a "read" do you get? The same as before.

No Answer. Zip. The question is not viable.

Except this. It was no coincidence. No way. It had all been plotted beforehand. It was all part of some large and bizarre drama. Author unknown. And he, David Drew, was only a pawn. He was being moved about on this stage like some actor. He was helpless, really, to do anything about it. Whatever happened next would happen. He knew there would be a next step. And a next. And a next. To some end. But to what end he did not know. He was no longer agitated about what was happening to him. On the contrary. He no longer felt any responsibility. He was now able to accept everything as it came. He awaited the next complication with a certain curiosity.

He thought about the *contessa*. Her beauty haunted him. It had haunted him when he had seen her as one of his TM images, as the young girl. And it did now, as he saw her in real life—older, to be sure, but still incredibly beautiful. Bianca Favretto. Bianca. The name had a certain ring to it, it set off small bells, it excited him. He spoke it aloud and listened to it fall from his lips. When he did, it stirred some fragment of memory; some tendril quivered.

Bianca Favretto and Teodoro Borsato.

They were all part of the mosaic. In time, they would both fall into place. Already, on the basis of what he now knew, he began to suspect, to conjecture . . .

But, of course, it was foolish, there was no way of telling, absolutely no way, it was all pure speculation . . .

First things first.

He wanted to know more about the Favrettos, much more.

A good place to start, he decided, was to go out and take a look at the Palazzo Favretto. He was about to go back into the hotel and ask the concierge for directions, when he remembered something. Something Adriana had told him. The family, at the time of the disappearance, had had a personal gondolier. Twenty-five years was a long time. But it was possible that the man might still be around, still be working at his trade. And if so, he could be a valuable source of information.

David walked to the gondola station on the lagoon. One of the gondoliers detached himself from the group and came forward. Apparently it was his turn to pick up a passenger.

"*La gondola, signore?*"

David shook his head. "What I want is some information."

"*Si?*"

"Do you know the gondolier who works for the Favretto family?"

The man nodded. "I know him. But he was discharged from the Favretto service a long time ago. Many years ago."

"What is his name?"

"The man you want, *signore,* is Bruno Savoldo."

"He still works as a gondolier?"

The man shrugged. "*Si.* Like all of us."

"Where can I find him?"

"His station is the Bacino Orseolo. You will find him there."

The gondolier told him how to reach the *bacino.* David thanked him, thrust some lire into his hand, and walked away.

It was no more than five minutes to the *bacino,* across the square and up a short street. The big basin, which was a kind of watery parking lot, was filled with black gondolas, bobbing slightly and gently bumping each other because of the backwash currents slapping up through the small waterways that connected the *bacino* to the Grand Canal itself.

Business was slow this morning, or perhaps it was too early for it to begin. But the *fondamenta* was lined with gondoliers, smoking and chattering. A few others slept in the bottoms of their boats. Still others lounged in their armchairs or were busy polishing the two little brass sea-horses on either side of the seats, or the pronged silver beak on the bow, the six-notched *ferro*.

As he approached, some of the men shouted at him, inviting him into their gondolas. But David's eyes swept the group, and finally he saw him.

Bruno Savoldo.

He was sitting in his gondola, lolling back indolently in the armchair and reading a copy of *Il Gazzettino*. He looked considerably older than the young face David had seen in his meditation, but he recognized the man immediately. There was the same peasant face, the hair now gray. The same hooked nose, the same large wart on the right side of his chin.

David shook his head at the hawking gondoliers and went through the motions of asking for the man he wanted.

"I am looking for Bruno Savoldo."

One of the gondoliers turned and yelled at Savoldo.

"Bruno. There is someone here who asks for you, personally."

Bruno Savoldo put down his newspaper, left his gondola, and came up to David. Like the others, he wore flared trousers, the traditional striped blue and white jersey, and the red-banded straw hat. Then, politely:

"*Si, signore?*"

"I'm interested in seeing the Palazzo Favretto. And I'm told you used to be the family gondolier."

"*Si, signore.* Of course, that was many years ago."

"If you're not busy . . . "

"Not at all," said Savoldo. "At your service, *signore*. At your service." He waved toward his gondola. "Please."

David took a seat in the red velvet armchair, and Savoldo shoved the gondola away from the edge of the *fondamenta* with a thrust of his oar.

"You are an American, *signore?*"

125

"Yes."

"But not an Italian."

"No."

"You speak a good Italian. A very good Italian."

"Thank you."

"If you ask to see the palazzo, then you must be interested in the Favretto case."

"Yes. I am."

"Where did you hear about it, *signore?*"

"I read about it in the newspapers."

"The American newspapers?"

"Yes," lied David.

"I'm not surprised. It's a very famous case, *signore*. Very. They keep printing it again, from time to time. People like yourself come up and ask for me all the time. Of course, nobody knows more about the Favrettos than I." Savoldo laughed. "I myself have become famous in a small way. The fact is, I was one of the last to see him before he disappeared."

They headed out toward the Grand Canal through a maze of smaller waterways. David found it interesting moving through the web of narrow canals, behind the palaces and the tall houses with their little Moorish windows and arches, their bases stained with green scum at the waterline. Somehow the city seemed more Oriental here, and much more quiet. Every sound seemed magnified—the steps of a lone pedestrian on the stone of an adjoining *calle,* the slap and swish of Savoldo's oar as he expertly maneuvered the gondola. Now and then, when he came to a blind corner around some building, he called out the traditional "*Oy*" to warn any other invisible gondola that might be coming around the same corner on a collision course.

Bruno Savoldo proved to be friendly and talkative. He went into the classic complaint of the gondoliers in Venice. The price of a new gondola was too exorbitant to think about. The gondolier was being squeezed out by the powerboats. Once, there had been ten thousand gondolas in

Venice. Now, there were only four hundred and fifty. All the Savoldos, the men in his family, had been gondoliers for almost two hundred years. But now none of them cared about continuing the tradition. They did not want to serve an apprenticeship of at least ten years before they got their license. They all took jobs in factories in Mestre.

"I really can't blame them, *signore*. You have to work like a dog and break your back, in order not to starve these days. Today, the Venetians don't use gondolas. Too expensive, they say. Or gondolas are for the tourists. So they take a damned *vaporetto* or *motoscafa*. And the tourists usually take only one gondola ride. Shortly after they arrive, or just before they leave." He paused for a moment to yell another warning "*Oy*" as he rounded the corner of another palazzo. "It's no wonder the gondoliers here are Communist to a man. What we need here is some sort of subsidy from the city. A guarantee of so many lire a week, no matter how bad business is. Otherwise, in a few years there will not be a gondolier left. And what will Venice be without the gondola? Eh, *signore?* I ask you that. You know the answer. Nothing. This boat you sit in now is the symbol of this city. Its heart and soul, *signore*."

They came out onto the Grand Canal. David had meant to ask Savoldo a few questions about the Favrettos, but he refrained for the time being. In the Grand Canal, the gondolier had his hands full. Cabin cruisers and power boats crossed and crisscrossed in front of him, whipping up waves and causing the gondola to pitch and toss. Zooming speedboats and the slower *motoscafi*, going in opposite directions, boxed them in and buffeted them with their wakes, while Savoldo bent his back to keep on keel. He shouted angry epithets, *criminali, assassini*. The plight of the gondolier was *disgraziati*. The speed limit, as he pointed out to David, for a gondola coming out of a *rio* onto the Grand Canal was supposed to be eight kilometers an hour. You could read it right there, on that red sign. But everybody ignored it. The damned powerboats had made a racetrack of the

127

lagoon and the canal. The gondolas take a terrible beating from their wakes. A man is lucky if he can keep one together for ten years.

And so on.

Finally, they left the Grand Canal and entered a quiet *rio*. David felt a stirring within him. This particular little canal looked familiar. It almost *smelled* familiar to him. He thought again of the *contessa* and the images he had seen in his TM, and he had the feeling that he was getting close now, very close. And he said to Savoldo:

"How long did you work for the Favrettos?"

"Well, *signore,* I went into their service when I was twenty-one. I inherited the job, you might say, from my father before me. I worked for the count ten years in all."

"Until he disappeared?"

No. Actually, I continued to work for the *contessa* for five years after he was gone. Then she married the family lawyer, Teodoro Borsato." Savoldo's voice turned bitter. "One of the first things he did was to tell me I was no longer needed. He forced me out after ten years of faithful service. The *contessa* tried to keep me on. But it was no use. Borsato simply took charge. He is a powerful man, a bull of a man, you might say, and he likes his own way. So, he forced me out on the world. I had to buy my own gondola and go into business for myself."

"I take it you don't like Borsato."

David could not see Savoldo, since he was at the oar behind him, but he could hear the anger in the gondolier's voice. "Teodoro Borsato is no good. An arrogant man, a *bastardo.* He could not wait to have the count pronounced officially dead. He married the *contessa* for her money, nothing more. Now, he spends her money, gambles it at the casino, and cheats on her with other women. Everybody in Venice knows he is a womanizer. Not that this is a crime, but he doesn't even have the delicacy to be discreet. In this way, he insults her. Teodoro Borsato. *Figlio di puttana!*"

David turned to see Savoldo just as he spat in the canal. The gondolier's face was livid in its anger.

"What about the *contessa?*"

"Eh? What about her, *signore?*"

"I mean, what kind of woman is she?"

"She is one of the most beautiful women in Venice. Perhaps in all of Italy. She was a beautiful woman when I worked for her, years ago, and she hasn't aged or changed much, as far as I can see. A gentle and sweet and very generous woman, *signore*. Herself from a noble family, the Gattis, very rich and very powerful. But Borsato treats her like dirt."

"I am told she rarely appears in public."

"This is true."

"Do you have any idea why?"

"It may be that she is still in mourning."

"For Count Favretto? But he died years ago . . ."

"Twenty-five years ago, *signore*. In September of 1954, to be exact. But you don't understand. About the way the *contessa* felt about Vittorio Favretto. She worshipped him. He was like a god to her. When he was gone, she was never the same again."

"Then he was quite a man."

"Not just a man. A great man. As noble as his name, generous, and madly in love with the *contessa*. And also—very rich. A handsome man, *signore*. Every woman in Venice had her eye on him, dreamed of sleeping in his bed, hated the *contessa*, jealous with envy if you follow me, *signore* . . ."

There was a pause. They were gliding up a narrow canal now, in complete silence, except for the dip and swish of Savoldo's oar. Finally David turned in his seat and looked at the gondolier.

"What do you think happened to him?"

Savoldo let the gondola coast a moment, shrugged, and then bent to his oar again.

"Who knows? All I can tell you is what happened that evening. He was on his way to San Marco to meet his friend Borsato. They were to have a drink and talk business. He told me he would not go by gondola, that he preferred to walk, and told me to take the evening off. He said goodnight

129

to the *contessa* and started to walk toward San Marco and—
that's it. He never got there. That's all I know."

"Just disappeared, then. No trace of a body, nothing."

"In a city like Venice, it is easy to disappear," said Savoldo.
"One can vanish forever without ever leaving this place.
With so many canals, you understand, it is easy to hide a
body. This has been a city of missing persons from the time
of the doges until now. From the Palazzo Favretto to San
Marco, there are many routes. The count could have taken
any one of them. If these canals could speak, *signore,* they
could tell some foul stories."

"Then you think he was murdered?"

"I think nothing," said the gondolier. "I simply do not
know."

They glided further into the maze. From a window opening onto a rococo balcony of a palazzo, someone began
plucking at the strings of a guitar. A little girl in a second-
story window lowered a basket on a cord, so that her mother
could fill it with provisions, and then pulled it up. They
passed under lines of washing stretched across the canal from
window to window. An old woman sat in an alcove under a
statue of the Virgin, patching a red nightgown. An old man
sat dangling his legs over the canal's edge and eating a huge
bunch of grapes. He waved to Savoldo and threw them both
a rheumy, toothless smile.

David watched all this as though in a dream. It was all
like some Renaissance painting. It all seemed unreal, in some
other time, part of some other world. The slight rocking
motion of the gondola lulled him into a kind of somnolence.
He was alerted again by Savoldo's voice.

"Here we are, *signore.* The Palazzo Favretto."

It was classic in its beauty. It had an elaborate facade,
handsome carved chimneys, sculptured columns, and exquisitely designed Gothic windows, typical of the fifteenth
century.

At the moment, the sun was dappling the canal with its
rays, and it threw up reflections of light that danced and
shimmered, running along the stonework and lighting up the

130

scrollwork, illuminating the dark corners of the loggias. To David, the whole effect was incandescent, luminous; the Palazzo Favretto seemed to almost float, an opulent and exotic fantasy.

The medallion hanging from the chain around his neck seemed suddenly hot, it seemed to burn against his chest.

There were two large heavy doors providing entry into the palazzo.

On each was embedded a great round disc of bronze, bearing the family crest.

It was a great maned lion, standing on its hind legs. And in each paw it held a scroll.

Later, back in his room, he began his meditation.

When he entered the PA stage, the young face of the gondolier, Bruno Savoldo, was gone. Again, he had met the flesh-and-blood version, and, as in the case of the *contessa* and her husband, the image, once seen in real life, vanished.

Now, the only faces left were those of an infant child and of the handsome young man with the black mustache.

Aside from these, the same strange object appeared again. It was still blurred, but a little less fuzzy than before. There was the same curved body, but now it seemed to curl more and thrust farther forward, and on the end of it there was a mass or lump that vaguely had the shape of some kind of head. Across this was a strange wavy, or dappled, effect.

The mantra crept in again and became stronger and stronger, louder and louder. Finally, it shut off, and he sat there, eyes closed, resting.

His fingers strayed to his chest and caressed the medallion.

Now, he knew that it, too, was part of the tapestry, the mysterious sequence of events that had brought him here. Out of eight million people, more or less, in the city of New York, *he* had walked past this particular shop window and seen this particular medallion, felt a craving to own it, and, against all logic, bought it. He knew it was no coincidence, it hadn't just happened.

Again, it had been planned.

He thought of the Palazzo Favretto. He had sat there in Savoldo's gondola for a long time, staring at it. It evoked in him a deep stirring of emotion, a poignant sadness. He knew this place, he had known it before. He had a picture of the inside. He wanted desperately to get in somehow, to see the interior, to affirm the image of it he already had in some deep corner of his mind.

He knew he would have to find some way. He had had a tremendous desire to step off the gondola onto the *fondamenta,* bang the knocker on the door, and ask to be admitted. He knew there would be this great *piano nobile,* and in the rear of the palace a lovely garden, with a fountain in the center, and a group of laughing little satyrs, sculpted in marble . . .

There was a knock on the door. He rose and opened it. It was a man from the hotel.

"Cable for you, Signore Drew."

"Grazie."

He tipped the man, shut the door, and ripped open the envelope.

The cable was from New York and signed by John Boyce. It was terse and to the point.

"You're fired."

Later, he sat at a table at Florian's, waiting for Adriana Manzoni to appear.

After receiving the cable, he had felt somewhat bereft, and he had called the travel agency on the off-chance that Adriana might be in. He now knew almost the exact time that she finished her afternoon tour, and he knew that she usually stopped in at the office for a few minutes to turn in her vouchers. He guessed right on the time and caught her just as she was coming in. She told him she could not spend the evening with him—she had other plans—but would be glad to join him on the square for a drink.

Waiting there now, David Drew felt a little numb.

There was the same evening parade on the square, the

same pedestrians, poodles, pigeons, peddlers, and photographers. Across the square, in front of Quadri's, the musicians were in fine fettle, the conductor more frenetic than ever. The band seemed hung up on old favorites tonight. Hoary old favorites. It played "Night and Day," "Hungarian Rhapsody," "I've Got You Under My Skin," and "O Sole Mio."

All this registered on David Drew's eyes and ears but only in a surface way. This evening, he was preoccupied with other things.

He had liked his job at Datafax, and he knew he had had a fine future there. Now, he had deliberately blown it. Not that he was particularly worried. He could always get another job, and he had a few thousand in the bank to tide him over until he did. He knew he would be staying in Venice, he *had* to stay, until he played out the string, until this weird scenario came to an end. He was committed, and there was no way he could do otherwise. He did not know how long it would take or what would be involved. But things were getting a little tight, he was running low on traveler's checks. Soon he would have to change to a less expensive hotel and cable his bank in New York for more money.

Again, he began to wonder, why has all this happened to *me?*

Of course, he was a believer now. He knew, now, that the soul of a human being was eternal, that it traveled through the ages, finding a home in one body, then, after that body turned to dust, seeking a new home in another. The reincarnationists gave this some divine purpose, said that it was ordained, and that, pursuing the karmic idea, it led to ultimate perfection, to nirvana, where finally, the soul would travel no more. You were responsible for what you did in this life. For good or evil, you paid your dues in the next life.

He still could not imagine why all this had happened to him. Out of billions of people in this world, why him? Was he supposed to give some message to the world? Had he

133

been selected to sell reincarnation, been tapped by some Divine Hand to preach it to the world? If so, there was no way he could ever make them believe it, no way he could prove it.

It boggled his mind just to think about all this.

He felt a little giddy, unreal. For all he knew, this great square might be an illusion, and all the people on it, and the musicians across the way. All this might be some wild dream, some gigantic fantasy. He knew he ought to stop that goddamn TM. Return to reality, whatever that was. Otherwise, he could go over the edge, lose control entirely.

But he knew he could not; he was committed.

"*Buona sera, David.*"

He looked up to see Adriana smiling at him. He had never even seen her approach. She sat down, and when the waiter came, she ordered a vermouth cassis. He ached, at this moment, to tell her about it. To blurt the whole thing out. But he restrained himself, for obvious reasons. Still, he was grateful for her presence now. It lifted his spirits, took his mind off the heavy stuff.

"I'm sorry you're busy later."

"I am, too. But, do you realize, we've spent a lot of time together lately? I mean, for strangers."

"I don't feel like a stranger. And I'll miss you tonight."

"*Caro,* there are other attractions in Venice."

"Not like you."

She laughed. "You know, you sound like a born Italian now."

"I do? Why?"

"An Italian boy knows how to flatter a girl. You know, pay her compliments. You're doing very well . . . "

"Okay. Maybe it's un-American. But I mean it."

"You're sweet, *caro.* And I think you do." Then, changing the subject quickly, she said: "What did you do today?"

He told her about his gondola trip to the Palazzo Favretto, and she looked at him curiously.

"Tell me something, David."

134

"Yes?"

"Why are you so interested in the Favrettos?"

"I don't know. The whole story about the count disappearing . . . "

"It isn't really that, is it?"

"What do you mean?"

She laughed. "*Caro*, it's so obvious. It's the *contessa* you're interested in, yes?" He started to protest, but she said: "Really, I don't blame you. She is beautiful. A woman with, how do you say it—mystique? But, of course, she's married, and old enough to be your mother, and she has nothing to do with tourists." Then: "Oh, I'm sorry. I'm being a cat now. No, that is not the word. Catty." She raised her hands, pointed her fingers at him. "See? I have sharp claws."

He took her hands in his.

"Adriana, what about tomorrow?"

"Tomorrow? Oh no. Tomorrow's Saturday. I am very, very busy. All day, and in the evening." She saw his look of disappointment. "But, if you wish, you can take me to the beach on Sunday."

"The beach?"

"The Lido. It has been very hot for early September, and I am taking the whole day off, and if you wish . . . "

"I do," he said. "I do. Very much. But that still leaves me tomorrow."

She thought a moment, then said:

"I *could* make a suggestion."

"Yes?"

"You've already seen the outside of the family palazzo. How would you like to see what it's like inside?"

He stared at her. Then, trying to sound casual: "Are you saying that can be arranged?"

"Yes."

"How?"

"Well, we've got this special tour at the office. It's scheduled for only one week, so you're in luck. It's called the Palazzo, Villa and Garden Tour. It lasts all day, it's by gondola, and you'll be charged double the usual fee, because it's for charity. You see, it's sponsored by a number of noble families here in Venice, and the proceeds go to a local orphanage. The Contessa Favretto is interested in this particular charity, and her palazzo is one of those included on the tour. It's really beautiful. One of the showplaces of Venice. Perfect fifteenth century."

He tried to keep his voice calm. "What time does this tour begin?"

"It starts at ten o'clock tomorrow morning. But be at the office at nine-thirty. It's a very popular tour, almost always fully booked. I'll call in tonight and make a reservation for you. That is, of course, if you want to go."

He told her he did, again trying to sound casual about it. Yes, he really would be interested, he'd appreciate her making this reservation, and finally she said *"Ciao"* and left.

After that, he sat there awhile, drinking his beer, trying to still the excitement welling up in him, and thinking again how precisely everything seemed to be arranged beforehand; the doors all seemed to open conveniently for him, whenever needed, one after the other, gradually filling in the missing pieces of the mosaic, bringing him closer and closer to—

To *what?*

PART THREE

II

THE Palazzo Favretto was the third to be visited on the tour.

The gondolas, of which there were several, lined up at the Fondamenta Narisi, one by one, to discharge their passengers. The guide assembled the group in front of the palazzo and said:

"Ladies and gentlemen, the Palazzo Favretto. Fifteenth century. One of the finest examples of Venetian Gothic—as Venetian, they say, as the waters of the Grand Canal itself. Originally built between 1420 and 1450 for the noble family Favretto, whose descendants still reside here. Our tour will be confined only to the *piano nobile*, or main-floor *portego*, which is on the lower level. The upper floors contain the private apartments of the family, and, of course, we are not allowed there. Please follow me."

The moment the doors closed behind them, David knew he had been here before.

He knew the great chandelier of spun Murano glass, the high ceiling ornately encrusted with gold, the airy loggia, the soaring pilasters and huge frescoes high on the wall, the great mirrors framed in swirling gilt. He had seen the sculpture before, in his meditation. A fallen warrior, in bronze. A lithe Ulysses, running in flight, also in bronze. A satyr and a nymph in marble, embracing each other. And the headless statues of two young girls, in the posture of the dance.

And, of course, there were the many paintings, ornate Baroque and Renaissance, some of them by the great masters—one of them, a Virgin and Child, by Giovanni Bellini, another by Carpaccio—a scene of a crowd, brilliantly dressed in velvet and damask, chatting and petting their lap dogs, outside a marble building.

"Now," the guide was saying, "as you see, this is a very impressive room, very big, very grand. But the family did not live here, did not use this great room except for state occasions, one might say. It was built to make a *bella figura* —how do you say?—to impress visitors on important occasions. Actually, the living quarters, no matter how grand or noble the Venetian family, were much simpler, both in furniture and decoration, and were located mainly on the floor above or below the *piano nobile*."

David saw the marble staircase with its red carpet pinned down at each step by shining brass rods. He knew where it led.

And he began to walk toward the staircase. He was drawn to it. It seemed to beckon to him.

He glanced at the tour guide.

The man had his back toward him. So did the others in the tour. The guide was pointing out the fine points of a painting by Paolo Veronese—a figure painting, another crowd scene with halberdiers drinking, a jester with a parrot on his wrist, a youth leaning over a balustrade, a gesturing nobleman in silk and satin with a tiny Negro page, dogs and cats . . .

David walked slowly up the staircase, the carpet dulling the sound of his footsteps.

140

He came to a long corridor at the top of the stairway.

The hallway was simple, almost barren, as he had known it would be. It was lined with Renaissance chests and red damask chairs, their wooden arms decorated with the carved and gilded heads and manes of lions. These same chairs, David knew, were spread through the living quarters, the reception room, the library, the parlor, the dining room.

The corridor was silent. Nobody seemed to be about. He heard no sound of stirring anywhere.

He knew where he wanted to go and what he wanted to see. He knew he was trespassing. But in another sense he was not.

In another sense, he was at home.

Unerringly, he headed straight for the third door on the left.

He opened it, tentatively, and peered through the crack. The room was empty. He opened the door wide and went in.

He stood there for a moment, hardly breathing, immersed in the room, enveloped by it, feeling part of it in a very special and intimate way, sensing that in this moment he had reached a high point in this weird drama he had been living...

Everything seemed exactly as he remembered it. The great bed, with its red velvet canopy and its red bedspread, the drapes, also in burgundy red, the still life on the far wall, a painting of a great bouquet of flowers in bright colors blooming out of its silver frame, the vanity table and bureau and chest, all in Renaissance style, the same Persian rug, now faintly threadbare with time. He did not part the drapes to look out of the window, but he knew what was below, he knew exactly what would be there. There would be an enclosed garden. In the center of this garden would be a fountain and a pool, and in the center of the pool an interesting little piece of statuary, a figure of Apollo, his right hip swung out, his left leg slightly advanced...

He detected the faint odor of perfume; it might have come from the flowers in the garden outside, but he knew it did not, because it was very subtle and very special and, again, intimately known to him...

Then, suddenly, he saw it.

The photograph.

He hadn't noticed it at first, because it was rather small, and it was on the end table on the opposite side of the bed, and his attention had been engaged by the room as a whole, rather than by details.

The framed photograph was that of a young man—very handsome, black hair, flashing black eyes, a small black mustache, and a wide, warm smile.

It was the face of the handsome young man he had seen in his meditation. Exact, to the smallest detail.

And on the photograph was written:

"Per mia moglie, Bianca. Con tutto il mio amore. Vittorio."
To my wife, Bianca. With all my love. Vittorio.

All along, there had been a growing suspicion in David's mind. But he had deliberately resisted it. He had refused to believe it. He had told himself it was impossible, it was all illusion, the fantasy of his own imagination. No matter how bizarre, there had been a reason, an explanation, for everything that had happened to him. He had clung desperately to that premise. If you didn't believe that, if you didn't stick to that belief, you could go over the edge, you could go mad.

But now he could deny it no longer. Now, he was sure. Now, he *knew*.

Once upon a time, he had been Count Vittorio Favretto, the man in the photograph, descendant of a noble Venetian family. Death had merely been an interlude, a kind of sleep. After that, he had been born again as David Tavish Drew, son of a hardware wholesaler, in Canton, Ohio, USA.

The same soul, but in a new body.

At the moment, he had no particular emotion. At the moment, he thought about it rather calmly, in a passive way. It was simply a point of information.

He picked up the photograph and studied it.

The face was young. About his, David's, age. He would estimate that at the time the picture was taken Favretto was about twenty-five. Then, David remembered. Something the gondolier, Bruno Savoldo, had said.

Vittorio Favretto had vanished in September 1954. And he, David Drew, had been born on October 3 of that same year. The period of death in between had been very short, only a few days, before the count's soul had found a new home.

Studying the photograph now, David wondered how he had died in his previous life. They had never found the count's body, it was true. But there was no doubt that Vittorio Favretto was dead. Otherwise, there would be no reincarnation.

"What are you doing here?"

He whirled, startled. In his surprise, he let the photograph drop from his hand. The *contessa* was standing in the doorway. She started to say something else, then stopped. She looked down at the photograph lying on the floor. Fortunately, the thick carpet had broken its fall, and the glass remained intact. The face of Vittorio Favretto looked up at both of them.

"I'm sorry," he said. "I know I shouldn't be here."

She did not respond. Nor, for the moment, did she come into the room. She seemed riveted in the doorway, watching him. There was absolute silence, except for a large bluebottle fly, buzzing around the window and bumping himself against the pane. He found the *contessa* just as beautiful close up as he had at a distance. He knew she was now in her middle forties. But, actually, she looked years younger. Her olive skin was still smooth, unblemished, and there was no sign of a wrinkle. Her hair was still black, alive, rich in texture. Her figure was that of a young girl. He caught the scent of her perfume. It was heady, it excited him. Her very nearness excited him. She was a woman of quality and elegance. But there was something highly sensuous about her, lushly feminine, sexual.

All this time she seemed a little confused, tongue-tied. But now she came into the room and said:

"I am Contessa Favretto. And I ask you again, what are you doing here? In my room. These are private quarters. They are not open to the public."

"Yes," he stammered. "I know. And I'm sorry. It's just that I was curious. I left my tour group and just began to wander around . . ."

"I must ask you to leave at once."

"Yes," he said. "Yes, of course."

Her eyes wandered away from his and then down toward the photograph lying on the floor. For a while, neither spoke. The big bluebottle fly stopped banging against the window. Now, from outside, they could hear the voice of the guide as he led the tour group into the garden. He began to explain that many of the palaces in Venice had elaborate gardens like this, in the rear.

David bent over and picked up the photograph. He put it back on the bedtable. He felt embarrassed.

"*Contessa,* I'm sorry. I realize I had no right to touch your personal possessions . . ."

He stopped. There was a sudden change in her. She had gone pale. Her eyes were wide, startled. They were fixed on his chest. She was looking at his medallion. It was a hot day, and he was wearing an open sport shirt. When he had leaned down to pick up the photograph, the big gold disc had fallen out over his shirt.

"Where—where did you get that?"

The medallion lay on his chest, face up. She continued to stare at it. Her voice shook a little. "Please, you must tell me. Where did you get it?"

"I bought it in New York."

"In New York?" She seemed upset, under some great tension. "Please." She reached out her hand. "May I see it?"

"Of course."

He lifted the chain up over his neck and gave the medallion to her. For a moment, she studied the insignia, the lion holding up the scrolls. Then, with trembling fingers, she turned the medallion over.

144

She saw it was blank, and she gave a long sigh. It seemed to be one of relief. She turned the medallion over in her palm again.

"You know, *signore* . . . "

"Drew. David Drew."

"This is the Favretto crest. You knew that?"

"Not until I came to Venice."

She looked at him, confused. "Then, it is a very strange coincidence. I mean, *signore,* your appearing in my house and wearing this medallion. You see, I gave one exactly like this as an anniversary gift to Vittorio." She hesitated. "Count Favretto. My first husband. For a moment, I thought, I almost believed . . . "

"That this had been his?"

"Yes." She returned the medallion, and he hung it around his neck, concealing it beneath his shirt again. She rubbed her fingers across her forehead. "Excuse me, *signore.* I am feeling a little faint. I know how absurd this sounds. But for a moment, I thought your medallion was his—and that, by some miracle, he was still alive. But, of course, it isn't true. Thank you for letting me see it. It reminded me so much of my husband . . . "

"Bianca!"

They both turned. Teodoro Borsato was standing there. He was staring at David. His face was hostile.

"Who is this man?"

"Oh. He is part of the tourist group, Teodoro."

"What's he doing up here? In your room?"

"It's my fault," said David. "I know I shouldn't be here. I was just curious and wandered in . . . "

The gray eyes under the beetling brows were cold. He came toward David, his lips in a thin, hard line. He was a big man, powerful physically, aggressively dominating in personality. And, clearly, he had taken an instant dislike to David.

"I think you are lying," he said. "Your instructions were clear. All the tour groups were told that the upper floors were private. You are trespassing here. Why?"

"I told you. I was just curious."

"And I told you, I think you are lying. I think you came up here to steal—"

"Teodoro!" said the *contessa*, shocked.

"Be quiet, Bianca. I will handle this."

"But you are being rude."

"I said be quiet," he said savagely, glaring at her. Then, his eye caught the photograph on the table. Suddenly, he seemed to forget David entirely. He went over and picked up the photograph. Then he looked at his wife angrily. "What is this? I *told* you I did not want his picture around the house!"

"This is my bedroom," she said defiantly. "I have a right to have anything I please in it."

"Not *his* picture. I am your husband, Bianca, not Vittorio. Vittorio is dead. He has been dead a long time, you have mourned him enough." He held up the photograph. "But, I see, he *still* takes my place in this house. I will not have it, Bianca, do you understand? I simply will not have it!" He flung the picture on the bed. "Now, get rid of this. Put it away somewhere. If I see it in this house again, I'll burn it."

She looked at him, distressed. "Teodoro, for the love of heaven, this is a private matter. There is a stranger here."

Borsato turned his attention to David.

"I ought to call the police. But this time I'll let you go. Now, get out, damn you."

"I'm sorry, *contessa*, for causing you all this trouble."

"It's nothing, Signore Drew. But please go."

"Get out," repeated Borsato.

David went downstairs. As he did, he heard Borsato's heavy footsteps stamping out of the bedroom and down the corridor above. The tour group was still in the garden when he joined it.

A minute or two later, the guide had finished and began to lead the group through the palazzo toward the *fondamenta* on the opposite side, where the gondolas were waiting.

Just before they left, David looked up toward a small rococo balcony on the upper floor.

The curtains had been parted, and he saw Bianca Favretto's face in the window, watching him.

They stood, looking at each other for a long moment, and then she closed the curtains.

He turned and followed the others into the palazzo.

After David had gone, Bianca Favretto lay on the bed for a while.

She still felt dizzy, a little faint. She told herself it was the heat. The bedroom was oppressive with it. But she knew it was more than that.

It was strange. The way this young American, this David Drew, had affected her.

Somehow, when she had walked into the room and first seen him, she had found herself at a loss for words. She had felt a certain confusion, experienced some deep and turbulent stirring of emotion. She did not know what it was, and she did not know why. There was nothing extraordinary about him. Certainly he was very attractive. He had blue eyes and straw-colored hair, a good chin, a nice mouth, and a warm smile. He was lean and wiry and quite tall; it would be easy to mistake him for an athlete of some kind. She was old enough to be his mother. Yet, she had found him strangely exciting. And more than that. She sensed that he, too, had in his own way felt the same vibrations.

It was all very baffling. She was under the distinct impression she had known him from somewhere before. But she could not, for the life of her, recall where. She knew she hadn't seen him in Venice before. If she had, she would have remembered. She had been to the United States, but she was sure she had never met him there.

Then *where?*

Finally, she decided it was all her imagination. She was a little distraught after the incident with Teodoro a few minutes ago. She wasn't thinking rationally. She had never met David Drew at all. They moved in different circles entirely. He was just a tourist passing through. She never expected to see him again. Here today and gone tomorrow. Yet, it was all so strange. So very strange.

The matter of the medallion, for instance.

There had to be some explanation of how this David Drew had come to possess it. Long ago the Favrettos had struck off a few of those gold discs bearing the family crest, for use by the male heads of the household. But again, that had been a long time ago, when these family symbols had meant something. Now, they no longer had any significance; the aristocracy was no longer really important anymore, either in Italy or elsewhere. And the practice of striking off the medallions had been discontinued many years ago. As far as she knew, there were only a very few left in existence. She had seen one, in the possession of a Favretto granduncle, and she had liked it and had one made for Vittorio in celebration of the first anniversary of their marriage.

The Favrettos had been impoverished during the last war, things had been hard for everyone, and it was possible that one of the family might have sold his medallion to an American soldier in exchange for food. Or some German might have stolen or liberated it and sold it later. Or perhaps an American had found it on a dead body on some battlefield. At any rate, somehow it had been brought to America and, years later, had come into the possession of this David Drew.

It was strange that he should appear in her bedroom, wearing it. Of course, it was only a coincidence, it had to be. But still, she felt a chill run up her spine. Coincidence or not, it was all a little frightening...

She rose, picked up the photograph of her husband, and looked at it for a long time. She realized that people thought her strange, a little off-balance. You mourned a dead husband a certain time, she had heard them whisper. But not for twenty-five years. She had married Teodoro Borsato, Vittorio's best friend, hoping for a new life in a new marriage. But it had turned out just the opposite. Her life with Borsato had turned her even more to the memory of the man she still loved, even if he was dead.

She placed the photograph tenderly under some lingerie in a drawer and closed it. It was the only picture she had left. And she knew that Teodoro had meant what he said. The sight of it had infuriated him, as it always did. He was perfectly capable of burning the photograph, even though it was hers and all she had left of Vittorio Favretto.

Later that night, she and Teodoro dined alone.

They said little to each other. Finally, he rose and said:

"If you will forgive me, my dear, I have a business appointment."

"Oh? When will you be back?"

"I'm afraid it will take the rest of the evening."

He came over to her side of the table and kissed her on the cheek. She turned her head away. It was perfunctory, a ritual between them. Everything, she thought bitterly, was a ritual between them, and had been for years. They were living a kind of empty charade. They slept in separate bedrooms, as they had for years. She knew he had no business appointment. She knew he was going to see his mistress. She had no idea who the latest one might be. But Teodoro also made frequent trips to Milan, to Rome, and to Geneva. All on business. In places where she knew he had no business.

Not that she cared. She had ceased caring years ago what Teodoro Borsato did. She, herself, in desperation, had had a few affairs during the years. But none of them had lasted very long. Teodoro knew she had had lovers. And he did not care. It was another ritual between them. What they had between them wasn't a marriage, it was a mockery, simply an arrangement. She had given a lot of thought to ending it with Teodoro, to getting a divorce. But, somehow, she couldn't bring herself around to doing so. It was a matter of inertia, a horror of going through the whole procedure.

Her own family, the Gattis, were violently opposed to even the thought of divorce. They were very conservative and very Catholic. Besides, she had no incentive; there wasn't any other man.

Yes, she had made a terrible mistake in marrying Teodoro after Vittorio was officially declared dead. It was a mistake that had condemned her to all these empty years.

About an hour after Teodoro had left, a messenger came to the door. He said he was from the Hotel Donatello, and he delivered a small package to her.

She opened it. In it, she found the Favretto medallion. And a message from David Drew:

"Dear Contessa: Please keep this. I want you to have it. David Drew."

I 2

THE morning promised a hot and blistering day.

When David got out of bed and opened the blinds to the window, he could feel the blast of the sun in a cloudless blue sky. Its glare seemed to shimmer the surface of the lagoon. Already, the Sunday crowds were heading for the beach. He could see them jamming up the platform at the boat station below on the Riva degli Schiavoni. They boarded the *diretti* marked "P. San Marco-Lido," which then headed across the lagoon. The boats were swollen with their human cargo, and they seemed ready to roll over and collapse from the sheer weight. People swarmed on the decks and shoved and pushed down the aisles, cramming every square foot of space, and piled in human mounds against the cabin. And when each *vaporetto* began to move away from the dock, there was always a latecomer or two who made a daring leap from the platform, grabbed a rail of the boat by his fingernails, and was pulled aboard by others.

David looked at his watch. He had a little over an hour before he was to meet Adriana. After seeing the water traffic, he wondered ruefully whether he and Adriana would survive the trip across to the Lido.

He closed the windows to shut out the noise and then the blinds as well.

Then he began his meditation.

Again, after a while, the mantra disappeared and he entered the PA stage, the euphoric world of No-Thought.

The faces of the principals he had seen before were all blanked out now. Including his own.

But the curled object, the sculpture that had always been blurred and unidentifiable, now came into focus.

It was a small carved head.

The face of the head was human. It had great round eyes, a pug nose, and, instead of a tongue in the thick-lipped lascivious mouth, it had fangs. The face was smiling. The smile was insolent, malignant, obscene, the fangs were bared.

It was interesting to note that the head was attached to the curling body of a snake.

The sculpture appeared to protrude from the edge or eave of some rooftop, and it seemed to be night. And again, there was that strange, rippling play of light and shadow across its face.

When David met Adriana, she had a pleasant surprise for him.

They did not have to take the public *vaporetto* at all. As an official guide, she had certain mysterious credentials. They boarded the private speedboat that belonged to the deluxe Hotel Excelsior Palace on the Lido, which was used to transfer its guests to and fro across the lagoon.

They sped across the lagoon, and in a few minutes they had landed, walked the short distance across the area that contained the casino and the various cinemas of the film festival, crossed the busy boulevard, alive with buses, cars, and horse-drawn buggies, and entered the hotel itself.

They walked through the elaborate lobby and through the sea entrance of the Excelsior, guarded by two Egyptian stone lions with human faces. Just below, on the beach, was a long series of cabanas, each with sloping awnings and each topped with a glass globe.

They rented two locker rooms and changed into their suits.

Adriana wore a white bikini, very brief and very interesting. She looked appealing in it and quite exciting, and David whistled his appreciation. She blushed a little, then laughed and took his hand, and they walked down to the beach itself.

David looked at the long pier with its signal flags flying, the sailboats, the people on the rock jetties, the lazy bathers lying on lounges in front of the cabanas. His eye swept the villas along the beach in the distance, and faintly he could hear the traffic on the Lungomare Marconi, above.

A group of three girls walked in front of them, strolling along the beach. David grinned. These young Italian beauties might have been American girls. They sauntered by, swinging their hips and buttocks, brown and bikinied, confident in their youth and their beauty, completely and sensuously at home in their bodies, like young animals, their hair awry, salt-streaked, and bleached by the sun. They walked in slow cadence, eyes straight ahead and yet somehow watching, knowing they were being watched, warmed by the sun, by their own admiration of themselves, and the admiration of others.

"*Caro.*" Adriana laughed. "Today, you are an Italian."

"Yes? In what way?"

"The way you look at the girls."

"I'm a girl watcher in America, too."

"Oh?"

"I might as well be at Jones Beach or Fire Island, or somewhere on the Cape. I mean, these girls are no different from American girls. Look just the same. You can't tell them apart without a scorecard."

She seemed puzzled by the expression.

"Without a scorecard?"

He explained, and she laughed and said she must remember it, this "without a scorecard," it was very interesting. They decided to walk along the beach for a little while, and she asked him how he liked the Lido now that he had seen it.

"Somehow," he said. "I can't believe this is part of Venice."

"No? Why not?"

"Well, Venice lives in the past. But everything's modern here. All of a sudden, we're in the twentieth century. There isn't any—well, any sense of history."

"Ah," she said. "That is where you are wrong. The Lido here is full of history. You are right, it does not look it now, but there is all the history you want here. Some of it traditional, some of it romantic."

"For example, what?"

She laughed. "As a professional, I should charge you for my services."

"I'll pay."

"It will be a special rate, since I am acting as a personal guide, and not for a tour. And on top of that, it will cost you double-time, since this day I am not supposed to be on duty at all." She cocked an eye at him. "You'll *still* pay?"

"Anything you ask."

"Well, then, it is true. The Lido is nothing at all like Venice. But it was not always this way. Once it was covered with pinewoods. The Adriatic here was alive with ships from everywhere in the civilized world, running along this coast, and some were wrecked on this shore. It was here in 1202 where thirty thousand knights prepared to embark for the Fourth Crusade. It was the port from which the fleets sailed to conquer the East, and where Venetians organized their defense in the most critical times of their survival." Adriana paused. "But all this is rather boring, I won't go into it any further, *caro*. The romantic history of the Lido is much more interesting."

"Yes?"

154

"It became a home for artists and lovers. Goethe and Shelley walked right where we are walking now. Byron rode horses along this beach and swam from the Lido here to the Grand Canal. George Sand and Alfred de Musset walked this beach, arm in arm. And you've read Thomas Mann's 'Death in Venice,' of course. Well, Gustave von Aschenbach sat on the Lido here, and yearned for Tadzio." She looked at him. "What do you think of all that?"

"I agree," he said. "It's very romantic."

"It still is," said Adriana. "Every Italian boy who feels romantic toward his girl takes her here to the Lido. It's a place for couples. As you see, couples, couples everywhere."

He grinned. "Just like us."

"Well," she said. "Not exactly. We're just friends, *caro*. As you Americans say, casual. In a few days you will go home. To her."

"Oh, I don't know. I—"

He cut off abruptly, as he saw her.

Bianca Favretto.

She was standing directly in front of him, at the water's edge, opposite one of the cabanas. She wore a sleek, one-piece, tight-fitting bathing suit. She saw him the moment he saw her, and her eyes widened in astonishment.

"Signore Drew. I did not expect—"

"Neither did I, *contessa*."

"I was going to telephone you at your hotel. I—" She stopped in some confusion, noticing that Adriana was with him. David introduced her to Adriana, who responded a little stiffly.

"*Signore*," she said, glancing at Adriana. "I know this must sound rude. I do not mean it to be. But I must speak to you, alone." Then, to Adriana: "Forgive me, *signorina*. I will be only a few moments ... "

"It's all right, *contessa*."

Adriana gave David a queer look and then, instead of walking along on the beach, ran into the water. The *contessa* looked after her, distressed.

"I'm afraid I have offended her."

"No," he said. "It's all right."

"*Signore,* I thank you for your lovely thought. It was very sweet and generous of you. But, of course, I shall return the medallion to you."

"No," he said. "Please keep it. I really won't miss it. And I know it means a lot to you."

"Thank you, *signore.*" She was very firm. "But really, I cannot accept it. I appreciate your thought in this, again, it is most generous of you. But that medallion is very valuable, and, after all, we're complete strangers."

"No," he said, abruptly. "I don't think we are."

For a while, they said nothing. Simply looked at each other. She was thrown off balance, confused by what he had just said.

"Look," he said. "I've got to see you again, talk to you."

"*Signore* . . ."

"Not *signore.* David."

"David. It is impossible. I am afraid."

"I'll telephone you tomorrow."

"No," she whispered. "It is better that I call you."

"When?"

"I don't know."

"*When?*"

"Wait. In a day or two. When the time is right. We must be careful." She sounded bewildered, incredulous. As though unable to believe herself. "*Dio mio.* What am I doing, what am I saying? I've only just met you."

For a single moment, he was tempted. To tell her who he really was. He had a tremendous urge to take her into his arms and tell her everything. But he resisted it. He knew he could not. Not now. But sooner or later, he knew, he would have to tell her . . .

"Oh," she said. She was looking over his shoulder, and her face was distressed. "My husband's coming. I did not expect him so early."

David turned to see Teodoro Borsato coming down the beach toward them, from the direction of the hotel. He wore white slacks and a blue slip-on shirt and carried a small bag. He came up to both of them, then smiled, and said:

"Well, if it isn't our inquisitive young American again." He grinned at the *contessa*. "Did you arrange this rendezvous, Bianca?"

"Teodoro, you're being very rude."

"Am I, *cara?*"

"Signore Drew was just walking along the beach. We met by accident."

"Ah," said Borsato. "Yes. Of course. By accident." He looked David up and down. "A new candidate, eh, Bianca? A new lover?" Then he laughed. "But why not?" He winked lewdly at David. "Be my guest, *signore.* There's room for everyone." Then back to the *contessa*. "But, *cara,* this one is very young. You are old enough to be his mother. Not like the others. Since when do you steal from the cradle?"

"Shut up, Borsato," snapped David.

"*Bastardo,*" said Borsato. He thrust his face at David's. His eyes were cold, gray marbles. "*Giovane bastardo.* You dare insult me?"

"Teodoro," pleaded the *contessa*. "Please. Stop it! You are making a scene."

"*Porco,*" said Borsato. "American pig . . ."

David's hand whipped out and grabbed Borsato's shirt. He pulled the Italian in close.

"You son-of-a-bitch," he said. "You crude son-of-a-bitch. You've got a big mouth. You've insulted your wife, and now you insult me. If I hear another word from you, one more word, I will smash your damned face in."

"Please, David." The *contessa* tugged at his arm. "Please. Let him go."

Borsato stared at him, his face a mask of hatred. He squirmed, trying to get free. But David had a firm grip on the older man. Finally, he pushed Borsato away. Borsato stumbled, almost fell.

"You'll hear from me," Borsato shouted. "Do you understand? You'll hear from me!"

David ignored him and turned to the *contessa*.

"I'm sorry about all this," he said.

Then he turned and ran into the water. Adriana was floating on her back when he joined her.

"Did you have a nice talk, *caro?*"

"Not very."

"You seem upset."

"It's nothing."

She sounded piqued. "You never told me you met the *contessa.*"

"I didn't think it was important."

"Still, you *might* have told me."

"I'm sorry."

"And it must be important if she had to speak to you alone." She waited for him to reply, but he did not. "It's all right, *caro.* It's all very personal, and it's none of my business, and you don't want to talk about it."

Adriana turned on her stomach and began to swim. They swam together for a short distance, without speaking. Then she stopped and floated again, her eyes closed against the sun.

"David?"

"Yes?"

"What are you doing in Venice?"

"I told you . . ."

"No. What are you *really* doing here?" He was silent, and she went on: "You know, you're beginning to frighten me a little."

"For God's sake, Adriana. *Come on!*"

"No, I mean it. There's something strange about you, *caro,* and about what's going on. Something secret. Something to do with the Favrettos. You seem involved with them—with her. I saw the way you two looked at each other. Like old friends. No. More than that. Like old lovers. If I didn't know better, I'd swear you'd met before."

"That's ridiculous."

His objection was a little too emphatic. She studied him for a moment, curiously.

"Who are you, David? Who are you really? And I'll ask you again. What are you *really* doing in Venice?"

"Adriana, I don't want to talk about it."

"I see."

"It's just that I *can't* talk about it," he said desperately.

She turned over on her stomach again and said:

"Let's go in. I'm getting cold."

13

THE next morning, during his prebreakfast meditation, something new appeared.

The human-headed serpent still held steady. There was still the rippling, dancing effect of light and shadow across the face. It was still, clearly now, a piece of sculpture jutting out from the edge of some roof. But its position had changed. It no longer appeared in closeup; it had receded. He had the impression now that he was looking up at it from somewhere below, standing on a street.

In addition, the roof had now become part of a blurred mass, which David knew was a building. And more than this. There were two additional blurs just below David's line of sight, which seemed to be human figures standing just in front of him.

David was fascinated by this change. He knew, from past experience, that the blurs would become clearer. And that they would tell some kind of story. Another piece of the mosaic which had led him to Venice and to Vittorio Favretto.

He knew that somewhere in the city this obscene head on its serpentine neck actually existed. But where, he had no idea.

He drew a sketch of the snake and head on a sheet of hotel stationery.

He had breakfast on the square and then walked to the Bacino Orseolo. He showed Bruno Savoldo the sketch on the off-chance that the gondolier might recognize this particular piece of sculpture and know its location. But Savoldo, after studying the sketch, shook his head and told David he had never seen it before. He showed it to the other gondoliers idling about, waiting for a fare. They passed the sheet of paper from hand to hand.

None of them had ever seen it, anywhere in Venice. And, as Savoldo explained:

"It would be very easy to miss something like this, *signore*. Venice is a very big place, *molte grande*. There must be hundreds of these, no, thousands in the city. You see them everywhere, on every *campo* and *campiello*, in every *vicolo*, every *calle* and *fondamenta*. They are on the front and rear walls not only of the palazzi but of many other buildings, public and private." Savoldo shook his head. "It is only by accident that you would find something like this." He noted the disappointment on David's face. "This is important to you, *signore?*"

"Yes," said David. "It is very important."

After that, he thanked the gondolier and left. Bruno Savoldo was by nature a curious man, and he had hoped this young American would elaborate on the reason for this unusual request. But since he didn't, Savoldo shrugged and went to gossip and while away the time with his companions.

Monday passed. Then Tuesday. David put in a call to Adriana. He asked her to lunch, but she refused, saying she was busy. He told her he would try again. She said that was fine. He thought he noted a certain coolness in her voice, but he couldn't be sure.

Meanwhile, he waited impatiently for Bianca Favretto to call. In a day or two, she had said. When the time was ripe. Finally, he decided that she had changed her mind. He was sure he would never hear from her again. The trouble was, he desperately wanted to see her again. He wanted to call her, but he did not dare.

On Thursday morning, when he had just about given up, his phone rang. He expected it to be from Adriana. He had phoned her the day before, but she had been out, so he left a message to call him back.

But it wasn't Adriana. It was Bianca Favretto. For the moment, she sounded different. Composed. Almost formal. Very much the *contessa*. And she did not waste any time in preamble.

"Are you free today, *signore*?"

"Yes."

"Then come to lunch, please."

"Where?"

She seemed surprised at the question. "Here. At the palazzo."

"The palazzo?"

"Why not?"

"I don't know," he said. "I just thought . . . well . . ."

"Signore Drew, there is no need to meet me in some dark rendezvous." He noted that it was "*signore*" and not "David." "I invite you for lunch in my own home. What is so wrong with that? Anyway, I do not care what people think. I stopped caring about that a long time ago."

"But your husband. What about him?"

"Teodoro? He's not here. He's on one of his business trips. To Rome. He'll be gone for two or three days." Then, almost brusquely: "Will one o'clock be convenient?"

"Yes. That'll be fine."

"Good. I'll expect you then."

At noon, he left the hotel, walked down the *riva*, turned right through the Piazzetta, and crossed the square, heading for the Bacino Orseolo.

He had decided to go to the palazzo by gondola again. It was an expensive way to go, and, of course, he could have walked. But in David's view, it was worth it. He wanted to know more about the Favrettos, and especially about the man he had once been, the kind of life he had once lived. Obviously, there was no better source of this information than Bruno Savoldo.

The gondolier was sitting on the edge of the *fondamenta*, dangling his legs over the basin and eating a sandwich, when David appeared. He stuffed the rest of the sandwich into his mouth, rose, and greeted David effusively.

"Ah. *Buon giorno, signore. Buon giorno.* What can I do for you today?"

"I'd like you to take me to the Palazzo Favretto again."

"Of course. Please." He waved to his gondola. "It really interests you, eh?"

"Yes."

As he poled the gondola away from its mooring place, and out into the basin, Savoldo said:

"*Signore,* may I know your name?"

David turned his head and looked at him.

"Why do you want to know?"

The gondolier smiled and shrugged.

"I don't normally ask. A tourist is a tourist, and, if he pays my price, so much an hour, I really don't care. But somehow, *signore,* you interest me. A young American who isn't even an Italian but who speaks good Italian anyway." He paused. "And there's something else."

"Yes?"

"Since you already know my name, why should I not know yours?"

David laughed and said that was only fair and gave Savoldo his name. Then:

"You like Venice, Signore Drew?"

163

"Very much."

"I am happy to hear that. There is no place like it in all the world. How long will you be here?"

"I don't know."

"Where are you staying?"

"At the Donatello."

"Ah. It is a very good hotel. First class."

David was amused. He couldn't help liking this grizzled old gondolier. There was something earthy about him, real. He was both garrulous and inquisitive. But somehow David did not find it offensive. Like many other Italians, Savoldo was curious about everyone he came in contact with. He was totally unabashed about it, he had no inhibitions about any invasion of privacy.

"Signore Drew."

"Yes?"

"May I ask your profession?"

"I'll let you guess."

"You are a *corrispondente* for an American newspaper. A *giornalista* interested in the Favretto affair. I think this, because you have more than just an ordinary interest in this case. Am I correct?"

"No."

"Then you must be writing a book, perhaps a *romanzo*."

David decided to let it go at that. He laughed and said: "All right, Savoldo. Have it your own way."

He led Savoldo into talking about the Favrettos. The result was a potpourri of information. Vittorio Favretto, when just a boy, had left Venice and gone into the hills as a guerrilla, fighting the Germans. He had fought with great courage and later had been decorated for it. His wife, the *contessa*, had been a Gatti, from another very old and noble and enormously rich Venetian family. They had married very early, and she had borne him an infant son, Ludovico. Their life was idyllic, anyone could see they were very much in love, and in the years he, Bruno Savoldo, had been in the Favretto service, he had never heard a harsh word between them.

As for Teodoro Borsato, he had caught the *contessa* on the rebound, so to speak. He had waited patiently until the verdict was official that Vittorio Favretto was dead. He had been the count's best friend, or professed to be, but all this was a sham. He had comforted the *contessa* in her grief, managed her affairs, and finally courted her. All with one object in mind, Savoldo insisted. To marry her money. He dominated her, he kept her under his thumb, he cheated on her outrageously. But he had told David this before, and it was well known.

David was curious as to why Savoldo was so hostile when it came to Borsato. He knew Borsato had fired Savoldo as the family gondolier, but he sensed it was more than that. He asked Savoldo about it, but suddenly the gondolier, so open about everything, closed up.

"*Scusa, signore.* It is true. I have no use for this *briccone.* It is a personal matter. And I cannot discuss it."

They arrived, finally, at the Fondamenta Narisi.

As Savoldo swung his gondola around in the canal, he lingered to watch the young American being admitted to the Palazzo Favretto.

He was still uncertain who this Signore Drew really was and what he was up to. He might actually be a writer of some kind, and he might not. But whoever he was, he was a pretty fast worker. Here he was, being admitted in a private visit.

And by the *contessa.*

He knew it couldn't be anyone else. Only yesterday, while on the lagoon, he had seen a speedboat zoom by, presumably headed for the airport. Borsato was the only passenger, and there was luggage piled up beside him. Obviously then, Borsato had gone out of town. Probably to spend a few days with one of his *amanti,* his kept women.

Again, he began to wonder about this young American. It was really very puzzling that he gained such ready entry. The *contessa* was almost inaccessible. She saw practically no one, except very close friends. And Savoldo knew she would never receive anyone interested in reviving the now-famous Favretto case, for the newspapers, or anything else. It was something very painful to her, which she preferred to forget.

The more he thought about it, the more he began to wonder.

14

THE servant who admitted David was an ancient crone, apparently some kind of housekeeper. She led David through the main floor of the palazzo and then outside to a terrace overlooking the garden itself.

A table was set for two, with gleaming silver and exquisite Murano glasses. Bianca Favretto was there, dressed in a long, loose-fitting, togalike robe of pale blue. She was with a young man, about David's age, slim, beautifully tailored, and strikingly handsome. They were chatting over a glass of wine when David entered.

"Ah." She rose. "Signore Drew. I am very happy you could come."

"Thank you for your invitation, *contessa*."

"This is my son, Ludovico," she said. "Ludovico, this is Signore David Drew. From New York."

"How do you do?"

"Pleased to meet you."

"Ludovico has been with us for two days," said the *contessa*. "But he is just leaving for Rome. He is studying law there."

They shook hands, murmuring the usual pleasantries. Ludovico's eyes were faintly curious. As though wondering what his mother could possibly have in common with a young American tourist like David and, more, why she would go to the trouble of having him to lunch. But he was too well bred to ask any questions on that score.

"I hope you are enjoying your stay in Venice, *signore*."

"I am. Very much."

The words came out of David Drew mechanically. He was shaken, trying hard to adjust to this grotesque situation. It was, of course, wildly incongruous. Weird. This handsome young Italian was his own son. *I was his father*, thought David, *and in a certain sense, I still am. Yet, we are just about the same age.*

He remembered the image of the infant he had seen in his meditation. That baby, of course, was the new Count Favretto, who stood before him now. That image had hung on after the others had gone, and David knew that after today's meeting, it too would vanish.

It was just too much to absorb. He stood there, still in shock. Suddenly, he was conscious that Ludovico Favretto was looking at him, in a puzzled kind of way, and David realized that he must have been staring rudely. He searched wildly for something to say. Then, lamely, he said:

"I haven't been to Rome as yet."

"You will like Rome," said Ludovico, politely. "It is a fascinating city." He looked at his watch. "Forgive me, *signore*. But I must leave now."

"You are all packed?" asked the *contessa*.

"Everything's in the speedboat. And Pietro's waiting to take me to the airport." He shook hands with David again. "Goodbye, *signore*."

"Goodbye."

Ludovico went to his mother, put his arm around her waist, and kissed her gently.

"*Ciao*, Mama."

"Take care of yourself, *caro*," she said. "And study hard." He smiled at her, kissed her gently, then turned and left.

"He's a nice-looking boy," said David.

"Yes. He looks very much like his father."

"Is he married?"

"No," said the *contessa*. "But he lives with some girl. Of course, they all do these days." She went to a small marble table in a corner of the terrace, on which a small package was lying. She picked it up and gave it to him.

"Your medallion."

"I wish you would keep it," he said.

"Thank you. As I told you, it was most generous of you, but . . . "

"Keep it, Bianca," he said firmly. He spoke her first name again, easily. "I told you, I don't care that much about it, one way or the other. But I know how much this might mean to you."

She looked at him, shaken. Still holding the box in her hand.

"David . . . "

"I insist."

"But it must have cost you a lot of money. If I could only—"

"No," he said. "It's a gift."

She looked at him for a moment. Suddenly, she seemed on the verge of tears. Then, impulsively, she put her hand on his cheek, caressed, it, then leaned forward and kissed him gently on the lips.

"You are a darling," she said, softly. "And I cannot thank you enough." Then, as though to cover her confusion, she turned abruptly away from him and went to the table. She picked up a tiny glass bell and shook it. The tinkling sound brought the old woman to the door of the terrace.

"Please, Rosalba. We will have lunch now."

"*Subito, contessa.*"

The luncheon was delicious. A first course of *spaghetti alle vongole,* followed by a *zuppa di pesce,* along with a fine white wine, a Verduzzo.

"You know, David, I keep looking at you . . ."

"And?"

"And there is something about you—I don't know. I have the feeling that, somehow, I know you. That somewhere we've met before."

"I feel the same about you," he said.

"I have been in New York a number of times," she said. "Perhaps it was there . . ."

"I suppose it's possible."

Then she shook her head. "No," she said, vehemently. "If we had *really* met, I would have remembered you. Perhaps I saw you somewhere on the street, in a crowd." She seemed tantalized, tormented. She could not take her eyes from his face. "*Dio mio,*" she said. "I *do* know you. But how? Where?"

It would have been easy to tell her then. But he did not. For the same and obvious reason that he had never told Allan Fischer, or Adriana, or anyone else. She would think he had gone off the deep end, that he was acting out some madman's fantasy. He *wanted* to tell her. He wanted to tell her that her husband, Vittorio Favretto, was still alive. In the sense that he, or his spirit, was still alive in his, David's, body. But of course, it was impossible. He still told himself that this whole experience, this experience of reincarnation, even though it manifested itself as the truth, could still be a fantasy, could still be a dream, and he would one day wake up to realize it.

And of course, there was no way he could tell Bianca Favretto until he could prove it somehow. Prove that he was who he used to be.

If he could do that, then he could tell the whole world.

"David," she said. "Tell me about yourself."

"There isn't anything to tell."

"No," she said. "I want to know everything. Who you are,

where you were born, what you do, the kind of life you have. I want to know everything, everything . . ."

He told her all about himself, right through the dessert, an ice cream and sherbet mold called *bomba campiello,* and she listened intently, watching him all the time, never interrupting. He was afraid he was being garrulous, but he could see that she was deeply interested and that her thirst to know all about him was really genuine. The coffee came, and then the old woman who had served them came in to clear the remainder of the dishes. She was just about to go back into the house when the *contessa* asked her to wait a moment. Then she said:

"Rosalba, you may take the rest of the day off."

David sensed that she had dismissed the woman on impulse; it was a spur-of-the-moment decision. The old woman's face showed nothing, but she glanced sidewise at David, then nodded and left.

"She will leave the house now," said the *contessa.* "And we will be alone."

They were both silent for a while. Then she said to him, almost in a matter-of-fact way:

"You knew it would come to this."

"Yes."

"So did I. I knew it, *caro,* even though we had hardly met. I am not a woman who gives herself to any man freely. And especially to such a recent acquaintance. But somehow I feel that I know you better than I knew any man—except Vittorio." She spoke very quietly now. "But Vittorio is dead, and I am still very much alive. And this—it seemed inevitable. Bound to happen. Almost—what is the word?— ordained." Then she hesitated. "Still, I feel strange about this—so strange. It is unnatural. Wrong . . ."

"Why? Because of your husband?"

"Teodoro?" She shook her head. "No. Not because of him. I do not believe he would care if he knew. No, it is because I am much older than you, David—twice as old. *Dio mio,* old enough to be your mother."

171

"I don't think of you that way . . ."

"I know. But it is the truth. When I saw you, a little while ago, standing there beside Ludovico, I thought the two of you could be brothers. Yet, I still wanted you, David. I still . . ."

He rose and came around the table to her and put his arm around her shoulder. She looked up at him, her lips parted, and he kissed her, and after that she rose from the table, took his hand, and whispered:

"Come, *caro*. Let us go upstairs."

He had never experienced any woman like her in his life, and he knew he never would again.

At first, when both their heads were side by side on the pillow, when both bodies came together, when arms and legs were entangled, he lay immobile, simply holding her, feeling the thrilling touch of her flesh, her warmth and closeness, tasting her lips gently at first, knowing his hunger, and sensing hers, but holding back, waiting a little while, making every moment last.

It was like lying deep in some long dream, sailing on some gentle, billowing sea, and yet he distinctly heard the sounds from outside her bedroom window, the slap of a gondolier's oar and the bump of his craft in some waterway beyond the garden, the voices of a man and woman quarreling as their steps clipclopped on stone, and, distantly, the faint sounds of the motor-driven boats moving up and down the Grand Canal.

Then, her arms tightened around him, and her breath came shorter, and he held her closer, and all the sounds of the city disappeared, and now his ears were attuned only to the small sounds of themselves, as their lovemaking built in tempo and intensity, and he heard their hearts thudding against each other, and in his ears there was a distant roaring, like the smash of sea upon the beach.

Her mouth was greedy, hungry for his, and his ecstasy was unbearable, he tasted her breasts, first one, then the other, and she writhed and cried out, and he continued to kiss

172

her body, and then she told him, wordlessly, that she was ready, she signaled him and let him know that the time had come, and when they had locked, he felt the long reaching of her stroke, and its deepening, and he thrust into her, and it seemed to become harder and harder as he did, it seemed to swell inside of her, and she moaned and sighed and made little noises, and tossed her body back and forth, her breath coming in agonizing gasps.

And just before she came, she cried out his name:

"Vittorio, Vittorio . . . !"

She moaned it over and over again, as he came with her, *Vittorio, Vittorio*. Then at last, they were done, and she made little kitten cries, and her eyes lost their madness and became soft in her perspiring face, and she whispered softly, "*Amore mio, amore mio*," and reached out to touch his lips with her fingertips and then to caress his cheek, beginning to murmur, "*bello, meraviglioso*," and she called him *amanti*, my lover.

Then her eyes widened, and she remembered. Even in the heat of her orgasm, she remembered, and her face reddened and she pushed him off and away from her, and they lay together, side by side. Then she cried out:

"*Dio mio! Dio mio!*"

"What is it, Bianca? What's the matter?"

"I am so ashamed." She put her hands over her eyes. "Oh, David, I am so ashamed. In the middle of our lovemaking, in the very middle, I called out *his* name. Vittorio's. Not yours."

"It's all right."

"No. I have insulted you. I have never done such a thing in my life. A thing like this is unforgivable."

"You must have loved him very much."

"More than my own life," she said. "But that is not enough." She hesitated. He was aware that she was looking at him strangely now. "I can only try to explain . . ."

"You don't have to explain anything."

"I must, David. Not only to you. But to myself. It is very strange. I do not understand it."

"Yes?"

173

"To lie in the arms of a man and cry the name of another —I know this is horrible, shameful. Yet—at the time, I thought you were Vittorio. The touch of you was like that of Vittorio. The smell of you, the way your hands caressed me, the little ways you make love, they were all Vittorio's. My God, you *were* Vittorio. When I called your name, you were he." She covered her face with her hands. "*Dio*, I must be going mad."

He stroked her face. "No. No, Bianca. It's all understandable."

"It was all in my mind, yes? I *wanted* you to be Vittorio. I imagined you to be him."

"Something like that."

"You're not angry with me, *caro?*" she beseeched him. "You won't be angry?"

He kissed her gently, on the lips.

"No. Of course not. I told you, I understand."

"No one has ever made love to me like that. Not since Vittorio. He was about your age, *caro*, when we were last together. It was so strange. A few moments ago. As though he had come back. Into my bed, into my life." Her voice shook a little. "David, I do not believe in ghosts. But I tell you again—I am frightened. I fear for my mind."

He comforted her again. Up to now, he had still had a few lingering doubts as to who he had been. He still hadn't been able to totally believe what was obvious. But now those doubts had gone. This radiantly beautiful woman, lying next to him, naked, had once been his wife. This had once been their bed, and this had been their room.

He thought of telling her. I *am* Vittorio. *But in another body, Bianca.* If I loved like him, it was not your imagination. It was because I *was* him. I have come back to you, not from the grave, but in another way.

But he said nothing.

She started to weep quietly. He held her in his arms until she stopped.

Finally, under his gentle prodding, she started to talk about her dead husband.

After all these years, she told him, Vittorio was the only man she had ever loved. She had realized that she could not go on mourning forever, and a year or two after he was officially declared dead she had married Teodoro Borsato. She had had a certain affection for him, thinking he was kind, someone she could lean on, someone who could be a good stepfather to her son.

But gradually she had been disillusioned. The marriage had turned sour. She realized, in time, that Borsato had been after the Favretto money. It was she who held the purse strings, and he was always demanding money. Money to invest in wild speculation in the market in Milan, money to gamble away at the casino, money to play the role of the affluent Venetian gentleman. He was inconsiderate and domineering.

"I'm really afraid of him," she said. "We hardly speak to each other now. We haven't been intimate for a long time. And Teodoro, of course, has his women."

"Women?"

"Yes. Not just one, but several. Not only in Venice but in Milan and Rome. He is always going on business trips to these places, where he has no real business, except his *amanti*. He has practically flaunted them in my face, but I no longer care."

"And you?" He was confused, thinking of some way to say it, delicately. "You've lived—well, like a nun?"

"I did for some years. Then I thought, why not? Vittorio is dead, and Teodoro is nothing, and, after all, I'm human." She turned her head to smile at him and then kissed him lightly. "As you very well know, *caro*. Anyway, Venice is full of attractive men. I took a few lovers. But only for a little while. Each seemed so pale—inadequate. No one took, or ever could take, the place of Vittorio. Until now."

He lay back on the bed, idly, watching her as she dressed.

He thought that if one word could describe her, in essence, it was "ripe." Her breasts, her mouth, her thighs, her hips, they were all lush and woman-ripe, the smoothness

175

of her skin, the curve of her back—all were tremendously sensuous, total woman.

They had tasted each other for a second time, and this time they had taken longer, lingered and dawdled, slowly arousing each other, dreamily, and this time, shortly before climax, in her ecstasy she had cried a name again.

But this time it was his, David, and not Vittorio.

Now he studied her, delighting in her as he watched, committing her to memory.

She sat before a vanity, totally naked, combing her hair. He kept watching her, amazed. She's old enough to be my mother, he reflected again, and yet she has the body of a young girl. Or, make that woman. The body is all woman, and there is nothing spare, nothing adolescent, nothing incomplete about it.

She picked up her brush now and tilted her head, as she started the long, rhythmic strokes through her gleaming, healthy hair. Stroke, and again stroke, each deliberate, each ritualized in a delightful, feminine way, each making a whispery sound, as the bristles rustled through the strands.

In the mirror, she saw him watching her, and she smiled, and with her free hand she blew a kiss at his reflection, and then she said:

"Please, please, *caro*. Now that I've found you, don't go away. Stay here in Venice."

"When shall we see each other again, Bianca?"

"I am free tomorrow night."

"Where?"

"Here."

"And after that?"

"Anywhere. Here, if possible. At your hotel. It doesn't matter. As long as we see each other. As often as we can."

He had just entered the lobby and was headed for the elevator when the concierge called:

"A telephone call for you, Signore Drew." The concierge waved toward the telephone booth at the far end of the lobby. "You can take it there, if you wish."

He went into the booth and lifted the receiver.

"Hello?"

"David, Adriana."

"Adriana, I've been trying to get you—"

"I know, I know. I'm sorry I haven't been returning your calls. I've been terribly busy . . ."

"Look, I'm free tonight. If you'd be interested in dinner . . ."

"I'm sorry, David. But tonight I am packing."

"Packing?"

"I'm leaving Venice in the morning. It isn't just that I'm returning your call. I wanted to say goodbye."

He didn't even try to conceal his surprise.

"What's happened, Adriana? Where are you going?"

"You remember I told you about Giorgio?"

"Oh. Yes. The engineer in Libya."

"Well, I got a cable from him. A few days ago. They're giving him a month's holiday. He's going to spend it in Morocco. In Marrakesh. He asked me to join him."

"I see. But I thought you and he—"

"I know." She sounded a little defensive. "I told you we were just friends. But then I thought it over. At first, I was going to say 'no' to Giorgio. But then, some things happened —well, I changed my mind. I decided 'why not?' It'll be good to get away for a little while."

"You're sure you want to go?"

There was a pause. "No, I am not really sure. But I'm going anyway. I know Giorgio isn't very exciting. What I mean is, he doesn't excite me. But he's attractive and amusing and he cares for me. That's important—more important than anything else. So I'll make whatever accommodation I can."

"I'll miss you, Adriana."

"And I'll miss you, David. You have been very nice. For a little while, I thought—" She laughed nervously, and then: "Never mind. As you Americans say—it is all water under the bridge. Now, I must go. *Addío, caro.*"

"Goodbye, Adriana."

He hung up and felt a genuine sense of regret. He had

enjoyed Adriana, and in a certain way he would miss her. They had developed an affection for each other, but they had both known that it would never really go anywhere from there. At least, he had known it.

And all he could think of now was one woman, and that was Bianca Favretto.

He went up to his room, undressed, and prepared to shower.

He was still stunned by what had happened at the palazzo a little while ago. He had been in love with Bianca Favretto once, in another time and as someone else, and now he was in love with her all over again. This had stayed consistent in life and through death and back to life again; only the body changed, the spirit remained constant.

His mind was in a whirl. He tried to think of the immediate future. *Where do we go from here?*

He decided to let it ride. Put it on the back burner for a while. He was too confused to think it through and make any decisions now. He took off his robe and turned on the shower. For a moment, he was reluctant to step under the water. He could smell her perfume on his body and, more than that, the perfume of her own flesh, and he hated to wash it off. It delighted him. It made him feel close to her, as though she were part of him. Many times, after going to bed with some girl, he was glad to shower, to wash off the scent. But not now. Not this time. This was different.

After he showered, he sat down to meditate.

The sound of the mantra came in high at first, as always, with a hard and steady beat. A series of vagrant thoughts floated across his mind. He thought of Cassie Knox and wondered what she was doing back in New York, and he thought of jogging with her in the early morning and making love to her. He thought of Allan Fischer and how he was doing in Iran, and he thought of the old job he had had at Datafax and all the people he had known there, and he thought that when he got back he'd have to start looking

178

for a job all over again, but then, good systems men were hard to find, and he shouldn't have any trouble, he really shouldn't.

His thoughts swung back to the present, and they were filled with Bianca Favretto, they centered exclusively on her, and the mantra became fainter and fainter.

Finally, it became a distant echo and vanished completely, and his mind was clear and at rest, completely free of any thought . . .

Now, it came into focus again.

The picture.

But now it was clear. Horribly clear.

Nothing was blurred any longer. There was the human-headed snake, with that strange, rippling effect of light and shadow.

It was on the roof edge looking down over the shoulder of a man. The man was standing in front of him. He was dressed in black. He had his arm raised high. In his hand was a knife, glinting in the light of the moon. The face of the man was twisted in a smile of hatred. His eyes shone with the lust of killing, and saliva drooled from his mouth.

The face of the assassin was clear in the moonlight. It was very clear.

It was the face of Teodoro Borsato.

15

THAT night, David Drew walked for what seemed to be miles. Trying to clear his head, to put it all together . . .

The image he had seen in his meditation haunted him. He sensed it was the last one he would see, that any memory of his former life had ended with his death. He kept seeing the smile on Borsato's face, the ugly, murderous smile, just before he plunged the knife home. It revolted him, cast him into a black mood. Now, he transferred what he saw on the assassin's face to Venice itself. A city smiling falsely. Yet, ugly.

It was low tide as he walked. The stink of the canal water, thickened by the city's effluvium, offended his nostrils. The green and brown slime around the painted mooring posts depressed him. The palaces had the look of decay, part of some doomed slum, old roués in flaking stucco and tarnished ornaments. In one of the narrow canals, he saw the remains of some dead animal floating against the base of a retaining wall in the middle of a clump of assorted garbage.

Finally, exhausted, he found himself on a bench in the gardens near the Capitaneria del Porto. He sat there awhile, staring across the lagoon to Santa Maria della Salute and San Giorgio Maggiore, trying to think it through.

In a sense, he reflected, this was the end of the scenario. He knew now who he had been and how he had lived and how he had died. If he had been sent here by some mysterious Hand on some mission to prove the eternal truth of reincarnation, it was so proved. But only to himself. There was no way to prove it to anyone else. He could shout it from the rooftops, but nobody would believe it. They might think him unbalanced. Another visionary, another life-after-death freak, a crazy.

His mission in Venice, then, whatever it actually was, seemed to be finished. It was time to go back home. He thought of Bianca Favretto. He thought of her with tremendous longing and regret. He knew what the truth was, and he faced it reluctantly. There was no way they could meld their lives together, as they had before. As Vittorio Favretto, he had been Bianca's age. As David Drew, he was now only half her age. He thought again of meeting her son, Ludovico. In a sense, his son. And yet, in terms of age, they could have been brothers.

He had to face it. He and Bianca were worlds apart. She lived in Venice, her whole life was here. But his life, his work, his friends, his future were all back in the United States. There was no place for him here in Venice. And obviously he couldn't stay here indefinitely. He couldn't afford it. Even now, his money was beginning to run out. Tomorrow he'd have to cable his bank for more . . .

Clearly, then, the thing to do was to say goodbye. Say goodbye to Bianca and to Venice, and go back to New York. Forget about this whole reincarnation thing, forget that it ever happened, put it aside like some nightmare, some dream. Find a job, find a girl, get back in the mainstream, where he really belonged . . .

This was all very logical. All good thinking; it made sense.

Yet, he knew he wasn't ready to leave Venice. Not yet. In his heart, he knew he couldn't, even if he wanted to.

There was still a reason to stay here. At first thought, he had convinced himself that the death of Vittorio Favretto was the end of the scenario. But now, he knew this was false. He knew the true ending was yet to come.

There was one more step to go.

Back in his room, before he finally drifted off to sleep, he spent an hour studying a map of Venice.

He traced the possible routes between the Fondamenta Narisi and St. Mark's, blocking out three or four in pencil. There were any number of them, a labyrinth of *calles,* canal bridges, alleys, and *campielli.* Vittorio Favretto, setting out to meet Borsato, might have taken any one of them.

And somewhere along one of them, from the edge of some roof, a human head on a serpent's body, carved in stone, looked down on the spot where Vittorio Favretto had died.

The next morning, with the map in his hand, he started from St. Mark's and walked a route to the Fondamenta Narisi, looking up toward the roofs.

He saw plenty of stone carvings, many of them small and hard to see. There were heads of nymphs, bearded prophets, lions, and more lions, the heads of cherubs, cupids, and angels.

But no human head on a snake's body.

From the palazzo, he took another route back toward St. Mark's.

And still nothing.

He spent the whole day in this fashion, walking back and forth, taking one possible route after another.

And still nothing.

That evening, just before he set out for the palazzo again, this time to see Bianca Favretto, he marked out further possible routes. All he could do was keep trying.

182

That damned human-headed snake was *somewhere.* And sooner or later, he knew he would find it.

After the first time, when they both lay side by side in the big bed, temporarily spent, he said:

"Bianca, there's something I'm curious about."

"Yes, *caro?*"

"It concerns your husband. Your first husband, Vittorio, I mean. But it may be too painful for you to recall . . . "

"No. It's been a long time now. Don't worry about it. What is it you want to know?"

"On the night, he—he disappeared. When did you see him last?"

"I was with him just before he left to meet Teodoro. I saw him leave for the Piazza San Marco—watched him go from the window." He turned his head to look at her. There was a faraway look in her eyes. "Do you know, *caro,* I did not want him to go. I tried to stop him."

"Yes? Why?"

"I don't know. I had some kind of feeling, a premonition. An intuition. Call it anything. But suddenly I was afraid, I did not want him to go. Then, thinking I was being foolish, silly, really, I changed my mind. If I had stopped him— well, who knows? He might still be here."

"Bianca, tell me. Did he often walk from the palazzo here to the Piazza?"

"Often."

"Do you know whether he took any particular route. I mean, was there any one way he favored?"

She looked at him, puzzled.

"Why, no. I don't think so. Of course, I don't know for sure. But Vittorio loved to wander, depending on his mood. I remember, now, his sometimes telling me that he had taken a longer route than necessary, just to see this particular church, or that *campiello.*"

"But he didn't say which way he was going to walk to San Marco that night."

"No." And again, puzzled: "Why do you ask all this, caro?"

"Oh," he said. "It's nothing. Just interested. Just curious." Then, after a pause: "How did you first find out Vittorio was missing?"

"Teodoro phoned. From Florian's. He wanted to know where Vittorio was, why he hadn't appeared to keep his appointment."

"I see. Teodoro called." Then a thought came to him, and he said: "Speaking of Borsato, Bianca."

"Yes?"

"There's something I wonder about. I meant to ask you before."

"What is that?"

"If you're so unhappy with him—why don't you divorce him? It's legal here in Italy now, isn't it?"

"Yes. It has been for some years now. Ever since 1960. Before that, a wife could not be free of her husband unless she could get an annulment from the ecclesiastical courts. The husband still kept the right to open her mail, forbid her to see people he didn't like, and, in some cases, to even strike her with his fist, legally. She could go to jail for adultery, while, if he were guilty of the same thing, he went free. We women have new rights, we have been liberated, as you say in America. But in Italy, this still does not mean much to many husbands. They are very slow to change, to accept the new ways. Teodoro is one of them. And my father, unfortunately, is another. This makes divorce for me very difficult."

He was puzzled. "I still don't understand."

"Oh," she said. "Of course. I have not been clear. You see, caro, I was a Gatti before I married Vittorio. The Gatti family is very old here in Venice, descended from one of the doges. I do not boast, I simply state facts. My family is very rich and very powerful, and it is also very conservative and Catholic. My father, Benedetto Gatti, who is head of the family here, does not like Teodoro. But he does not like divorce, either. He regards it as an offense against the

184

Church. I have spoken about it to him, and he is strongly against it. He and all my uncles, and my two brothers. They do not want scandal in the family. Mud on the Gatti name, they all say, would be unthinkable. So—I have respected my father's wishes. Up to now."

"Up to now."

"Yes," she said, softly.

She smiled up at him, and her lips parted, and he leaned down and kissed her, and they began again.

Shortly after dawn, David Drew left the Palazzo Favretto.

He did not notice a gondolier poling his craft along the canal. But the gondolier, who was returning from an all-night assignation of his own, noticed him. His name was Carlo Grapiglia, and it so happened that his regular station was at the Bacino Orseolo.

Carlo Grapiglia recognized the young American. He had seen him before, when he had come to the Bacino asking for Bruno Savoldo.

He laughed softly, as he watched David striding down the *fondamenta*. He found it very amusing, really. Here was the Contessa Favretto, this fine aristocratic bitch with her nose always in the air, with a reputation as the purest of the pure, aloof and unapproachable, sleeping not with one of her noble friends, but with an ordinary tourist. And one half her age, at that.

The fact that the *contessa* was being stuck between the legs by somebody other than her husband was a juicy piece of gossip. And in a few days, no, in a few hours, it would be all over Venice. And why not? That was fine with Carlo Grapiglia. He was a Communist, and so were the other gondoliers, those he knew. It was nice to be able, even in a small way, to kick these rich capitalists, these aristocratic *bastardi*, right in the *coglioni*.

And the man who would be particularly interested in this romantic rendezvous, he knew, would be his close friend and fellow gondolier, Bruno Savoldo.

The next two days, David went through the same routine.

He walked from the palazzo to St. Mark's, taking a new route each time. And each time he craned his neck until it was stiff, studying the eaves and rooftops.

Still nothing.

It was particularly difficult, since, while he could see the roofs on the opposite side of a *calle* or *fondamenta,* it was almost impossible to make out those on the same side of the passageway where he stood, since he had to look straight up. The angle of sight was vertical, and, therefore, anything almost directly overhead, particularly anything small, like this particular piece of sculpture, was very hard to see.

He was baffled by his lack of success. He knew that human-headed snake was somewhere between the Fondamenta Narisi and St. Mark's. It was sticking its evil face out from somewhere.

But where?

He thought again of the obscene stone sculpture, curling from some roof, and then remembered that it seemed to have wavy lines moving across it—shimmering, erratic stripes of light and dark, as though it were reflecting something . . .

Then, suddenly, it hit him.

Water. Of course.

He swore at himself for not thinking of it before. The human-headed snake was reflecting the play and flow of water, which meant it overlooked some canal. He had seen the same shimmering effect on the sides of buildings, windows, and so on, when the moon shone on the canals. But up to now, the connection had escaped him.

All of which made his job much simpler.

There were only three or four canal routes leading from the palazzo to St. Mark's.

And the best way, the easiest way, to find that obscene stone grotesque was by gondola, where he could clearly see the roofs of the buildings on both sides.

186

16

In the morning, David went to the Bacino Orseolo. He saw Bruno standing in the center of a group of gondoliers. They were in the midst of an argument. Not that this was unusual. The gondoliers of Venice, David had discovered, always seemed to be arguing, shouting at each other, discussing politics, women, and how hard life was in general. Certainly, it was understandable. Waiting around idly for a fare, sometimes for hours, was boring. They had to blow off steam somehow.

They broke off suddenly, as they saw him approach, and turned to stare at him. They watched him silently, their faces amused. He realized that, for some reason, he had become the center of their attention. He had no idea why. But it made him a little uncomfortable. Savoldo came out of the group to greet him. He was cheerful, beaming.

187

"Ah, *buon giorno*, Signore Drew."

"*Buon giorno*, Bruno." Then: "I'll need you this morning. If you're available."

"Certainly," said Savoldo. "Certainly. It will be a pleasure to serve you." He tried to keep a straight face. "To the Palazzo Favretto, I suppose?"

"No. Not this time."

David took the tourist map from his pocket. He had marked, in red pencil, all the canals crossing through the area between the Fondamenta Narisi and St. Mark's. "I want you to take me down each *rio* you see here on the map."

Savoldo studied the map, then returned it to David.

"This could mean all day, Signore Drew."

"That's all right. I'll pay whatever you ask."

The gondolier looked at David, puzzled. To hire a gondola for a whole day took many thousands of lire. He wondered why the young American was so extravagant. And his curiosity got the better of him.

"Excuse me, *signore*. I know this is not my business. But is there some purpose in this?"

David explained that he was looking for the human-headed stone snake he had discussed with Savoldo before and thought it might possibly be on one of the roofs bordering these particular canals. Savoldo still had no idea why it was so important and did not really care. All tourists were half-crazy, he had decided long ago, and especially Americans. He needed the lire, and if this Signore Drew wanted to throw his money away, why it was fine with him.

As he edged the gondola out in the basin, he studied the back of his passenger's head. It was incredible that this American, in such a short space of time, had been able to bed down the *contessa*. More than that. To think she would even let him come anywhere near her. *Per amor di Dio*, really, it was unbelievable.

The young American, he had to admit, was very handsome and personable. Clearly, he was attractive to women. The

188

miracle was that he had taken the *contessa* in such a short period of time. The gossip was that she and Borsato had a very formal marriage, they did not sleep together and had not for years. Of course it was only gossip, and nobody could prove it. Gossip in Venice was a sport; everyone indulged in it. Still, it could be believed, it might just be true. The fact that this Signore Drew was much younger than she, young enough to be her son, did not matter. The Venetian aristocrats, in their amours, weren't fussy about matters like this. Old crones in some of the palazzi had been known to sleep with boys when it suited them. That, among other things. Also, it was very convenient for the *contessa* that he was a tourist. He would be gone soon. He wouldn't be around long enough to matter.

Bruno Savoldo chuckled. It would be interesting to see Borsato's reaction when he found he was wearing horns. Probably, he did not care who his wife slept with, as long as it was kept private. But to face your friends as a cuckolded husband—that was something different. Already, he relished Borsato's humiliation.

Well, Teodoro, he thought gleefully, you have a surprise waiting for you. But it isn't enough. I hope, he thought savagely, you, Teodoro Borsato, will come home with a fine dose of the *sifilide*. I hope one of your expensive *puttane* in Rome or Milan will send you home with an even more malicious disease, so that you will walk straddle-legged, and your teeth will fall out, until finally, you go blind.

For the injustice you have done me, Teodoro.

David had plotted a possible route which Vittorio Favretto might have taken on the last walk of his life. It began on the Fondamenta Narisi, then along the canal, Satupurtego Narisi. From there, Favretto would have crossed a canal, taking the bridge, the Ponte del Pestrin, then proceeded along the Calle del Pestrini into the Campo Francesco Morosini, and from there through the Calle del Spezier, and over another canal by way of the Ponte San Maurizio.

All that day, Savoldo piloted the gondola up one canal after another, crisscrossing this general area. Some of the canals were very narrow and passed through little-traveled areas.

Still, neither David nor the gondolier saw anything remotely resembling a human-headed snake peeking out from the roof of some building.

By late afternoon, as they came down a canal called the Rio de la Malvesia Vecchia, David was thoroughly discouraged. He knew it was somewhere, it had to be. But still, it eluded him. There was the possibility that they had actually passed by it without seeing it. It might have been hidden by the particular angle of a roof, which blocked it out from a gondola view. It might have been temporarily hidden by laundry hanging from clotheslines stretched between buildings. There was also the possibility that the snake head had been taken down or destroyed while the building on which it had stood was being remodeled. And, of course, the most probable reason was that he had not proceeded up the right canal.

He was just about to call it a day and tell Savoldo to take him back to the hotel when he saw it.

It was peeking out from a roof overlooking the canal.

There it was, the obscene face set on the serpentine body, wearing the same leering, malignant smile, the thick-lipped mouth baring its fangs.

Exactly as he had seen it in meditation.

"Bruno," he said.

"Yes?"

"Stop the gondola here."

"*Here, signore?* But why?"

David pointed upward. He was fascinated by the sculpture, and he did not notice Bruno Savoldo's face. He was busy now, reconstructing what had happened on the night he, as Vittorio Favretto, had died.

He looked at the *fondamenta* bordering the canal and recognized it as the one he had seen in his meditation. It was here, just at the edge of the canal, that Teodoro Borsato

190

had plunged the knife into his body. A few feet away, David saw a narrow street running under a building—what the Venetians called a *sottoportico*—and the sign read: *Sotoportego e Calle Lavezzera.*

It was probably under this *sottoportico*, thought David, that Borsato had hidden in the darkness, waiting for his prey to pass by. Somehow, he must have known that Favretto would be coming this way. Perhaps he had walked it with Favretto before and knew it was his favorite route. He, David Drew, did not have the answer to this. But the fact remained. The assassin simply lay in waiting, sure in his knowledge that his victim would come this way.

It was reasonable to suppose, too, that Borsato, after murdering Favretto, had disposed of the body right here, at this point in the canal, the area over which the gondola now floated. There would be no point in taking the corpse elsewhere. The Rio de la Malvesia Vecchia was not only handy, it was a perfect grave.

Now, David looked down over the side of the gondola.

He stared into the murky depths for a long time.

He shivered, knowing that he was looking down into his own grave.

Somewhere on the bottom lay whatever remained of Vittorio Favretto. He was sure that Borsato had weighted the corpse down somehow. The assassin would know that a body, unweighted, would come to the surface, be found, and after that there would be an investigation, in which he, Borsato would be questioned. And all this could be dangerous. No, Borsato would make sure his victim would never be found. And he hadn't been.

What was left of the corpse could lie on the bottom here forever, completely hidden by many feet of dirty water.

Then, thought David, Teodoro Borsato, having murdered his best friend, and certain that he could never be accused, had waited until Vittorio had been officially proclaimed dead, and then courted and finally married the *contessa* . . .

Twenty-five years ago, this was the way that he, then

known as Vittorio Favretto, had died, this was the obscene way his life had ended, before he was born again.

He looked up at Savoldo.

"Bruno."

"*Si?*"

"How deep is it here?"

Savoldo stared at him. "Why? Why do you ask, *signore?*"

"Just curious. How deep is it?"

The gondolier took some time to answer. Then he said: "To tell you the truth, *signore,* I don't know."

"You must have some idea."

"It would be only a guess."

"Then guess."

The gondolier was watching David closely. His old ebullience had vanished completely. He seemed to be in some kind of trance. His answer came in a halting way.

"It depends on the tide. At high tide, it might be nine feet. At low tide, six. But as I said, *signore,* it is hard to guess." Then: "But you have not told me. Why is it so important?"

David sloughed off the question. He had no intention of making a confidant of the gondolier.

"It's not important. I was just curious."

They drifted over the area for a minute or two. Finally, David gave the order to leave. Savoldo seemed relieved at this. He propelled the gondola down the canal quickly, away from the Fondamenta de la Malvesia Vecchia.

When they arrived at the gondola station near his hotel, David paid Bruno Savoldo. It came to a small fortune. But the gondolier did not count the money, he did not even look at it. He simply thrust it into his pocket.

"*Grazie.*" Then: "You will need me tomorrow, *signore?*"

"No. I don't think so." Then David said:

"Bruno, before I go. A question."

"*Si?*"

"Where can I find police headquarters?"

192

Bruno Savoldo sat in his gondola for a while, watching David Drew's retreating back.

He felt ill, nauseated. His body had broken out into a hot sweat. His shirt was soaked with it.

Yet, he felt cold. He began to shiver.

Finally, he got out of the gondola and walked rapidly down the Riva degli Schiavoni.

He looked for the nearest bar and, finding it, ordered a *grappa* to steady his nerves. He drank it quickly, gratefully feeling its fire burning down his gullet and warming his stomach.

He saw his reflection in the mirror behind the barman. His face was ash-white, deathly pale.

He ordered another *grappa*, downed it at a gulp.

Then, fortified, he fumbled in his pockets, looking for coins. He went to the phone. The phone was attached to the wall, and open. There was no booth. He had to be careful what he said; there were people about.

Finally, after a ring or two at the other end, he heard the voice he wanted:

"Hello?"

"Teodoro, this is Bruno."

"Bruno?"

The name didn't seem to register for a moment. Savoldo hadn't talked to Borsato in a long time. For years. *Bastardo,* thought Savoldo, grimly. *How easily you forget.*

"Bruno, as in Savoldo."

"Oh." A long pause. Then: "What the hell do you want? The usual? More money?"

"Teodoro, I must see you."

"Oh," jeered Borsato. "You must see me. Why, *amico?* To try to blackmail me again? Well, you know that won't work. Now don't call me again. I tell you now, as I've told you before, it's useless."

"Teodoro," he interrupted, quietly. "I did not call to ask for money. Not this time. You had better see me. And at once."

193

There was a pause at the other end. Borsato had been caught by something in the gondolier's voice.

"What is this, Bruno? What are you talking about?"

"Teodoro, someone knows."

There was a long pause from Borsato. Then he asked: "What are you talking about?"

"I'm trying to tell you. Someone knows."

"About—about—?"

"Yes."

Again, there was a long silence, before Borsato said, "You're mad, Bruno. That's impossible. It's completely impossible. You're losing your mind."

"I think I am, Teodoro. Maybe I am going crazy. I know it's impossible, as you say. Twenty-five years, and it's long forgotten. Or so we thought. Who would ever know? And the answer to that is, somebody does. Somebody knows, Teodoro."

He waited awhile for Borsato to speak. And finally, calmly, Borsato said: "All right, Bruno. Where shall we meet? And when?"

They made arrangements to meet late that evening at a cafe called Da Sebastiano. It was a place Savoldo knew, near the Old Ghetto, an area in which neither of them was apt to be known or recognized.

When the gondolier hung up, he went to the bar.

Agitated, he ordered another drink.

He stared at himself in the mirror, and now it all came back. That night twenty-five years ago. Borsato had told him what he intended to do and that he needed help; he had promised Savoldo an enormous amount of money, half beforehand and half on delivery, after the job was done. At the time, Savoldo had been cruelly pressed for money. His wife had been in the hospital, desperately sick; she had been there for weeks, and he had been drained of every lira. And he heavily owed the moneylenders, besides. He had nothing against Count Favretto—he liked his employer—

but his back was to the wall, with a spike driven through it, and so he had swallowed his conscience and gone along.

Borsato had assured him that there was no chance, no possible chance whatever, that anybody would ever know.

He had planned the whole thing perfectly. At the time, Borsato lived in an apartment on the Campiello dei Calegher. He had phoned Vittorio Favretto to stop by at his place, and together they would walk to the Piazza San Marco. The *campiello* was just beyond the Fondamenta de la Malvesia Vecchia, and in order to reach it, Favretto would have to pass it. There was no other possible way he could come.

So, they had dressed themselves in black and waited in the darkness under the *sottoportico*, and they had heard the ring of Favretto's footsteps and seen him coming in the moonlight that filtered down through the gap in the buildings lining the *fondamenta* and the canal. They had agreed that they would not attack if, by chance, some other pedestrian appeared. But there was none; the *fondamenta* and the entire area around it were deserted.

After that, they leaped on their quarry and did what they had planned to do, and they lowered Favretto's body into the canal, and the weights they had attached to him dragged him down, and he was out of sight forever.

But not out of mind.

For years after that, Savoldo had recurring nightmares of that evening, and his conscience had eaten into his soul, and he cursed himself bitterly for ever having been involved. Especially since Teodoro Borsato had never given him the other half of the sum on which they had agreed. At first, it was promises, promises, and then, even after he had married the *contessa* and come into her money, it was still more promises, until he realized that Borsato never intended to pay him. And, to add insult to injury, Borsato had fired him from the family service, as well.

And so, through the years, Bruno Savoldo had nursed his bitterness against Borsato. That had always stayed alive. But as the years passed, he had managed to shove that long-ago September night back into the recesses of his mind, so that it became a kind of dream, a fantasy, which had never really happened.

But now, it had all come back with this young American, David Drew.

He twirled the liquor glass in his fingers, staring at the fiery brandy as he swished it around. Then he downed the *grappa* with one gulp.

His head was spinning now. Something monstrous is going on here, he thought. But what? Who is this Signore Drew? Who is he, really?

Madonna mia, what does he know?

17

THAT evening, David was unable to get very deep into his meditation.

He tried to relax, but it was no use. The mantra continued to beat without diminishing. One thought after another crossed his mind and spun around and around. All of them concerned Vittorio Favretto.

Finally, he came out of it. A few moments later, his phone rang.

"David, it is Bianca."

"Yes, Bianca. Yes."

"I miss you, *caro*. And tonight, I am free."

"Where shall we meet?"

"At your hotel." She laughed. "You're sure you want to see me?"

"You know how I feel, Bianca."

"Yes," she said. "I think I do. It is the way I feel."

197

"When shall I expect you?"

"It will take me a little time. I am calling from the airport."

"The airport? What—"

"I'll explain later. Please, David—give me your room number. I don't want to ask the concierge."

"It's three-oh-two."

"I love you, *caro*," she said, softly. "I love you very much."

Then she hung up.

Later, when she came into his room, she explained that she had set out for an overnight trip to Milan. To do some shopping, see some friends.

In the airport, just before she was going to board the plane, she thought of him and wanted to be with him so badly. Then, she had told herself, why not? The evening was hers, Teodoro would think she had spent the night in Milan, he would never know the difference, and as a matter of fact, she did not care too much, at this point, whether he did. She realized it was stupid to spend a very dull night in some hotel in Milan, when she could simply stay in Venice and be in his arms all night. It was one thing to sleep briefly with a lover and then see him go home. But to spend the whole night with him and wake up to feel him still next to you, to see his face on the pillow when you first opened your eyes in the morning, to stand in the shower with him, to have breakfast with him, well that was different, that was something lovely, exquisite . . .

Later, just before she came to climax, and totally unaware, as she had been before, she cried out his old name again:

"Vittorio! Vittorio!"

Sebastiano's was a noisy and dingy place, reeking with the odor of greasy food and cheap wine and loud with the conversation of the workers who frequented it.

Bruno Savoldo was sitting at a table in the rear of the place when Borsato came in. After they had each ordered a glass of wine, Borsato looked about him sourly.

198

"You might have picked a better place than this."

"I'm sorry if it offends your aristocratic nose, Teodoro. But it is better that we are not seen together. And nobody knows us here."

"All right, Bruno," said Teodoro, curtly. "You asked me to come to this miserable place. Make it short. What is all this nonsense you spoke of?"

"Teodoro," said the gondolier. "Be careful."

"Of what?"

"Don't talk to me as if I were dirt."

"Just get on with it."

"*Bastardo*. You still owe me, and you've never paid me."

"Listen, my friend. I did not come here to quarrel with you. Or to go over another one of those boring discussions about some imagined debt I owe you." His eyes narrowed as he studied Savoldo. "You stink of *grappa*." He began to rise. "As a matter of fact, you're drunk. Imagining things . . ."

"Sit down, Teodoro."

"Listen, I don't have time to—"

"*Sit down.*"

Savoldo's voice was commanding. His eyes were very cold. Borsato hesitated and then sat down.

"Very well. I suppose I ought to listen."

"You had *better* listen."

"You said someone knows. About Vittorio."

"Yes."

"May I ask who?"

"A young American. A Signore David Drew." Savoldo saw his companion react. "You know him, Teodoro?"

"I have met him, yes. But what's he got to do with all this?"

Savoldo then told him what had happened. This American, Drew, had made him stop his gondola directly over the spot where they had dumped the body overboard. He had seemed to know exactly where it was by spotting a sculpture in a roof overlooking the *fondamenta*, where they had am-

199

bushed Vittorio Favretto. Drew had then stared down into the water. He had asked how deep the water was over Favretto's grave. Then, finally, he had asked directions to police headquarters. He, Savoldo, had asked the American what was going on. The man Drew had been evasive, simply saying that he was curious.

Borsato listened, fascinated. After Savoldo finished, there was a long silence. Then:

"Bruno, it's impossible."

"I tell you it happened. Just as I told you. He *knows*, Teodoro."

"But he can't. This was twenty-five years ago. All this happened before this man was born. Or perhaps when he was a year or two old."

"I know that. Yet, there it is."

"Who is he? Do you know anything about him?"

"Nothing. Except to know this, he must be an incarnation of the devil."

"Where is he staying?"

"At the Donatello."

"I wonder if he's ever been to Venice before?"

"No. He told me this was his first visit." He paused, then said: "You know, Teodoro, I've often thought—" He hesitated.

"Yes?"

"I've often thought that perhaps that night—there was a witness."

"You're seeing ghosts, Bruno."

"Still, it's possible."

"No. It was dark. There was no one else around. But, for a moment, let's assume you're right."

"Well?"

"Why hasn't this witness ever come forward and told the police?"

"You have a point."

"I have a point, because there wasn't any witness."

"Then how does *he* know?"

Borsato shrugged. "I have no idea. As you say, he may be an incarnation of the devil. But I doubt it."

"I told you he's going to the police."

"What of it?" said Borsato calmly.

Savoldo's voice became shrill. "How can you sit there and act as though—"

"Keep your voice down, you fool. You want everyone in this miserable place to hear you?"

"All right." Savoldo shook his head. "I admit it. I'm frightened. I don't like it. I feel trouble coming. I feel it in my bones."

"Calm down. There's nothing to worry about."

"No?"

"Bruno, you are a very stupid man. The police will think he's crazy. They'll throw him out of the office. Even you can see that."

"All right. Maybe they would. But there's still that damned question. How did he *know?*"

"I don't know. It's absurd. We really don't know *what* he knows. If anything." He studied Savoldo closely. "Bruno, are you sure you didn't just imagine this?"

Savoldo looked at Borsato coldly. "Now and then, during my lifetime, Teodoro, I have been a fool. Especially when I have dealt with you. But don't take me for a fool about this. I have told you exactly what has happened. He knew exactly what he was looking for. He knew all about that carving on the roof, something that I had never even noticed myself, even though I've gone by it a hundred times. Personally, I'd feel a lot easier if this American, this Drew, would leave Venice. He makes my skin crawl, Teodoro. I have a feeling he could be dangerous."

"It would help to know more about him. Who he really is, what he's doing here, how long he intends to stay."

Savoldo leaned back, watching Borsato. Then, savoring his words:

"There's one way to find out, Teodoro."

"Yes?"

"Ask your wife."

Borsato looked at him, startled.

"Bianca?"

"She knows him very well." Savoldo grinned. "In fact, I have it on good authority that she is very close to him."

Borsato's face froze into a hard mask. He stared at the gondolier.

"Now, what does that mean?"

"Surely, Teodoro, you can guess."

"I don't believe it."

"It's all over Venice, *amico mio*. By this time, everybody knows you are wearing horns."

"You lie."

Suddenly, he reached over and seized the gondolier by the shirt collar. He squeezed it around Savoldo's neck. His eyes were blazing. "Damn you, Bruno, you lie."

"Let me go, Teodoro."

"I ought to cut out your lying tongue."

"I said, *let* me go!"

He tore Borsato's hand from his throat and pushed him back into his chair. He smiled at the anguish on the lawyer's face. This was something he had looked forward to with great relish. *For the injustice you have done me, Teodoro.*

He knew Borsato, knew the kind of man he was. He knew Borsato cared nothing about his wife's affairs, as long as they were private. The rich in Venice, as well as those in Rome or Milan or anywhere else, were not above playing musical chairs with each other's wives. It was part of the *dolce vita*, an antidote to boredom. But the word was *discreto*. Discreet. Once it became public, then it was another matter. To Teodoro Borsato, it meant a tremendous loss of face. To sit on the Piazza, to go to the theater, to gamble at the casino, to know that everywhere he went people were gossiping about him, laughing and whispering, saying he had been cuckolded by his *contessa*. And by whom? Nobody important. Trash. A young American tourist half her age. They would even sympathize with her. The implication

202

would be clear. Her husband simply wasn't taking care of her in bed. Clearly, she needed a young stud. And this tourist would be just right. Young and virile. Uncomplicated. Here today and gone tomorrow, and nobody the wiser.

"I still think you're lying," Borsato was saying.

Savoldo shrugged. "Think what you like."

"You'll have to prove it to me."

Savoldo told him how he knew. His friend, his fellow gondolier, Carlo Grapiglia, had recognized the young American hurrying out of the Palazzo Favretto just after dawn. And he concluded:

"Certainly, my dear Teodoro, it must be clear to you that Signore Drew did not spend the night in your home sleeping with your old housekeeper."

Borsato was silent for a while. Then, he rose.

"Excuse me, Bruno. I'll be back in a minute or two."

Borsato went to the bar, changed some money, and then went to a pay telephone in the rear of the establishment. He put in a call to the Cavalieri, the hotel in which Bianca always stayed when she went to Milan. In fact, he had heard her phone for a reservation there, just before she had left. He asked for the reception desk and said to the clerk:

"I'd like to talk to Signora Borsato, please."

There was a pause. "I am sorry, *signore*. The *signora* is not registered here."

"But she had a reservation for tonight."

"Yes. That is true. But she telephoned us from Venice and canceled it."

Borsato hung up and walked slowly back to the table, where Savoldo was waiting for him with a malicious smile.

"You made a phone call, I see."

"Yes."

"Did you find it interesting?"

"That, Bruno, is none of your damned business."

Savoldo shrugged. "As you wish. But there is something that is my damned business."

"Well?"

"The money you owe me."

"I owe you nothing."

"We made a bargain, Teodoro. Even if it was twenty-five years ago. Half before. And half after. You never paid me the second half."

"We've gone into this many times before, Bruno. I am tired of it. I've said it before, and I'll say it again. I owe you nothing. I paid you well for what you did."

"Teodoro, I'm a poor man and have been for years. I needed that money then, and I need it now. I'm sorry I ever got into this with you, I'm sorry I ever let you talk me into it."

"You have my sympathy," said Borsato sarcastically.

"*Ladro*. I ought to go to the police and tell them everything."

Borsato laughed. "Now *you're* going to the police, eh, Bruno? Say that again and listen to how stupid it sounds. The first thing they'd ask you is how you knew about all this. Implicate me, and you implicate yourself, you fool. You'll be giving them your own confession and signing your own death warrant as well." He laughed. "You've threatened me before with this old chestnut. Really, I'm tired of hearing it."

"So you think you've got me by the *coglioni*."

"Put it that way."

"Don't squeeze too hard, Teodoro. Some day we'll have an accounting."

"You really are an imbecile, Bruno," said Borsato, as he rose from his table. His face mirrored his contempt. "You always were, and you always will be." He threw some lire on the table. "Just to show you how generous I am—the wine is on me. If you want to call this filth wine."

"How can I help you, *signore?*"

The policeman at the desk, David decided, was a Venetian version of a desk sergeant, or even less, a minor functionary, a kind of clerk. He'd be wasting his time trying to tell his business to this man. And probably to anyone else here. He knew he shouldn't have come, it was insane, but he had to try. There was always a chance, however desperate, that someone might listen and perhaps take him seriously. And, at least, he would be on record with what he knew.

"I'd like to talk to someone who is acquainted with the old Favretto case."

"Ah." The man smiled. Apparently he was familiar with this, he had heard this kind of request before. "You are a *giornalista, signore?*"

"Yes."

"We have had others here. *Giornalisti, scrittori,* writers of all kinds. The man for you to see is the *tenente*, Lieutenant Cozzi. He knows something of the case. He was a young *poliziotto*, attached to the investigation at the time. If you will wait, I will ask him if he can see you. Your name?"

"Drew. David Drew."

"And where are you from, *signore?*"

"New York."

The man picked up the telephone and asked to speak to Lieutenant Enrico Cozzi. After a brief conversation, he hung up and told David that the *tenente* would be glad to see him. He was, however, busy at the moment, but if the *signore* could wait a half hour, no more . . .

David said he would be glad to wait and sat down on one of the hard benches lining the wall of the reception area. And again he thought, *what am I doing here, who is going to believe me?*

Finally, he was admitted to a small office. It was hot and stuffy, furnished in a spartan way. File cabinet, desk, a somewhat dilapidated sofa and chair. The man behind the desk was about fifty-five. He had gray hair, his face was pockmarked, and he was built like a tank, squat and solid with broad shoulders. He needed a shave, and his tie and collar were loosened against the heat of his small office. Somehow, he did not look like a Venetian. He was unprepossessing, but his smile was warm as he rose to greet David. Then he said, in heavily accented English:

"Good morning, Signore Drew. I am Lieutenant Cozzi."

"Buon giorno, tenente. Placere di fare la vostra conoscenza."

"Ah." Cozzi's black eyes lit up. "You speak Italian, then. Good. That will make it easier." The lieutenant had a stack of papers on his desk; he fumbled with them a little, and David had the impression that Cozzi was busy, that he was merely being polite in granting this interview, and that he proposed to make it as short as possible. "Now, Signore Drew, I understand you are an American journalist, and you would like me to give you what information I can on the old Favretto case."

"Lieutenant," said David, quickly. "I must be honest with you. In the first place, I'm not a journalist. It was just a pretext, an excuse to get in to see you."

"Yes?" Cozzi's dark eyes studied him curiously. "And why would you need an excuse, *signore?*"

"Because your man at the desk would never have let me see you if I told him the real reason I'm here. He'd think I was insane. And I'm afraid you're going to think the same, after I'm through. But I felt I had to come in and tell you what I know, anyway."

"I see." Cozzi reached for a cigarette and offered David one. But David refused. "Well, then—just what do you know, *signore?*"

David took a deep breath. "I know where you can find the body of Vittorio Favretto. I know who killed him and how it was done."

"I see." There was a long silence. Cozzi's face lost its animation. It became a mask. His eyes narrowed a little as they watched David. Then he repeated, slowly: "You know where you can find the body of Vittorio Favretto. You know who killed him and how it was done."

"Yes, sir."

"Forgive me, *signore*. But how old are you?"

"Twenty-five."

"And you have been to Venice before?"

"No. This is my first visit."

"And you are really going to give me all this information on something that happened about the time you were born? In a place you've never been?"

"Lieutenant Cozzi, I know you're skeptical . . . "

"Forgive me, *signore*. I do not wish to be impolite, but I am a very busy man, with much to do. If you will excuse me . . . "

"Please," said David, desperately. "Hear me out."

"As I said, I really do not have the time . . . "

"Give me a chance to tell my story, Lieutenant. I'll make it as short as I can. I know you're not going to believe it, I'm a fool for coming down here in the first place, but hear me out anyway."

Cozzi looked at David. He seemed undecided whether to humor David by listening or to throw him out of the office. Finally, he leaned back and lit a cigarette. His face said, *What the hell, might as well listen to this crank and get him off my back.*

"Very well, *signore*. I am listening."

David told him everything that had happened. He left nothing out. It was the first time he had revealed what he knew to anyone else. He studied Cozzi's face as he spoke. It was impassive. David could read nothing in it. Even as he told the lieutenant about his TM meditations and the images he had seen, he realized how insane they must sound. Yet, he continued anyway. He could not account for how or why this had all happened to him, he told Cozzi. But there it was and it was the truth. And, finally, when he had finished, Cozzi said:

"This is all interesting, Signore Drew. Very interesting." He studied David, then took a long breath. "Let me see if I understand you. This is so bizarre, I must be clear in my own mind. You say you once lived in Venice as Vittorio Favretto."

"Yes."

"And you were murdered by Teodoro Borsato. Or rather, Count Favretto was. And his corpse has been lying on the

207

bottom of the Rio de la Malvesia Vecchia for twenty-five years. And all this, you know through certain—what shall we call them?—visions?"

"Yes."

The lieutenant smiled politely. It was plain that he considered David some kind of lunatic. Harmless, but crazy.

"Signore Drew, I appreciate your coming here and telling me all this. But, really, I cannot take any of it seriously. Visions are for saints or prophets or other characters in the Bible. But not for pure ordinary humans like us. If you have seen visions, fine. That is your business. But they make very poor evidence in an investigation."

"You don't believe me, then. You don't believe a word I say."

"I am sorry, *signore*," said Cozzi. "I am a good Catholic, and I believe the soul survives, after the body is gone. But it goes either to heaven or hell, and not into the body of someone else. Dead is dead."

"Then you're not going to do anything?"

Cozzi spread his hands. "What is it you would want us to do?"

"Reopen the investigation."

"On the basis of your visions? Because you claim to be Vittorio Favretto, once removed? Please, Signore Drew, let us be realistic. How can I go to my *capo*, the commissioner, with *that?*"

"If you'll only take the trouble to drag that canal," said David, pleading now. "There's a chance to find the remains of Favretto."

"It's out of the question."

"All I ask is that you try. What can you lose?"

"Signore Drew," said Cozzi, patiently. "We are not in the business of dragging or draining canals on the basis of, well —fantasies. Venice happens to have a hundred and fifty canals, more or less. And in the centuries this city has been in existence, hundreds of people have disappeared mysteriously, from the time of the doges on. Murdered and

208

thrown in some canal. The point I'm making, *signore,* is that we could drag the bottom of every canal in Venice and perhaps get some interesting results. But unless we have some hard evidence—well, surely you understand." He stood up. "And now, if you'll excuse me. I have work to do."

Just as David left, a sergeant, carrying a sheaf of papers, passed him in the corridor and walked into Cozzi's office. He found the *tenente* leaning back in his chair, bemused, shaking his head incredulously.

Cozzi waved the sergeant to the chair which David had just vacated.

"Sit down, Emilio," he said. "I've been a policeman for thirty years, and I thought I'd heard everything. But this is one you won't believe."

18

AT the Palazzo Favretto, during dinner, Teodoro Borsato asked his wife, casually:

"Did you have a nice trip to Milan?"

"Yes."

"You stayed at the Cavalieri, of course."

"I always do."

"What did you buy in Milan, *cara?*"

She stiffened a little, watching him.

"Why do you ask?"

He shrugged. "Just curious. You went on a shopping trip, did you not, my dear Bianca?"

"Yes."

"Then I ask again. What did you buy?"

"Why is it important?"

"Usually, my dear, when you go to Milan, you come home with an armload of packages. This time, you came home with nothing. I saw you unpack. I saw nothing you might have bought in the shops on the Via Monte Napoleone. No dresses, no shoes, no new jewelry."

"Just what are you trying to say, Teodoro?"

"I say, my dear, that you are a liar."

"Oh?"

"I say that you have taken this young American, David Drew, as a lover. I say you spent a night with him, here in our house, and that last night you never left Venice at all, but slept with him at his hotel. There may be other times, for all I know."

"And?"

"It *is* true, then."

"Suppose it is," she said, coldly. "Do you care?"

"Not particularly," he said. "You have your private life, and I have mine. I question your taste, in seducing a boy young enough to be your son, Bianca. Really, I'm disappointed in you. But then, I suppose he's virile in his own way, and a stud is a stud, when you need him."

She began to rise from the table.

"I don't care to continue this discussion."

"But I do."

"I think you've said enough, Teodoro."

"Not quite. You asked me if I cared. The answer is I don't. I don't care a damn how many times this young American stabs you between your legs. As long as it's kept discreet—a private matter. But I *do* care when it becomes public, *cara*. All Venice apparently knows of it. And you understand, of course, I cannot tolerate this. It's a matter of my honor."

"Your honor," she said. "Sometimes you make me ill, Teodoro. What is your honor? Where has it been all these years?"

"I am still your husband. You are still my wife."

"I know. But those are lines from some farce, Teodoro. Some low comedy. This so-called marriage of ours should have ended years ago."

211

"Come, Bianca," he said. "I'm not going to quarrel with you now. But I *am* curious. About this American, this David Drew. Who is he? What is he really doing in Venice? Did he tell you how long he expects to stay?"

She did not even bother to answer. Her face was set and cold. She got up from the table and left the dining room.

An hour later, the phone rang, and Borsato answered it. It was Savoldo.

"What do *you* want, Bruno?"

"Don't shout at me. I don't like it, Teodoro."

"What is it this time?"

"You had better listen to me, and listen carefully."

"Well?"

"This American, Drew, *did* go to the police. He talked to Lieutenant Cozzi."

"Cozzi? Cozzi?" Borsato searched his memory. "Oh. Yes. I remember him."

"You should. He was involved in the original investigation."

"How do you know he went to the police?"

"I have a friend who is a *carabiniere*—the brother-in-law of a gondolier I know."

"All right. This man Drew went to the police. What of it? What could he possibly tell them?"

"That he knows where the body is."

"And you still think the police would listen to some wild fantasy like this?"

"I don't know ... "

"Use your brains, Bruno. I *told* you, they'll laugh at him. Throw him out. There's nothing he can prove. Absolutely nothing."

"All right. Maybe you think he's a big joke. Maybe the police will. But I don't. There's something about this man Drew. He sends chills up my back. I tell you, he's stirring up some kind of witch's brew." Savoldo's voice changed to a bewildered croak. "He's some kind of devil, Teodoro. Think about it. How could he know where Favretto is? The exact spot where he lies. How? How? Answer that!"

"I don't know."

"Teodoro, I tell you he's dangerous. He knows more than just this. I feel it in my bones. We'd better do something about him."

"What do you suggest?"

"I leave that to you, Teodoro. *You're* the clever one."

Again, David could not get down to the PA stage in his meditation.

The beat of the mantra remained high, a parade of thoughts swamped his mind.

It had been stupid to go to the police. He should have known they would laugh at him. Still, for some crazy reason, he had felt impelled to report to them anyway. They had judged him to be a kook, a crazy, and, actually, he didn't blame them.

His thoughts continued to float across the mantra. I have found out who I was. How I lived and how I died and when. This must be the end of the line. There's no use in pursuing it further. What good would it do? To me? To anybody else? To the world itself? It's like removing the cover of an old sewer and looking down into its dank, stinking interior. There is only evil within.

Let it go. There's no way you can prove Teodoro Borsato did anything. Let it die right here. Leave Venice for good, go back to New York, look for a job. Forget about the *contessa* and who she was to you. The whole thing is impossible, there is no future for either of you. Go back and look up Cassie Knox, or find another girl. Lead a normal life. Forget this whole trip. Think of it as a bad dream, put it in the back of your mind forever . . .

The phone rang. Abruptly, he was jarred out of his meditation. He picked up the phone.

"Signore Drew?"

"Yes."

"Teodoro Borsato here."

"Oh?"

Borsato's voice was pleasant, very cordial. "I think it is time we had a little talk."

David hesitated for a moment.

"I don't think we have anything to talk about, Borsato."

"Please, *signore*. I ask you not to take offense. I know I have been rude to you, and I apologize. It was very stupid of me, those remarks I made at the Lido. There was no reason for the way I acted, no excuse. Suppose we meet for a drink at Quadri's? At five, say? Just for a little chat."

"About what?"

"It really isn't something one can discuss on the phone, *signore*. Let us just say—it is a personal matter."

At five o'clock, David arrived on the square.

Quadri's cafe was tremendous. Its chairs and tables were symmetrically lined in long rows, extending out into the Piazza itself. He took a minute to run his eye over the rows, but he did not see Borsato.

He took a table in the first, or outer, row.

He could guess why Borsato wanted a "little chat" with him. He knew the encounter between them was bound to be unpleasant, and he did not look forward to it. But he tried to prepare himself for it. Borsato would accuse, and he would deny everything. He knew Borsato's cordiality over the phone had been a fraud. The man had disliked him on sight, hadn't even bothered to conceal his hostility.

It was interesting, now, to speculate about why. It was possible that Borsato had hated Vittorio Favretto long ago. Hated and envied him because Favretto had a noble and respected name, because he had Bianca and the palazzo, and because he was very rich. Men had murdered other men for much less than this. But now, in the light of what David now knew, it was possible that Borsato disliked him purely by instinct, without knowing why.

In any event, it wasn't important. It really didn't matter

214

what Borsato had to say to him. He was about to leave Venice for good. Tomorrow possibly. Or the next day at the latest.

He had played out the string, this was dead end, and his only regret would be leaving Bianca Favretto. His reunion with her had been short-lived, but he would remember her for the rest of his life, the way it was when they had been together. But now her husband had stepped in, and, of course, it had to be over, there was no way he could continue to see her.

He sat there at his table, in a kind of dreamy trance, staring out at the sight that now had become so familiar to him, hearing the familiar sounds . . .

A man at the next table was arguing with a waiter. He was convinced that there was some mistake in his bill. Either that, or this was a ripoff. He'd been to places like New York, London, Hong Kong, and Berlin, and nowhere had he been asked to pay this much for ice cream and coffee. The waiter shrugged and said, this is Venice, *signore.* The tourist swore and slapped down some money, told him he could shove it, and walked away.

He saw the usual stalls, their owners hawking beribboned straw hats, striped gondolier jerseys, souvenirs of Venice in every form, bandanas on which maps were printed, miniature gondolas made of metal, and others, more elaborate, made of glass and illuminated by batteries. There were the postcard vendors and the watercolor vendors, the guidebook vendors and those who sold glass paperweights in the shape of the campanile, and still others selling fake antiques, which, they swore by the blessed Madonna, were, in fact, *Signore e Signora, originalissimi.* Every free seat to this spectacle was occupied by those who could not afford or did not wish to pay the outrageous prices at Quadri's or Florian's. People rested their tired bodies and planted their rumps firmly on any step or balustrade they could find, on the ledges at the bottom of the campanile, around the flagstaffs, near the two columns of the Piazzetta.

And of course, there were the guides, shepherding their little groups, raising their colored umbrellas or candy canes, babbling in German, French, English, and Japanese, and people, people, people everywhere.

People sitting in the cafes, crowding the shaded arcades, buying glass and leather and lace or merely looking, people standing high and distant in the campanile belfry, others looking down from the clock tower, or the Palace of the Doges and swarming about in the square itself, wearing sensible cottons and sensible shoes and slacks and bright shirts, carrying cameras and guide books and chattering among themselves.

And then, as David watched, the hour struck, and, as usual, the bell rang on the corner of the Basilica, and the famous Moors, rigidly athletic as they swiveled from the hips, banged out the hour. Beside the old clock, the three Magi, led by the angel, came out from behind the shutters, bowed with great dignity to the Madonna, tiptoed stiffly around her, then vanished behind the shutters again, the little doors creakily closing behind them.

"*Buon giorno, signore.*" David came out of his reverie to see Borsato smiling down at him. "I hope I have not kept you waiting."

"No. You're right on time. I'm a little early."

Borsato took a chair. He was immaculately and rather formally dressed, in the manner of many upper-class Venetians. Gray suit, gray tie, white shirt. He studied David for a moment. He smiled again and said pleasantly:

"I watched you a moment before I spoke," he said. He nodded toward the square. "You seemed to be enjoying our little spectacle."

"I was."

"The Piazza at this time of year is great entertainment," said Borsato. "It is tourist time and, therefore, a fascinating circus. But it is not the true Venice. To see that, you must come in the winter."

"Yes?"

"Then you would see the Piazza when it is empty, and therefore truly beautiful. Especially when the snow falls. The fogs roll in, many of the hotels close, the restaurants are empty. No one sells souvenirs in the Piazza, the arcades are empty, the tourists have all gone home. Then it becomes *our* city—" He broke off as the waiter approached, waited expectantly. "Ah. Here we are. What will you have, *signore?*"

"A beer."

"A beer," said Borsato, cheerfully. "And a vermouth cassis for me." When the waiter left, he said: "They rob you outrageously here. But still, one always pays for the best seat in the house." He leaned back and lit a cigarette. "I hope you're enjoying your stay here, Signore Drew."

"I am."

"Will you be in Venice long?"

The remark was innocent enough. And very casual. Too casual. He sensed that, for some reason, the answer was important to Borsato.

"I don't know," he said, carefully. "That all depends."

"Yes. On what?"

"On some personal matters."

"Oh. I see. On some personal matters. But perhaps, *signore*, what you really mean is only *one* personal matter."

"Yes?"

"My wife."

Borsato's face was bland. He made the statement in a matter-of-fact way. He showed no sign of anger.

"I don't know what you are talking about."

"Come, come, *signore*. You were seen coming out of my palazzo just after dawn a few days ago. Surely you were not sleeping with my housekeeper, who is old and ugly. Moreover, I have it on good authority, namely one of the employees at your hotel, that my wife, the *contessa*, spent last night with you at your hotel, rather than in Milan, which was presumably her original destination. There is no need for either of us to wear masks. You are much younger than I, but we are both men of the world. We can speak of this

217

to each other in a civilized way, as one gentleman to another. Agreed?"

David was silent. For the moment, he could not fathom Borsato. He had expected outrage, some kind of flamboyant histrionics from the man. But he saw no sign of it. If Borsato was indeed angry, he was a consummate actor. Or else he was playing his cards close to his chest.

"All right," said David, finally. "So you know. I'm sorry it happened—but it has. I don't have anything else to say. Except that I'm not going to apologize for it."

Borsato spread his hands. He seemed injured at the very suggestion.

"My dear *signore*," he said. "There is no need to apologize. I understand perfectly how all this happened. You are a handsome man, virile and young, and someone different in Bianca's experience, an American. Clearly, you have a certain charm for women, and I compliment you on this. We Italians think we are great lovers but, to use your native expression, I take off my hat to you, *signore*. I do not hesitate to say that it is not every man who can attract my wife. When it comes to a choice of lovers, she is very fastidious. The fact that she brought you into her bed so quickly is a real feather in your cap. Frankly, I found it astonishing. But, then, my wife can be unpredictable. She is very disturbed, unstable, highly—how do you say it?—highly neurotic. But she is beautiful, and you are very young—and, of course, it was easy for her to seduce you."

"You're wrong about that, Borsato."

"Am I?"

"She didn't seduce me. It was my doing."

"Bravo," said Borsato. "Well said. I cannot say I am fond of you, Signore Drew. But I respect you as a gentleman. Still, there is no need to be gallant. I think I know my Bianca better than you."

"I think you've said enough. I think we both have."

"No," said Borsato. "Not quite. First, there is something you must understand. Bianca and I have an arrangement, an understanding. It is quite common here in Italy, among our upper classes. And perhaps the same in every country, including your own. She has her private life. I have my own. I ask her no questions, she asks me none. Neither of us interferes with the other."

"If that's true, you're interfering with her now, aren't you?"

"True. But I have a reason for this, *signore*. A very important reason. It is why I have asked for this talk with you."

"Yes?"

"If your affair with my wife had stayed private, I would have no objection. My head would be turned the other way. But unfortunately it has become known. Publicly, I mean. The gondolier who saw you coming out of my house spread the word immediately among his friends. These *porci*, these *bricconi*, are the scum of the earth. They will stop at nothing to embarrass their betters. At any rate, now the affair has become public, and the gossip has spread everywhere. And you have no idea how venomous gossip can be in Venice, *signore*, how exaggerated and twisted it can become. Now, the moment an affair like this becomes known, the rules change, *signore*. I am going to change those rules now."

Borsato's bland expression had disappeared. Slowly, his face hardened. David knew the threat would not be long in coming now, and he stiffened.

"You said you are going to change the rules."

"Yes."

"How?"

"You understand, *signore*, I am now the victim of your indiscretion, and Bianca's. My friends have begun to humiliate me with their snide remarks. My enemies are tearing my dignity to shreds. I am now a cuckold, a husband who wears horns in public, so to speak. I do not like people whispering when they see me or laughing behind my back. I am a Venetian, Signore Drew, an Italian. There is one thing an Italian like myself—or of any other class, for that matter—cannot stand. And that is to appear to be the fool. To be made to look ridiculous. Especially when it comes to his woman. You understand?"

"Yes. I can see that."

"Therefore, things will change in this way. First, you will, of course, never see Bianca again. Second, I must ask you to leave Venice immediately. To be specific, tomorrow. If you do so, people here will forget. They will view this affair as something temporary, a small dalliance with a stranger But if you stay, it will become very complicated. And for me, personally—quite unbearable. So, I am asking you to leave Venice for good, in the morning. No, I demand it."

"And if I refuse?"

"You would be very unwise, *signore*."

David stiffened. I'll be damned, he thought, if I let him run me out of town. Actually, he had planned to leave Venice in a day or two anyway. But, of course, Borsato did not know that. If he *did* leave, as planned, the Italian would think he had bluffed him out. He did not propose to give Borsato the satisfaction. Moreover, he wanted to see Bianca again, no matter what Borsato thought. The gray eyes were on him now, cold and ominous, under the beetling brows, waiting for some kind of answer. David was aware that Borsato wasn't playing games, that he was serious. He, David Drew, was fully aware that the threat was there, that this man could be dangerous. Very dangerous. Yet, the situation, as serious as it was, was almost amusing. It was stilted, a set ritual, a plot done a hundred times in grade-B westerns. The stranger is given twenty-four hours to get out of town.

"Borsato, there is something you must understand."

"Yes?"

"I am my own man. I come and go where I please. There's no way you can order me to do anything."

"Do I understand that you propose to stay?"

"As long as I have business here."

"In that case, you must take the consequences."

"I don't like threats, Borsato."

"I have tried to be reasonable, *signore*. But you have failed to see my point of view. My personal honor is at stake here. You have degraded it. I tell you again. I cannot tolerate your presence in Venice another day. You will leave, or else."

"Or else what?"

"Signore Drew, I am an *avvocato*, a lawyer. Let me tell you something about Italian law. In our code, the family is sacred, the heart of our whole society. Violate the sanctity of the family, and you have committed a crime. You have seduced my wife—"

"I thought you said *she* seduced me."

Borsato ignored him. "You have seduced my wife," he repeated. "In Italy, a husband whose honor has been soiled in this way has a certain moral right to redress. He can kill the seducer of his wife or his sister, the despoiler of his family, and he will be arrested and tried in court. But in almost every case the court will deal kindly with him, it will be very lenient. You have not heard of Article 587 of the Penal Code, I presume."

"No."

"This article recognizes that revenge taken for this reason is a matter of honor and not passion. Generally, an outraged husband who kills his wife's seducer serves only a light sentence. The judges interpret this article very liberally, and, in many cases, the husband simply goes free. Again, it is not considered a crime of passion at all. Merely settling an account, like settling a butcher's bill."

David was shaken, although he did not show it. Borsato might be bluffing. And then, he might not. David had played it cool with the Italian so far, but the anger was beginning to rise in him. He would be damned, he thought, if he'd let Borsato run him out of town, like a dog with his tail between his legs. He looked straight into Borsato's eyes. What he read there was plain. Borsato expected him to cut and run. Suddenly, a memory drifted across David's mind. A movie he, and almost everyone in America, had seen years ago. *High Noon*. Gary Cooper toughing it out, standing his ground. He wasn't any Gary Cooper, he was no hero. But this was High Noon in Venice. He almost laughed at the absurdity of the situation. He knew it was serious, deadly serious, but here it had a touch of comic opera, Italian-style.

And, of course, it was insane. Here was Teodoro Borsato, having murdered him once as Vittorio Favretto, now threatening to dispose of him all over again.

"Let me understand you clearly, Borsato. If I do not leave Venice by tomorrow, you threaten to kill me."

"Let me answer by saying that I cannot tolerate the dishonor that has threatened my home. That, as an outraged husband, I am fully capable of doing so."

"Yes," said David. "I know that already. I know it only too well."

Borsato stared at him.

"What do you mean by that, *signore?*"

"Take it any way you like."

"I demand you explain this." Borsato's voice rose. "What do you mean by that statement?"

"You know what I mean," said David.

Borsato rose. Suddenly, he reached across the table and seized David by the jacket. His eyes bored into David's. They were blazing with anger. And yet, mixed with this, a flicker of fear. He started to say something. Then he stopped.

"Let go, Borsato, said David, quietly. "And let go now. Otherwise, I'll have to knock you down."

Slowly, Borsato released his grasp. They both became aware that the chatter around them had abruptly stopped. The people at the other tables were watching.

Finally, Teodoro Borsato turned and walked rapidly away.

19

THE next morning was bright and hot.

David lay in bed, trying to think things through. He decided to stay in Venice until he heard from Bianca once more. Until he saw her once more. He knew that sooner or later, just as soon as she was free, she would get in touch with him. It might be today or tomorrow or the next day. But the call would come.

He did not underrate Borsato. He had good reason to know that the man was dangerous. But he couldn't be intimidated by him. He had to take the chance that Borsato was bluffing. He doubted very much that Borsato would be crude enough to walk up to him in the middle of St. Mark's Square and stick a knife into him, in front of God and everybody. That wasn't his way. If he did carry out his threat, if he really was serious, he'd plan it carefully, wait his chance. The way he had with Vittorio Favretto. And that would take time.

It was frustrating that he couldn't *prove* what he knew. Lieutenant Cozzi hadn't believed him, and, in all fairness, if he'd been in Cozzi's shoes, he wouldn't have believed such a ridiculous claim either. But the proof was lying there, or, at least, he thought it was, if there was some way of getting to it.

Suddenly, he sat upright.

The idea came from nowhere, and it stunned him. He turned it over and examined it. He decided it was impossible, completely mad. There was no way it would work. He lay down again, staring up at the ceiling.

Still, it was interesting.

He got up, put on a robe, sat down to meditate.

The beat of the mantra was loud and steady. The PA level was far beyond him this morning. The new idea clogged his mind. He started to plan it, detail by detail. Look at it from any angle you liked, it was still very far out, a hope and a prayer.

And maybe not even that.

He started to dress. But differently this time. He put on his swimming trunks instead of his shorts. And over them he wore his jogging suit. It was the one he had bought when he met Cassie Knox; he had had some idea that he might do a little jogging in Iran. He wore it now because it was zippered and easy to slip on and off.

He did not bother to have breakfast. He walked to the boat station on the *riva* in front of the Doges' Palace and took a *diretto* across the lagoon to the Lido.

After making some inquiries, he found a shop that sold and leased water sports equipment in one of the hotels. He rented a scuba diving rig, flippers, tank and mask, and a big diver's flashlight, as well as a big canvas bag in which to carry the equipment.

Then he took a boat back across the lagoon to Venice.

He carried the bag through the Piazzetta and then across the square itself. The bag was heavy and ungainly, and it was a long walk to where he wanted to go. He decided the simplest and easiest way to get there was by gondola. Bruno Savoldo had almost become his personal gondolier of late. And he might need Savoldo's help in what he was about to try.

He came into the Bacino Orseolo, carrying the heavy bag over his shoulder. He set it down. Savoldo was in the midst of an argument with another gondolier. They were like a couple of roosters, standing toe to toe, nose to nose, shouting at each other. When Savoldo sighted David, he abruptly stopped. He spread his hands to the other gondolier and shrugged apologetically. He was sorry, it seemed, to break off the argument. But business was business. They could resume where they had left off, at another time. The other gondolier understood and nodded. He agreed. Business was business.

"*Ah, buon giorno, signore.*"

"*Buon giorno, Bruno.*"

Savoldo stared at the canvas bag curiously. Its drawstrings were pulled together so that he could not see what was within.

"And where shall we go this morning, *signore?*"

"To the Rio de la Malvesia Vecchia." Savoldo stared at David. His mouth dropped open. He looked at the big canvas bag again. "To the same spot where we were before. You know where it is."

"Why should you want to go there, *signore?*"

"Just take me there, Bruno. You'll see when we arrive. I may need your help."

On the way, the usually garrulous Savoldo said nothing. He was strangely silent. As it turned out, David was grateful. He needed to concentrate, to think. This could be a fool's errand. The chances were very good, almost certain, that it was. And in what he was going to try, he was certainly going to be conspicuous. Still, there was no getting around that. He had thought of trying this at night, and then quickly discarded the idea. He needed all the light he could get. And the chances were that even in daylight there would be

225

little light, if any. He'd have to depend mostly on the big flashlight he carried in the canvas bag.

Finally, they came to the spot in the canal he wanted. Under the human-headed snake. He directed Bruno to bring the gondola up to the edge of the *fondamenta* and tie up there. He heaved the heavy bag onto the *fondamenta* and then climbed out of the gondola onto the stone walk.

He zipped off his jogging suit, kicked off his sneakers, and stood there, dressed only in his swimming trunks.

He was aware that Bruno Savoldo, sitting in his gondola, was staring at him, fascinated. He knew what the gondolier must be thinking.

Crazy American.

Well, he couldn't say that he blamed Savoldo. Very few American tourists went swimming in Venetian canals. He felt like a total idiot, standing there. And almost in an instant, a curious crowd began to gather.

For a moment, he considered abandoning the whole thing. I can't go through with this, he thought, it's insane. But then, he reflected, he had come this far, and he might as well go ahead and make a complete damned fool of himself.

Quickly, he slipped his feet into the flippers, strapped on the harness that held the air tank to his back, and attached the regulator to the tank valve.

For a few moments, he stood there, staring down at the water. It was filthy, opaque. Its stink assailed his nostrils. Its surface, roiled a little by a motorboat up the canal, washed against the sides, which were coated with slippery green slime. While he stood there, he saw bits of garbage float by—melon rinds, half of a rotted squash, orange peels. And on the opposite side, caught in a small niche where the canal met the wall of a building, was the body of a dead cat. Its head alone seemed to be caught in the niche. The rest of its body floated slowly to one side, then to the other.

He felt a little sick. He hesitated another moment. He realized that, in a sense, he was looking down into his own grave. It would be cold down there. Cold, and very dark . . .

He was aware that a large crowd had gathered. He heard

their muffled whispers. Some laughed openly, some jeered. They thought this was some huge joke. This crazy tourist, they were saying. He is *pazzo, demente,* some kind of *imbecille.* What was he trying to prove, anyway?

He caught a glimpse of Savoldo's face. He was sitting in his gondola, watching David. His face was deathly pale.

Quickly, David put on his face mask, turned on the air, and checked his breathing. Then he strapped the big underwater flashlight to his wrist, making sure it was secure.

Now, he was ready.

Well, he thought, *here goes nothing.*

He let himself fall into the canal, in the classic entry of the experienced scuba diver, feet spread wide, so that his gear would stay intact.

He kicked himself into a downward dive and headed straight down, until his hands touched bottom. He judged the depth there to be about ten feet.

He had done a lot of scuba diving and appreciated the fact that he did not have to worry about either water pressure or temperature. This was a shallow-diving situation, and the water was not too cold.

But the water was dirty, it almost seemed to crawl on his skin; he could feel its slimy embrace. In the world of scuba freaks this was called "blind diving." David judged his visibility to be about three feet, no more. Still, blind diving was not totally unfamiliar to him. He had done a lot of spearfishing as well. It was a fascinating experience to dive in the clear waters off the Bahamas or the Florida Keys. But you would find very little to hunt there. For spearfishing, you had much better luck in "dirty" water. This murkiness was caused by plankton, which was the basic food consumed by forage fish, such as anchovies, sardines, and herring. And they attracted the bigger fish. Because of this, he had spent much of his underwater time in this so-called dirty water.

Now, swimming very slowly, with his belly only a few inches from the bottom, he turned on his flashlight with one hand and groped into the bottom with the other.

The bottom was soft. Muck, and silt, and slime. Gooseflesh popped out all over his body, and it was not from the cold of the water but from his revulsion at the touch and feel of it. He knew the stench of it must be unbearable. He was grateful for his face mask. Without it, he knew he could not have stood it.

He continued to grope, pushing his hand deep into the muck, covering a foot at a time. He knew that what was left of Vittorio Favretto must be somewhere in this area. He was not sure that there were any remains of the corpse left at all. Twenty-five years was a long time. But if there *were* anything left, it would be buried deep under the muck and slime. With the ebb and flow of the tides, a great amount of silt could form on the bottom in a quarter of a century.

Down here, it was cold and eerie. It wasn't anything like the swimming he had done in other waters. This was like swimming through some watery grave. And that was what it was. The beam of his flashlight revealed a bottom littered with objects that had found their last resting place. There were bottles, rusted tin cans coated with slime, bits and pieces of jagged metal, broken tools, cracked pieces of building stone. There were what appeared to be a discarded sewing machine and a heavy piece of sculpture with a leg broken off and the face smashed in. In groping under the soft ooze, he found other jetsam of the same kind. Apparently, the Venetians found their canals very convenient places to get rid of anything they did not need.

Out of sight, out of mind.

Foot after foot, he explored the bottom. His groping hand came upon nothing except more bottles, more rusting tin cans. He had no sensation of depth and very little sensation of time and direction. He floated in a cold and eerie limbo. Dig with the hand, point the flashlight. Its beam was a cold yellow eye, crawling over the mucky desert of what seemed to be another planet.

He was getting cold now. The chill was starting to penetrate his flesh, seeping into the marrow of his bones. He checked his watertight watch. He had been under for fifty minutes now. His air cylinder was a standard tank holding a little over seventy cubic feet of air, and now, in reading the gauge attached to his regulator, he saw that he had only about ten minutes left.

He continued to probe. He turned up nothing but muck. He became desperate now. He debated whether he should even bother using up what air he had left. It was foul down here, filthy, and now his body was aching with the cold. It was time to give up this obscene mission and go to the surface. He had gambled and he had lost, and he had been all kinds of a damned fool for even thinking of trying it.

Suddenly, his hand, probing beneath the layer of soft muck, gripped something.

He pulled it up to the surface and turned the yellow spot of the flashlight on it.

His fingers were wrapped around the rusty link of some buried chain.

He pulled on the link. He knew immediately that it was attached to something heavy. He yanked on the link. Slowly he dragged a rusty chain from the muck. A chain still connected to or wrapped around something.

Whatever it was, it gave heavy resistance to his pull. He secured the flashlight into the chain on his wrist, and now he used both hands to pull. His muscles bulged with his exertion. And slowly, it came out of the muck, like some emerging Halloween fright.

A skeleton.

The remains of Vittorio Favretto.

In the murk of the water, it looked like a ghoulish apparition risen from Hell. The flesh had long been gone, but the skeleton remained intact, although the bones were eroded thin. The skeleton was still locked in the embrace of the rusty chains, from which heavy iron weights hung. The same iron embrace that had been curled around the living, breathing flesh a long time ago.

Propelled by the slight movement of the water, the skull teetered back and forth on its cervical vertebrae. Around these vertebrae, where the neck had once been, hung a chain, from which dangled a gold medallion.

He rubbed the scum from its surface with his finger. The medallion was pure gold and had not corroded. He brought the flashlight up close and peered at the medallion from a few inches away.

On it was the lion. Standing on its hind legs and holding up two scrolls, one in each of its upraised front paws.

His head whirled as he stood there, holding the skeleton. Standing in his own grave, holding the last remains of someone who had once been himself. Staring into the sightless eyes that had once mirrored his own soul. He felt faint. Nausea caught him in the throat. He wanted to vomit. He wanted to push that gaunt and grinning skull away from him, to bury this grotesque bag of bones back into the muck where he had found it. He wanted to shoot to the top, rip off his mask, retch, and then breathe the clean air again. Leave everything as he had found it. Put everything back in the grave he had desecrated.

Instead, he began to work off the chains in which the skeleton was entangled.

It was slow, excruciating work. He had to slide them off very gently, one by one. They were heavy and rusty. Once or twice he bumped some of the links against the bone. A piece of bone, separated from a weakened joint, broke off, then another. First a shinbone, then part of an arm.

His air, he knew, would run out at any moment. Even now, the gauge on his regulator registered zero. He hoped and prayed that the people at the sports shop had added a little extra air to the cylinder, just to allow for emergencies, to give the diver an extra break if ever he should need it. They sometimes did. But, of course, he had no way of knowing.

He began to work the last chain off the skeleton. The results of running out of air in a scuba situation could be extremely unpleasant and sometimes fatal. Then, just as he had almost managed to extricate the last chain, with its hanging weight, he ran out of air.

He held his breath now, as he worked. It seemed forever. It seemed his lungs were ready to burst when he finally managed to pull the chain clear. He embraced the skeleton with both arms and shot up to the surface, remembering to exhale as he did.

He broke water to look up at the staring faces of a big crowd. They were frozen in shock as he boosted the skeleton up onto the *fondamenta*. The skeleton rattled, and several pieces of it broke off as he did so. No one stepped forward to help. Many simply stood there, stunned.

He clambered up onto the *fondamenta*, ripped off the harness holding the air tank, kicked off his flippers, and took off his mask. He kneeled over the skeleton, staring at it. He looked at the medallion again, wound around the bony throat.

He fingered it a moment, then turned to look at the other side. He rubbed off the dirt and the scum, to reveal an inscription. *A Vittorio. Mio Amore. Mio cuore. Bianca.*

He stood up and looked at the crowd. It was still silent. The faces all had questions, but he volunteered no answer. He looked for Savoldo's gondola, in order to pick up his clothes and get dressed.

But the gondola wasn't there. His clothes had been thrown onto the *fondamenta*. He looked down the canal. Bruno Savoldo was racing the gondola away, sweeping his paddle hard, putting his back into it.

A *carabiniere* was standing in the crowd. Now he stepped forward:

"What are you doing, *signore?* What is the meaning of this?"

David noted that the man had a police walkie-talkie hanging from his belt.

"Will you please get in touch with Lieutenant Cozzi? And when you do, tell him to get here right away. Tell the *tenente* I've found him."

"Found who?"

"He'll know."

20

Lieutenant Cozzi sat at his desk, staring at David. Then he spread his hands.

"What can I say, *signore?* What can anybody say? Except that you have made me a believer." He paused. "I look at you, and I know it is true, and I tell myself this man sitting here across my desk was once Vittorio Favretto, or at least, his body carries the soul of Vittorio Favretto—" He broke off, shaking his head. "I am a good Catholic, and all my life, *signore*, I have been taught as an article of faith that a man's soul goes on, but it goes to heaven or hell, according to his behavior on this earth." He shook his head. "And all I can ask is—why you?"

"I don't know. I honestly don't know."

"*Reincarnazione*," said Cozzi. "I say the word, and still I find it incredible. You are the living proof of it and have shown its existence beyond all doubt, proved that men do not die forever, that they are born again to live another life, that someday they return from the grave as someone or something else. I have always known, *signore*, that millions, perhaps billions, of people on this world believe in it. People in the East, people in India, the Hindus and so on. But here, in the Western world, in the Christian world, only those who are dreamers, or complete madmen, the kind whom we keep in insane asylums . . . "

Cozzi fell silent. David could see that the man was still trying to absorb all this, still confused, caught between what he had already seen and what he had always believed.

"Lieutenant Cozzi." Cozzi did not seem to hear. He seemed to be lost in his own meditation. Finally, David repeated, louder:

"Lieutenant Cozzi."

"Oh? Yes, *signore*?"

"What happens now?"

"Happens?" said Cozzi, blankly.

"I presume the case will be reopened. That there'll be some kind of investigation."

"Oh," said Cozzi. "Yes. Yes, of course."

"I've already told you who the murderer is."

"Teodoro Borsato."

"Yes. I suppose you'll be talking to him."

Cozzi shrugged. "In time. There is no hurry."

David stared at him. He was surprised at Cozzi's seeming indifference.

"No hurry?"

"There are certain procedures, *signore*." Cozzi's eyes seemed to shift just a little. "They take time. And, of course, there is an obvious difficulty, when it comes to Borsato. We have no evidence."

"But I know he did it. And you know he did it."

"True. But no court in Italy or, for that matter, in the world would accept the vision you had as hard evidence. The chances are, *signore*, you would be laughed out of court.

233

And if we even made this public, you would most surely be the defendant in a countersuit by Borsato for slander and defamation of character."

"But there has to be *some* way of proving it."

"Not unless Borsato confesses. And, knowing the man as we do, that is a very remote possibility." Cozzi sighed. "Of course, we'll try. Naturally. But twenty-five years. It is a long time."

David studied Cozzi for a moment. He had a vague and somewhat uneasy feeling that Cozzi was being evasive. That certain wheels were turning in the lieutenant's head. That everything wasn't as obvious as it seemed.

There was a knock on the door. Then it was opened by a sergeant.

"Contessa Favretto is here to see you, *tenente*."

"Show her in."

Bianca's face was pale. She looked first at Cozzi, then at David.

"Please sit down, *contessa*," said Cozzi. He waved to a chair. "I am sorry to have to ask you here, at a time like this. You have been told, of course, what has happened."

"Yes."

"I know it is a shock to you."

"If I could see Vittorio's body, Lieutenant."

Cozzi shook his head. "There would be no point in it, *contessa*. You have the right of course, but there is nothing left to see. You realize, after twenty-five years, there is— nothing but a few bones."

"Then how do you know? How can you be sure?"

Cozzi reached into a drawer. He took the medallion out and laid it on the desk before her.

"This was found wrapped around the neckbone of the— the remains, *contessa*. We need you to make a positive iden- tification of it. Just a formality, for our police report."

She picked up the medallion. She turned it over, read the inscription. Tears sprang to her eyes.

"It is his," she said. "It was my gift to Vittorio on—on our first anniversary." Then she stopped. Her face was chalk-white. She looked at both of them.

"How did it happen? How did you find Vittorio? How did you know . . . ?"

"They were both silent. Then, after a while, as Cozzi seemed ready to speak, David said, quietly:

"Let me tell her, Lieutenant."

On the way back to the palazzo, in the family speedboat, David told her everything. The servant at the wheel, piloting the boat, could hear nothing. He was standing forward, and the noise of the motor was too loud.

She listened silently, never interrupting. He told her every-thing—who he was, how he had gradually found out that he had once been Vittorio Favretto, how the man she loved had died at the hand of her present husband, and how he, David, had finally found Favretto's last resting place. When he had finished, he said to her, gently:

"Do you believe me, Bianca? Do you believe that I was once—Vittorio?"

"I believe you," she said. Then she leaned her head on his shoulder. "Oh, my God, Vittorio, my God, you've come back."

"Bianca, you must understand. I am not really Vittorio. I am David Drew. The only thing left is Vittorio's spirit. Or his soul. It lives in my body . . ."

"To me, you are Vittorio," she said. "Lying in bed with you, making love to you, I thought of you as Vittorio. You loved me in the way he did, your hands, your mouth, your touch, the words you said, everything was his." Then he took her in his arms, as she started to cry:

"Vittorio, Vittorio. *Mio amore. Mio cuore.*"

The call from Bruno Savoldo was urgent. It was more than that, it was hysterical. He asked Borsato to meet him at a cafe on the Calle Larga, near the Ponte delle Ostreghe. Borsato was not to waste a moment. He was to come at once.

When Borsato arrived, Savoldo had already downed two or three *grappe*. He told Borsato not only that Favretto's remains had been found, but how. He had heard, through his pipeline to police headquarters, that this crazy American was not only claiming that he had been Vittorio Favretto at one time in some previous life but that he had also named Teodoro Borsato as his murderer.

After he had finished, Savoldo crossed himself fervently, and Borsato stared at him.

"You must be mad, Bruno."

"I am telling the truth."

"He actually claims he was Vittorio Favretto?"

"He must have been. How else would he know?"

"This kind of thing is for the insane, Bruno. You find madmen like this in asylums. They think they were Napoleon, or Caesar, or Alexander the Great, or . . ."

"Then how could he know, Teodoro? Eh? I ask you again. How could he possibly know? Perhaps he is really the incarnation of the devil, *il diavolo* himself. Perhaps he is Vittorio Favretto, come back to another life, under another name. I'm ready to believe anything now."

"I tell you it's impossible."

"Impossible?" Savoldo's voice rose shrilly. "I was *there*. Do you understand, Teodoro? I was there when he brought that damned skeleton up from the bottom. From the bottom of the Rio de la Malvesia Vecchia. Just where we had dumped him."

"Shut up, you fool." Borsato glanced around at the chattering crowd, then glared at his companion. "Keep your voice down. Do you want the whole world to know?"

"Teodoro."

"Well?"

"Suppose the police believe him?"

"They won't."

"How do you know for sure?"

"Because they can't prove anything. They have no evidence."

"But this man Drew—"

"Do you think some kind of wild dream, some vision from a madman like this American, is proof?"

"But he may have some other way."

"How?"

"I tell you, he has some kind of supernatural power. He's already accused you by name. Somehow, he may really be able to prove that you did it."

"Not I," said Borsato softly.

"Eh?"

"We."

"We?"

"Come, come, Bruno. You were there, remember? You held his arms while I gave him the knife. You helped to sink him."

"But my name isn't in this. He hasn't accused *me*." He stared at Borsato. "Wait a moment, Teodoro. There's something I'm not quite clear about."

"Well?"

"If they really caught you, nailed you to the wall as the assassin, you'd implicate *me*?"

"Why not?"

"Even if you didn't have to?"

Borsato shrugged his shoulders, then said, with a bleak smile:

"We are in the same boat, *amico mio*. Whatever happens to me happens to you. Believe me, I don't ever expect this to happen. In fact, it never will happen. But if I ever had to go to prison, there is no reason I should have to go alone. I am a man who loves company. I do not particularly like yours, but it is better than nothing."

"*Figlio di puttana*," said Savoldo. His eyes burned with hate. "May you rot in hell."

"Lower your voice, Bruno. If you don't, we may both do just that. Now, I tell you to stop worrying. There is absolutely nothing to worry about. They can prove nothing. Nothing. So go home, get drunk, beat your wife or sleep

237

with her, or whatever you feel like doing. But again, I warn you. Keep your mouth shut. There's nothing to be afraid of, my friend. Absolutely nothing."

Finally, they left the cafe and walked toward the square.

They did not know they were seen by the subject of their discussion. He was having a *cappuccino* at the counter of a small cafe on the Calle Larga, as they passed. As he watched them through the window, they were talking in animated fashion.

Knowing how Savoldo felt about Borsato, David found this very strange. And of more than just passing interest.

When Borsato arrived at the palazzo, Bianca Favretto was waiting for him in the sitting room.

Her face was set, cold. It might have been carved out of stone.

"Sit down, Teodoro," she said. "I have something to say to you."

"Look, *cara*, I am tired. Some other time."

"I have something to say to you *now*."

He stared at her. She was trembling a little, trying hard to control her anger. Her eyes were hard. Borsato was surprised. He was taken aback by her imperious tone. Always, he had been able to overwhelm her, dominate her. But now she showed absolutely no fear of him. By the way she had commanded him to sit down, he sensed that this was a new and determined woman he was facing. Expecting an attack, he stiffened to meet it. He was confident that, whatever it was, he was able to handle it, to contain it. He always had.

"Very well, Bianca," he said, wearily. "What is it now?"

"I know, Teodoro."

"You know what?"

"That they found Vittorio. And that you murdered him. And threw him in the canal."

He stared at her. Tried to look incredulous.

"My God, Bianca, what are you saying?"

"The truth."

"You must be mad."

"Why did you do it, Teodoro? Why?"

"Bianca, you don't know what you're saying. *Madonna mia,* Vittorio was my best friend."

"*Bugiardo,*" she said, coldly. "Liar. You hated him. You wanted the palazzo, the Favretto money, you wanted me. Damn you, Teodoro. Damn you!"

"*Cara,* don't be ridiculous. You must be insane, making a charge like that."

"Damn you," she cried. She began to beat at his chest with her fists. "I loved him so much. And you—"

He took her hands and flung her back roughly.

"Control yourself, Bianca. You're hysterical. You say *I* killed Vittorio? What the hell are you talking about? What proof have you got? Who told you that?"

"He did."

"Who?"

"David."

"Oh. Yes. The American," he jeered, then laughed. "The crazy one. The madman. The one who sees visions. I know that he went to the police with these wild claims. And that they practically threw him out. Can you imagine? He claims he was Vittorio once upon a time. Really, Bianca, that's a little too much." He laughed again. "You know who I was, once upon a time? I was Caesar. Would you believe that? And after that, well—let me see. I became the reincarnation of Bismarck. And after that, well—would you believe I was Gandhi?"

"Teodoro," she said. "I have already told you. I know. You made the appointment with Vittorio that night. You asked him to stop and pick you up at your house, before you went on to the Piazza. You knew exactly where to attack him. You knew he would have to come along the Fondamenta de la Malvesia Vecchia. There was no other way. You lay in wait for him and then murdered him. In the darkness, Teodoro, in cold blood. And then threw him in the canal."

239

"Bianca, you're insane. All this is pure fantasy. There's nothing you can prove."

"No," she said. "I have no proof. Not the kind I could give to the police. But I know you have the blood of my husband on your hands. No matter what your mouth says, I see it in your eyes. And from this moment on, I am finished with you."

He laughed.

"Oh? Indeed? *You* are finished with *me?*" He snapped his fingers. "Just like that?"

"Yes."

"Tell me, *cara*. Exactly what does that mean?"

"I want you to leave the palazzo tonight. I don't even want you to wait long enough to pick up your clothes. I'll have them sent along to you. I want a divorce, Teodoro. I want you to get out of my life. And out of Venice. I never want to see you again."

"Surely you're joking."

"Believe me, I am not."

"My dear Bianca, think a moment. Say what you just said and hear how foolish it sounds. There is no way you can order me to do all this. I am your husband and, by Italian law, I have certain rights. These rights—"

He stopped abruptly, as three men suddenly walked into the sitting room. They had apparently been waiting in the other room, and they had surely heard everything through the open door. Borsato stared at them, open-mouthed. One was Bianca's father, Benedetto Gatti. The other two were younger men, her brothers, Luigi and Niccolo.

"In this house, Borsato, you no longer have any rights."

The old man stood facing Borsato. He was the spokesman; the other two stood silently, their hard eyes fixed on Borsato's face. Benedetto Gatti was an old man, his body was arthritic, and he carried a cane. He wore a mane of white hair, and the eyes in his seamed, hawklike face were cold blue. He was formally dressed in a blue suit, white shirt, and blue tie, as were his sons. It was as though they had dressed for some ritual, some ceremonial occasion. Benedetto Gatti had a very quiet voice; it was almost a whisper and very hard to hear. But it carried authority, and it carried weight.

"You no longer have any rights in this house," he repeated. "Because you forfeited them long ago, Borsato. You have squandered much of the money left to my daughter by her late husband. You have brutalized and insulted her. You have flaunted your mistresses in her face and openly boasted of your *puttane* to your friends. You are not a gentleman, and you never were and never can be. You are *sporcizia*, dirt, a liar and a braggart, and not fit to associate with decent people."

Borsato's face turned red. He started to protest:

"Look here, you can't—"

"Be silent, Borsato. I have not finished."

"But I'm not going to stand here and—"

"I said, *be silent*." The old man snapped out the words. His eyes were blazing. "I am speaking, and you will listen. Do you understand, *animale?*"

Borsato said nothing. He simply stared at the old man.

"Now," continued Gatti. "As you know, my daughter here, Contessa Favretto, has spoken to me many times of her desire for a divorce. Notice, Borsato, I use the name Favretto." Then, acidly: "I have never addressed her as Signora Borsato, even though she became your wife, because I have never considered it an honor. But, to go on. She has told us all about Vittorio, the fact that his body has been found, and so on. And the fact that she believes you murdered him."

"There is no proof of that."

"Precisely. No formal proof. But Bianca believes it. I believe it. And so does the rest of the family. But because there is no exact proof—hard evidence, so to speak—we cannot be absolutely sure. Therefore, we have decided not to take, shall we say—harsher measures. Listen to me well, Borsato. These are your instructions. My daughter will start a suit for divorce. You are not to contest it, in any way. And you are to leave Venice within a week."

"This is an outrage, Benedetto."

"My name is Gatti. Do not address me in any familiar way."

"You cannot force me to do any of this."

"Let us just say, Borsato, we *advise* you to do as we say. We strongly advise you."

"I have my rights. There is law in this country. If there is a divorce, there is a matter of property rights—"

"You have no property rights, *animale*. According to the law, private property in Italy at the time of marriage remains the property of the individual partner. And anything earned jointly after that would be owned jointly. But you have produced nothing but pain and disgrace. However, the family has decided not to make a hard point of this. We shall decide on a sum of money, a very modest sum, I assure you, and give it to you. On the premise that you will need some money to get out of Venice, and, we hope, out of Italy itself. And, legally, to buy out any claim you may try to institute later. And, to conclude, you have one week to get out of Venice. Is that understood?"

Borsato tried to bluff it out.

"It is understood. But not accepted."

"I see."

"I'm still standing on my rights. On my legal rights." Borsato spoke defiantly. "I am a lawyer, and I know how to assert them."

"You are not simply a lawyer, Borsato. You are also a fool. A reckless fool. I do not care what your legal rights are. I am talking about a law that is above the law you will find in the Italian courts. Now, we Gattis are Venetians, we are not from Calabria or Sicily. We do not propose a vendetta; it is not our way. Still, you must understand that our family goes back to the times of the doges. In those days, my ancestors had occasion to protect the family honor or position by simply, shall we say, liquidating its enemies. It is conceivable that a few of these enemies ended up in some convenient canal, during the dark of night. In the same way you disposed of Vittorio Favretto. Now, of course, the old custom has died out. We Gattis have long abandoned the technique of violence." The old man shrugged. "Still, who knows? There is a matter of redress involved here, Borsato. You have violated my daughter in a hundred different ways. Sometimes, one finds it necessary to revive an old custom. And we have never hesitated to do whatever is necessary to preserve the family honor. Personally, I do not have the time or the stomach to follow innumerable procedures through the courts, to deal with judges and lawyers and bureaucrats of all kinds. In matters of this kind, my inclination would be to look for a quicker solution. I'm sure my sons agree with this, as well." He looked at Bianca's brothers. They both nodded, their black eyes fixed steadily on Borsato. "We are offering to let you escape with your life. It is a very generous offer, Borsato. Take it or leave it. Which shall it be?"

Borsato stood there for a long moment, staring into the eyes of the old man. Then he said, in a low voice:

"All right. I'll do as you say."

"Very good," said Benedetto Gatti. "Insofar as you have an instinct for survival, Borsato, you are a wise man. You may thank Bianca here that you have this chance. She begged us not to take blood for blood; she did not want yours on her conscience. Now get out!"

21

T HE following morning, Borsato called Savoldo. He asked the gondolier to meet him at the same cafe bar; it was urgent.

As soon as they were seated at a small table at the rear of the cafe, Savoldo asked anxiously:

"What is it, Teodoro? What's happened?"

"I've been thinking over what you said yesterday."

"And?"

"You may be right, Bruno. Maybe this man Drew does have powers we do not understand. The fact is, he did find Vittorio Favretto's body. And if he's capable of doing that, then he's capable of anything. Of delivering us to the police, for example. He's already named *me*. So—I agree. This man is very dangerous. And he could destroy us."

"What can we do about it?"

244

"There's only one thing to do. Destroy *him*."

There was a long silence. Then Savoldo said flatly:

"No."

"We have no choice, Bruno."

"No. I will not become a partner in this. You talked me into this once, Teodoro. I've lived these years to regret it."

Borsato's face was a mask of naked hatred. His eyes were feverish, unnaturally bright. To Savoldo, he suddenly seemed a little unbalanced in his intensity:

"Imbecile. Don't you see? Can't you understand? This American, this vulture, is simply waiting to feed from our remains. Sooner or later, Bruno, he will find out, he will *know*, for sure. We must stop him and stop him now. Otherwise, we'll never sleep another night again." He reached out his hand suddenly and grabbed Savoldo by the shirt. His eyes glittered. "You want to go to prison, Bruno? You want to rot there the rest of your life? Do you? Do you? Because I tell you once more, if I am named and I am convicted, then I will name you as my accomplice."

"You keep playing that same tune, Borsato," said the gondolier softly.

"Only because I find it necessary to make you see clearly who your *real* enemy is."

There was a long pause. Savoldo drained his beer slowly. Then, brushing the foam off his lips, he said:

"All right, Teodoro. What must be done, must be done. On one condition."

"Well?"

"You pay me the rest of the money you owe me. To be exact, three million lire."

Borsato paused. Then:

"And if I don't?"

"You'll have to do it yourself."

"Bruno, you're a fool. You're in no position to bargain."

"Neither are you."

"You walk away from this and you dig your own grave."

"I'll take my chances." The gondolier decided he wasn't

going to let Borsato bluff him out. He rose, as if to go. *"Buon giorno, amico."*

Suddenly, Borsato grabbed him by the sleeve.

"All right. Sit down."

"It's a bargain, then?"

"A bargain."

"Cash in advance this time."

"You're a greedy man, Bruno."

"And a wiser one, since the last time." Savoldo ordered another beer. "Now, what do you suggest we do?"

"Well, let us begin with a premise. It may be possible that this Signore Drew has supernatural powers. But it is also certain that if one should stick a knife in his belly, he would bleed. Do you agree?"

"Yes."

"There is a certain irony to this whole thing, Bruno. If the American was once indeed Vittorio Favretto, as he claims, and he has risen from the dead, then we shall have to kill him all over again."

"And this time make it permanent."

Borsato laughed. "Very good, Bruno. I have never credited you with a sense of humor. Yes, by all means, this time we'll make it permanent."

"How?"

"We'll have to work swiftly. I've done a little thinking, with that fact in mind. And I believe I've found a way that will be quick, quiet, and foolproof. Nobody will ever know. After that, we won't ever have to worry again."

"Tell me about it," said Savoldo.

When Borsato had finished, he asked:

"Well? What do you think?"

"It's brilliant. You're a very clever man, Teodoro. You've missed your profession, you know. You should have lived in the time of the Borgias."

"Thank you, Bruno. I suppose I should consider that a compliment."

"Anything else?"

"No. I'll make all the necessary arrangements. Just be ready when I call you."

After they walked out of the cafe and parted, Teodoro Borsato walked to his bank.

He drew out three million lire in cash. The withdrawal just about wiped out his personal account.

Then he walked across the street to an outdoor cafe, ordered an espresso, and, for a while, watched the world go by.

He had taken a room at a hotel, and, when his things were sent from the palazzo, he would make arrangements to leave Venice. He had no idea where he would go. Rome, Milan, Genoa—it wasn't important now. The important thing was that his life here had been ended, he had been ignominiously kicked out in disgrace from the place in which he was born, the place he had always called home. And, once away, he knew he could never return, not in the face of the Gattis.

Well, then, he was going into exile.

But there was this matter he had to settle first. It was a matter of blood, a thirst for revenge, something he knew he must finish. He knew that, if he did not, it would eat away at his intestines for the rest of his life, like some cancerous tumor. He had been degraded, reviled, and spat upon. And one man was responsible for this.

Not only that. As long as this man lived, he would always be a threat.

The English had an expression for it. What was it? Ah, yes. The trick was to "kill two birds with one stone." Well put, he thought. Very clever. Kill two birds with one stone. The one he hated, who still remained a threat; and the other, the one whom he simply despised.

He smiled to himself, a bitter smile. Really, he thought, he had been very persuasive. Bruno Savoldo had really taken the hook in his mouth.

Borsato pictured what would happen. He would give

247

Savoldo the money, as promised, beforehand. Then, after they had finished off the American, he, Borsato, would watch for his opportunity. Probably it would come when Savoldo was leaning over to help push Drew into the canal.

A quick thrust in the back with the knife, and it would be over for Savoldo, too. Then he would take back his cash and leave both his victims for the tides. After that, there would be no one left to worry about. Only one person would be left who really knew what had happened to Vittorio Favretto.

And that would be himself.

He thought of Bruno Savoldo. He hoped he could give him the knife face to face, somehow. He wanted to see the expression on the gondolier's face when he felt the cut of the blade and realized what had happened.

It would really be something to see.

Savoldo was really an *idiota*. A simple, gullible fool. Borsato sighed. What could you do with people like this? Except use them. Once a stupid man, always a stupid man.

He patted the fat envelope in the pocket of his jacket, just to make sure it was there. From now on, he thought bitterly, he would need every lira he could get.

He drained the last of his espresso, down to the dregs. It tasted bitter, more so than usual.

He paid for it, walked down the street, and crossed the Ponte San Moise, into the busy Salizzada San Moise, which led directly onto St. Mark's.

At the entry to the square, there was a newspaper kiosk. Borsato bought a copy of *Il Gazzettino* and scanned it eagerly.

There was no story at all on the front page.

Finally, he did find it, buried on an inside page.

The story was only two paragraphs long. It mentioned the fact that an eccentric American tourist had been skin diving in the Rio de la Malvesia Vecchia. A curious crowd had gathered to watch this strange event. The skin diver had discovered sunken treasure at the bottom of the canal.

An old skeleton. No one knew whose skeleton it was. But it had been buried there, on the bottom, for a long time. The police were, naturally, conducting a routine investigation. But according to the *Questura,* they had absolutely no idea as to its identity.

No names were mentioned at all. Neither Drew's, nor Vittorio Favretto's, nor, in particular, his own.

But Teodoro Borsato was not fooled. The fact that the newspaper had treated the story so lightly, he knew, was only a ploy. They were deliberately underplaying it, so as to lull him, Teodoro Borsato, into a sense of false security. He knew they knew that the skeleton had once been Vittorio Favretto. And they had heard the American accuse him, Borsato. He had no doubt that, given time, this man Drew would come up with some kind of proof. And this time, hard proof.

All the more reason he should move swiftly. In fact, immediately.

He hurried across the broad Piazza, driven by a sense of urgency. He had certain arrangements to make. And they would take time.

"Signore Drew is here to see you, *tenente,*" said the sergeant.

"Ah, yes," said Cozzi. He leaned back in his chair and with his handkerchief wiped beads of sweat from his forehead. "I've been expecting him, Emilio. Send him in."

When David entered, Cozzi rose to greet him.

"*Buon giorno, tenente.*"

"*Buon giorno, signore.*" Before David had a chance to say anything further, Cozzi smiled and raised his hand. "I know. I know. It is written all over your face, *signore.* You are here to ask me about the investigation, how it proceeds . . ."

"Yes."

"There is an interesting turn to it, *signore.* But it is too hot to discuss it here in my office. Too hot and stuffy and, besides, we are apt to be disturbed by this phone call or that. I like to get out of this cell whenever I can. There is a *campo* just a minute from here, and on this *campo* a small cafe, and I thought perhaps we might sit outside and have a glass of wine and talk there."

"That's fine with me."

"*Va bene.*" He turned to the sergeant. "I'll be back in an hour, Emilio."

They walked down a narrow passageway and came to the *campo*. It was a small one, smaller than most. There was a wide canal on the opposite side, on which a church fronted. David and Cozzi took seats at a small table under a yellow awning in front of the cafe.

"I like this place," said Cozzi. "Whenever I can, I discuss official business here." Then: "If you will excuse me a moment, *signore*."

Cozzi rose and walked toward a fruit and vegetable stand set up in the *campo*, only a few yards from the cafe itself. It was a small stand, shaded by an awning. It was loaded to overflowing with red and white grapes, apples, pears, golden peaches, purple eggplant, zucchini, carrots, and onions. Cozzi bought a bunch of white grapes from the old woman who was the proprietor. She apparently knew what he had come for; she cut the bunch of grapes and had it ready for Cozzi even before he reached the stand. Apparently this was some kind of daily ritual. David watched as Cozzi strolled over to the *campo* fountain. It consisted of a small and exquisite sculpture of a nymph, torso leaning back, arms spread wide and head back, enjoying the rain of the fountain. From her small breasts, two more streams of water poured. Cozzi washed his bunch of grapes carefully in the stream flowing from the left breast and walked slowly back to the cafe, as though he had all the time in the world.

"These come from the Veneto, to the north and east. Or perhaps from the Valley of the Po. They are delicious. May I offer you some, *signore?*"

250

"No, thanks."

The waiter came. David ordered a cappuccino, the lieutenant a glass of white wine. Then, Cozzi said:

"Signore Drew, I believed you were crazy when you first spoke of your visions. A madman, harmless, of course, but still mad. But now, as you know, I believe. In reincarnation. With all my heart and soul, I have tried to resist this belief. It goes against all my religious training, everything. But you have proved it, and so I am a believer. I say words now, only for your ears and mine. This is a confidence. You understand?"

"Yes."

"I believe that you were once Vittorio Favretto. And on the basis of what you have already proved, I believe that Teodoro Borsato is indeed the murderer. Certainly, he had enough motive. The *contessa* was a beautiful woman, and still is. He wanted her. He wanted the money, the palazzo, the position."

"The question is—how to get the evidence. The hard evidence."

"Ah, yes," said Cozzi. "That is the question."

There was a queer look on Cozzi's face. He seemed to avert his eyes. He acted almost guilty of something. Suddenly, David was disturbed.

"Lieutenant, what's happened?"

"Happened?"

"To the investigation. Have you questioned Borsato? Tried to cross-examine him, break him down?"

"No."

"Then what have you done?"

"Nothing."

David stared. "*Nothing?*"

"Absolutely nothing," said Cozzi.

David was bewildered. "Lieutenant, I don't understand."

"Signore Drew, you remember I told you back at the office that there has been an interesting turn to the investigation?"

"Yes."

"Well, the interesting turn is simply this. The investigation has been ordered to die. The case is closed."

David looked at Cozzi, stunned.

"Closed?"

"More than this. The whole thing is to be kept quiet. Suppressed, if necessary. There is to be absolutely no publicity."

"I *thought* there was something funny about that story in *Il Gazzettino* this morning," said David. "I was about to ask you . . ."

"Now you know. *Il Gazzettino* had its orders, too."

"From whom?"

"From—well, shall we say, a high authority. A very high authority."

There was a silence. David studied Cozzi. The lieutenant plucked off one grape after another, put it in his mouth, and then spat out the seeds. He was very deliberate about it. He seemed in a thoughtful and meditative mood.

"All right, Lieutenant," said David. "Suppose you stop being vague. Suppose you tell me all about it now. And I'll start with my big question. *Why?*"

"First, nothing has really changed. We have no evidence to present to any court. We could question Borsato, yes. But he knows we can prove nothing. And, certainly, he would admit nothing."

"In that case, there's someone else you might work on." Cozzi looked at him in surprise. "Yes? Who?"

"This gondolier. The one who used to work for the Favretto family. Bruno Savoldo."

"Ah, yes. I remember him." He stared at David. "But why Savoldo?"

David then told him of Savoldo's unusual and what seemed to him suspicious behavior. The way he had gone pale when he, David, had discovered Favretto's grave. The way he had left the scene, poling his gondola swiftly away in panic when David had raised the skeleton. Then, David had seen

252

them together, though Savoldo had told him he despised Borsato.

"I never really thought one man could handle this assassination alone," said David. "I'm sure Savoldo was in this with Borsato. Maybe it's a straw in the wind, but if you really went after him . . ."

"Your information is interesting, *signore.* But useless. As I have already told you, the case is closed. The police will go no further with it, no matter what the evidence. You still don't see why?"

"I'm sorry. But I don't."

"Think about this, *signore.* Suppose we pursue this investigation. Then the whole question of reincarnation would have to be brought up and pursued. You, for example, would have to testify as to how you knew where to find Vittorio Favretto. You would therefore prove reincarnation valid. But your doing this would create a tremendous furor. And it would strike at the roots of the established Church, not only here but throughout the world. It would, in fact, establish a whole new religion. I do not need to remind you that Italy is a Catholic country. Catholics, and most Christians, believe in the soul, it is true. But they also believe that when the body dies, the soul goes to heaven or hell. And is not transmitted to another body in later life. You agree that all this could happen?"

"I suppose it is possible. Yes."

"I am not a religious man, *signore.* I rarely go to mass and never to confession. I did not see the consequences of all this. But my superior, the commissioner, did. He is a man who says his beads, and his brother is a priest. He took this problem immediately to the patriarch here in Venice. The patriarch, who is also a cardinal, was seriously upset, aware that this was an immediate and dangerous threat to the Church, perceiving that any proof of reincarnation would strike at the very tenets of the Church, perhaps at its very life. Naturally, he communicated directly to the Pope, personally, on the situation. The Vatican was in an uproar. It reacted swiftly, *signore,* as you can well imagine. Papal orders flew in all directions. Secret orders, of course. The police were directed to suppress the investigation immediately, close the case. The newspapers were directed to give the affair no publicity of any importance, name no names, never mention the word 'reincarnation.' " He paused. "You are not a Catholic, *signore?*"

"No."

"Then you might not fully conceive the consequences of any action against this directive. It was implied, though not directly stated, that *Il Papa* would excommunicate anyone who did not comply, and that, of course, included myself, Enrico Cozzi. And, my friend, I am not about to fight —what do you Americans call it?"

"City Hall."

"Ah. Exactly. I am not about to fight City Hall." Then, he said with a smile: "Believe me, *signore,* you have been an embarrassment to the Vatican. I almost think it would like to see you—"

"Dead?"

"I did not say this. You did."

"Then maybe I can find some way to tell the world myself."

"You can shout it from the rooftops, *signore.* It is your privilege. But nobody will believe you. Not unless we cooperate and document your claim. And, of course, that is out of the question. If you persist on your own, our orders from the president of the republic himself, as well as the minister of the interior, are to declare that, in our opinion here in Venice, you are mad, unbalanced, insane. That the body is not that of Vittorio Favretto at all. That, in some eccentric gesture, you dove into a canal and brought up an anonymous skeleton from the bottom."

"I see. A real snow job."

"Snow job?" Cozzi looked puzzled. "What is that?"

David explained what it was, in precise and pungent terms, and Cozzi laughed.

"Listen, my friend. Let it lie, let the whole thing die. Forget it, and go home. It is better to keep the cat in the bag for a hundred reasons. If the truth got out, it would be the death of Venice—this city would be destroyed forever."

David stared at him. "I don't see what—"

Cozzi went on. "This is a city of churches. There are over a hundred of them. One for every two hundred inhabitants. I am speaking only of Venice proper, you understand. They are all Christian churches. If reincarnation is actually proved, then I repeat, it will become a religion, as it is, I understand, in India and other parts of the world. It will replace Christianity itself. And what will happen to the churches? They will all become warehouses, restaurants, whorehouses, or what have you. Most of them would be torn down. There are any number of monasteries and convents that would suffer the same fate. There are almost two hundred and fifty priests in Venice, and, of course, this would create massive unemployment." Cozzi smiled. "I do not even mention all the great works of art on Christian themes, the great paintings and sculpture of the Last Supper and the Madonna and the angels and saints and all the other subjects. What will become of them? And surely, *signore*, you can see that under these circumstances who would want to come to Venice? Our tourist trade would die and, therefore, the city itself. I talk only of Venice, of course. But you can imagine the effects of the death of Christianity, as we know it, and the introduction of this new religion throughout the whole Western world."

Cozzi leaned back and lit a cigarette. He seemed both amused and bemused, as he watched David's face.

"All right, Lieutenant. You've made your point."

"I've made it reluctantly, *signore*."

"But there's something you forgot."

"Yes?"

"There's still the matter of justice. We both know Borsato is a murderer."

"Ah, yes. I have given that some thought."

"And?"

"And, to ease your conscience, and perhaps mine, I would say that justice has already been done."

"How?"

"Perhaps not the ultimate justice, but for a man like Teodoro Borsato, almost as severe. Gossip seeps from every wall in Venice and travels fast. Already, Borsato has been terribly punished. Yesterday, as the story goes, the *contessa*, who holds the purse strings, has kicked him out of the palazzo and will file for divorce. She is backed by her family, the Gattis, who have warned Borsato to leave Venice and never return. All this, because she is convinced that what you told her is true. So, Borsato is not only to be exiled, he will be bankrupt or, at best, with very little in funds. Say what you will about him, he was a Venetian. He loved this city. He loved the life of the Venetian gentleman, of the husband of a noble lady like the *contessa*. Now he loses all this, and his pride and dignity besides. Now he has become nothing."

"What about the gondolier? Bruno Savoldo. I'm almost sure he's involved."

"Perhaps. But nobody is going to prove it. And if he is guilty, if he was indeed Borsato's accomplice, he will be punished anyway. Ultimately, and in time."

"What do you mean?"

Cozzi smiled. "I am a simple man, *signore*, and I do not do much reading, especially of books. But since I have met you, I took the trouble to go to the library. They had one or two books on reincarnation. I was much impressed by the whole idea of karma. If he is guilty, we both now know that he will not go to hell, he will not burn in eternal flame, the devil will not stab him in the backside with a red-hot pitchfork. No. He will live through this life, and die at his appointed time, and return in some future life. But his karma will be very bad. According to its law, he will have to suffer in his next life. He will have to pay his dues for the sins he was guilty of in this one."

David stared at Cozzi. Cozzi smiled blandly back at him. Much of what he had said was tongue-in-cheek, and much was serious. The trouble was, David was never sure which was which. But he liked Cozzi and decided the lieutenant was a much deeper man than he had first thought.

They sat in silence for a moment. Then their attention was attracted by something that was going on in front of the church across the *campo*.

The beginning of a funeral was in progress. It seemed somewhat elaborate, and apparently the corpse had been a fairly important personage. The canal in front of the church was lined with black gondolas. The priest stood there solemnly, the breeze ruffling his surplice. The mourners, all dressed in black, shook hands and kissed each other and lined up to step into their respective gondolas. The funeral barge itself was large, elaborately gilded, on its bow a golden lion, and on its stern a golden angel. Two smaller golden angels guarded the casket, and the barge itself was rowed by four boatmen, all dressed in black livery and wearing black hats.

For a while, David and Cozzi watched the mournful cortege as it began to move slowly up the canal. Then Cozzi said:

"You know, *signore*. I was just thinking. About the man in that black box. The casket."

"Yes?"

"I wonder if he might have died easier if he knew he would get another chance, that he would be born again."

"I don't know. But I think he would have."

"So do I, *signore*. Death would surely become less painful. The most painful thing about it is its finality. Still, I have a confession to make, even as a good, although not a strict, Catholic."

"Yes?"

"I have never really believed that death was forever. Not in my heart, *signore*, not in my soul. I think the human mind simply cannot comprehend the idea of forever, of eternity. All my life, deep in my heart, I have really believed that somehow, somewhere, I would be somebody again, something. That there was no such thing as 'forever.'"

"You know something, Cozzi?"

"Yes?"

"I've always felt that, too."

"Only you've proved it."

"To you and to me. But what good is it, if the whole world doesn't know it?"

Cozzi shrugged. "Maybe it's better. Maybe not. I am not wise enough to know. And maybe nobody is." Suddenly, he grinned at David. "A question, *signore*."

"Yes?"

"If you had your choice as to your next life, what would you want to be?"

David grinned back.

"I don't know. I haven't given it any thought. And you?"

"I am a man of small ambition and appetite, *signore*. If I had my choice, I would like to be my superior, the *questore*, and give orders to someone like me."

They both laughed, and Enrico Cozzi said that he had business back at the office and it was time to go. As they rose from the table, he said to David, casually:

"By the way, *signore*, when do you plan to leave Venice?"

"Tomorrow. Or perhaps the next day at the latest."

"Good. The sooner the better. If there is one man Teodoro Borsato must hate, it is you. As a policeman and, I like to think now, as a friend, I will feel much better when you have left Venice."

"I appreciate that, Lieutenant."

"*Arrivederci,* my friend."

"Goodbye."

They shook hands, and then Enrico Cozzi turned and walked swiftly away.

22

DAVID spent some time at CIT, arranging for air reservations back to New York the next day. He made them tentative, knowing that he would not leave Venice without saying goodbye to Bianca Favretto.

He was tempted to stay longer. But he took Cozzi's warning about Borsato seriously. The man must really hate his guts now. As far as he, David, knew, Borsato was still somewhere in Venice. And what Borsato was capable of doing once, he was surely capable of doing again. It would be insane to underrate the man.

There were other reasons why he was ready to leave now. He knew that if he lingered he and Bianca would become more and more attached to each other, and later it might be very difficult to break away. It was better to break clean and do it now.

Moreover, he knew the strange chain of events that had brought him here was over. The scenario had come to an end. He would never really know why he had been featured in his particular role, why he had been chosen. He tried to see some reason for it. He had proved the truth that reincarnation did, indeed, exist. He had proved it to a few others. But there was no way he could sell this truth to the world.

Then what was the point?

It was something he would never know.

Anyway, he was through with Venice, and it was through with him, and he wanted to go back home and forget all this, forget who he had once been, wipe it from his mind forever, and once again become David Drew—status: bachelor; nationality: American; profession: systems analyst and operations research specialist; presently unemployed and available; and last employed by Datafax Corporation, a major supplier of digital-stored computers. He wanted to become who he really was again, the way he had been before he arrived here, his own man, and not the walking repository of some other man's spirit or ghost.

Yes, definitely. His affair with Venice was over, and he was really ready to leave.

He had planned to telephone Bianca when he got back to the hotel. Or he had half-expected a message saying that she had called. Instead, there was a sealed note in his box.

The concierge gave him the envelope, and he tore it open. It was from Bianca, on her own stationery. It was urgent. And full of terror. The letter was being delivered to his hotel by hand, by her gardener, Antonio, whom she trusted implicitly. She wanted to see him, but she was deathly afraid of Teodoro Borsato. He had come back to the palazzo in a rage. He had sworn he would not be kicked out of his own house, he was defying the Gattis. She had been unable to phone. He had been watching her all the time. She begged David not to phone. He could not go to the palazzo, and she could not go to his hotel. It was too dangerous, Teodoro was in a murderous mood. Still she wanted to see him, she had to see him. She would slip away and meet him at ten, inside the Church of San Trovaso. After that, they could spend the night somewhere together. Somewhere where Teodoro could not find them. She wanted so much to be with him, in his arms again. And she signed it: To my love, Bianca.

David looked at the concierge.

"When was this delivered?"

"About an hour ago, *signore*."

"Can you tell me where I can find the Church of San Trovaso?"

"Why yes, *signore*. It is a church that has temporarily been opened all night, during the tourist season, for those who wish to worship late." The concierge whipped out a map and spotted the location for David. "You will find it here. In the Dorsoduro district. On the Rio di San Trovaso."

At the San Marco station, near Harry's Bar, he took a *motoscafo* and got off at the Accademia.

He found the Rio di San Trovaso and followed the course of the canal for a short distance. He passed a grim-looking sixteenth-century palace, and then another, on the opposite side, its ogee windows and flamboyant coat-of-arms, done in Gothic style, glinting in the moonlight. The surface of the canal shone pale yellow, then went dark, then yellow again, as the moon ducked in and out of the clouds.

Finally, he came to the church.

He looked at his watch. It was just ten. He opened the door and stood in the entrance for a moment, staring into the interior.

He did not see the shadowy figure, dressed in black from head to toe, pressed against the wall and hidden behind the door he had just opened.

The interior of the church was dimly lit, ghostly. A small lamp over the high altar threw eerie shadows. It gilded the cross and the artifacts on the altar, tinted the silent saints who brooded along the walls of the church. They almost seemed alive, waiting, pensive, and brooding.

There was no sign of Bianca. As far as he could see, the church was deserted.

He hesitated a moment in the doorway. His skin prickled a little. Somehow, the interior of an empty church at night bothered him. It turned him off. It had the same effect as a graveyard. He wondered why Bianca had chosen this as a place to meet. He assumed she must have had good reasons.

He was right on time, but probably she would be a few minutes late. It was silly to simply stand there in the doorway. He walked into the church.

The light played weirdly on a painting of the Last Supper on the right wall of the sacrament chapel. In the chapel on the other side of the chancel hung a great Gothic painting, a noble-looking man dressed in the fashion of an early-fifteenth-century knight and mounted on a charger in rich trappings, both looking ready for battle. Dimly, David could make out, in front of the altar in the west side of the south transept, the carved figures of angelic musicians holding the instruments of the Passion. Their childlike bodies, dressed in swirling draperies, looked alive. At any moment, he almost expected them to go into animation and fill this eerie and deserted place with heavenly music.

Suddenly he saw her.

Bianca.

He had concentrated his attention on the carved figures and, in the gloom, had missed her entirely. She was kneeling in front of the altar, head bowed and hands clasped in prayer. Her back was to him. A scarf was wrapped tightly around her head, and she was wearing a red cloak. He recognized it as the same one she had worn when she came down to the police station to identify the medallion.

He drew a long, deep breath. He was enormously relieved to see her. He had been getting a little edgy, waiting here alone. And, to tell the truth, a little leery, and beginning to wonder . . .

He came toward her. She did not seem to hear his approach; she was deeply involved in her prayer.

262

"Bianca."

Suddenly, she turned and rose to her feet.

He looked into the grinning face of Teodoro Borsato. He looked grotesque, obscene, standing there in his women's clothes.

"*Bastardo*," he said.

David saw the knife shining in Borsato's hand. Borsato slashed at David's neck. Some instinct, some quick and automatic reflex, saved his life. He ducked low, an instant before Borsato began his thrust. The knife whished over him.

He grabbed his assailant around the waist and flung him against the altar, knocking Borsato off balance just before he could get his knife hand free again.

Then David turned and ran for the entrance.

Borsato ran after him. He began to shriek:

"Get him! Kill him!"

He was on David's heels, only a few feet behind him, brandishing his knife. He continued to scream at his accomplice to finish the job. The man in black, wearing a nylon stocking over his face and hiding behind the entry door, stiffened. His hand tightened on his knife.

He timed his move beautifully.

Just as David began to rush through the door, he stepped out. He let the American pass and waited for Borsato, running just a few feet behind him. And just when Borsato started through the door, realizing something was wrong now but unable to stop his momentum, the man in black plunged the knife into Borsato's belly.

Borsato gasped and staggered out of the church, holding his belly with both hands. He tried to say something, but his voice was only an agonized croak. His accomplice glanced at the American running down along the *fondamenta* bordering the canal.

Then he turned his attention to his victim.

Borsato had stopped. He stood there, stooped over and crying softly, still holding his belly with both hands. Blood seeped through his fingers. His assailant walked to him, and spun him around. Then he said, softly:

"I *told* you, Borsato. Some day we would have an accounting."

He pulled the stocking from his face so that Borsato could see it. He wanted his smile to be the last thing Borsato saw in this life. Then, he turned his victim around and plunged the knife into Borsato's back three times.

Borsato fell to the pavement. His assassin leaned over and dragged him to the edge of the canal. Then, with a contemptuous shove of his foot, he pushed the body into the canal.

Bruno Savoldo crossed himself. Then he walked to his gondola. He poled it out into the middle of the canal. He took the chains and weights he had gathered, on Borsato's orders, and threw them overboard.

After that, he moved the gondola rapidly up the Rio di San Trovaso, working his paddle hard.

Opposite the Fondamenta Nani, he passed a *squero,* or yard where gondolas, *sandali,* and other boats were built and repaired. A worker had built a bonfire beside one of the gondolas, in order to burn the paint off its hull. The smell of wood smoke and hot tar tickled Savoldo's nostrils. It reminded him that it was time to bring his gondola into the *squero;* its hull needed to be scraped and tarred. He patted the fat envelope in his pocket and had another thought, this one far more exciting. He wanted a new gondola badly; he needed one.

The lire in the envelope would be a good start to this end. Very helpful, indeed.

His heart continued to pound against his chest; he was still high, exhilarated.

Finally, he moored his gondola in front of a cafe frequented by his colleagues.

He sat at a back table and had three *grappe,* downing one after another, hardly taking a breath between.

Finally, he began to relax. He felt good now, very good. It was over with, and done.

He remembered Borsato's stricken eyes, as he looked up into his, Bruno Savoldo's, face for the last time, the slavering mouth, still open in surprise. He laughed aloud. It reminded him of the face of a dying fish when you were about to strip him from the hook.

He had to assume that Teodoro Borsato had planned to get rid of him as soon as they had finished the American. First, because Borsato would always see him as a threat. And, second, there was all that money, now safely secured in his own pocket.

They had both had to gamble on the fact that the church would be empty of some nocturnal worshipper. The gamble had succeeded, and the stage had been set. But the play, as far as Borsato was concerned, had turned out quite unexpectedly.

Now, he, Savoldo, was the only witness as to what had happened to Vittorio Favretto twenty-five years ago. He wasn't worried about Signore David Drew. The American hadn't seen him in the dark, back there at the church. And suppose he *did* have another one of his crazy visions and told the police that Bruno Savoldo was one of the assassins?

Well, what of it? He could prove nothing. Visions were for saints, prophets, devils and angels, or crazy people in insane asylums. True, he had envisioned Vittorio Favretto lying at the bottom of the Rio de la Malvesia Vecchia. But again, without actual proof, there was nothing to worry about.

He glowed in self-satisfaction. Teodoro had always thought of him as a simple and stupid man. Sometimes stupidity, or the appearance of it, paid dividends.

In this case, the old expression could be changed a little. A fool and his life are easily parted.

He rose from the table a little unsteadily, went to the bar, bought a smile from the bartender with a tip of a thousand lire, and walked out.

23

THE plane gained altitude, circled over Venice once, and lost the city in the cloud cover as it set its course.

He sat at a window seat and saw the city slip under white fluff, finally watched it vanish, and he knew that this was the last time he would ever see it. He was hypnotized by the way the city below was slowly obliterated. It was as if it had existed only as a dream, and the dream had been wiped out by wakening, until finally it was over.

And, he thought, perhaps that's all it ever was. A dream.

The night before last, as soon as he could get to a phone, he had telephoned Lieutenant Cozzi. Cozzi had been working late, and David had caught him in, and he quickly told the lieutenant what had happened at the Church of San Trovaso. Cozzi sounded laconic. The police would investigate it, of course. He was too busy to come himself, but he would send someone over. He assumed the assassin, who,

David said, was Borsato's accomplice, had dumped the body into the canal. And, of course, they must recover the body first, before they could really proceed. And that might be difficult, if not impossible.

No, it would not be necessary for David to remain in Venice. No, he would not be needed to testify, he had already adequately reported everything over the telephone. There was absolutely no reason whatever for Signore Drew to stay. In fact, said Cozzi, pointedly, the police would prefer to have the *signore* leave. For reasons already stated.

"Once again, my friend," Cozzi had said. "*Addío*. Have a good trip home."

And that had been that.

He had postponed his departure, and he had spent all of yesterday and last night with Bianca Favretto. In fact, he had just left her bed to make this flight, and the delicate perfume of her body still clung to his skin, reminding him of the delight he had deliberately walked away from.

At dawn, when they were both exhausted, they had rested, faces turned toward each other on their pillows. And suddenly, he had said:

"Bianca, I'm not going."

"But we agreed. You must."

"I've changed my mind. I can't leave you."

She had reached out her hand then and stroked his cheek tenderly.

"I know. I love you for saying this, *caro*. I don't want *you* to leave. Believe me, it is the last thing I want, in my heart. But of course, you must."

"But why? I can stay here. I don't *have* to go back."

"*Caro*, listen. Venice is not your world. You do not belong here. What would you do here? Your work, your future, it could never possibly be here. There would be nothing for you to do. You have your own special work, your career, you are so young, there is so much ahead for you. You must go back where you belong."

"Then you can come back with me."

"No," she said. "My place is here. There is no future for us together, David. We have known this all along. I am old enough to be your mother. A year, perhaps two, it might work for a while. But then as the years passed ... you would see me differently. You could not help it, it would be only natural. I want you to go now, while I can still bear it. I want you to remember me as I am now. Not when I am older. Not when my hair is gray and I have wrinkles and am getting fat. And I want to remember you as—not as Vittorio Favretto, *caro*—but as the man you really are— David Drew. My young American, possessed with the soul of the only man I really and deeply loved. I could not bear to see you every day and think of you as Vittorio and know that this is just an illusion, that Vittorio Favretto is really dead. And you would not want me to think of you that way."

They were silent for a while, and then he said:

"I'll be back."

"Please, *caro*, no. It is over. We must never see each other again. It is best that way. To keep the memory as it is—not to spoil it. But even though this is the last time we shall see each other, there is still a way in which I want you to remember me ... "

She slid her naked body out of bed, padded to her bureau, and took something from the top drawer. It was the inscribed medallion he had found on what was left of Vittorio Favretto.

He had been wearing the medallion he had bought in New York. She sat on the bed, leaned over, unhooked it from his neck, and put it to one side. Then she put the new medallion around his neck.

"Wear this," she said. "After all, it really belongs to you."

Then she leaned over and kissed him, they got dressed, and she took him to the airport in her own speedboat; they said goodbye, and that was the end of it.

Except that throughout the night she had sometimes called him David and sometimes Vittorio; she seemed confused according to her mood. He was encased in another man's shadow or, rather, it was contained in him. He wondered how she would really remember him. But he knew how he had to regard himself from now on. He had to forget that he had ever been Vittorio Favretto.

Vittorio Favretto was dead and gone and had been for twenty-five years, and he had to remember that. And, although his widow was still alive, he had to think of her as dead and gone as well, and he knew this would take time and he would have to work on it.

At the moment, his identity was blurred, but in time he knew he must see himself, and think of himself, and know himself as one man, David Drew. Period.

Put it all behind him.

Otherwise, he could go mad.

The morning after he got back, he did all the usual things. He went through his mail, called his cleaning woman to tell her he had returned and she could come in on her usual Monday.

Then he called Allan Fischer's extension at Datafax, to find out where he could reach his friend in Iran. To his very great surprise, a familiar voice came on the phone:

"Fischer, C Section, Programming."

"Allan, David."

"For God's sake."

"For God's sake yourself. I thought you were in Iran."

"I was. Till the day before yesterday."

"What happened?"

"Mission aborted."

"Yes. But why?"

"Who knows? The shah threw the whole deal out. Maybe he decided to use the money to buy another superduper, supersonic, radar-defying stratospheric special for his air force. Or one of our new smell-sensitive homing missiles that targets in on borscht and caviar. Or it could simply be that one of our competitors intercepted our pass, came up with more money than we did in the right place, and took the ball over for a touchdown. Like I said, who knows? But never mind at all. When did you get back?"

"Yesterday. How about lunch today?"

"Why not? I'm free."

"Say one o'clock? At the Input?"

"Good deal."

He showered, toweled himself dry, and then stood before the mirror, studying his reflection for a moment. The medallion still hung around his neck. He unhooked it, took it off, and put it in a heavy manila envelope, chain and all.

Shortly before his appointment with Allan, he went out into the street. There was a bank about a block away from his apartment.

He had no account in this particular bank, but he walked in and made an application for a safe deposit box.

The girl led him into the bank vault, slid out the box, and gave it to him.

He took it into a small booth and closed the door behind him.

He opened the envelope and took one last look at the medallion. Then he put it back into the envelope, shoved it into the steel box, and called for the girl to lock it up.

She gave him two keys. She explained that if he lost one, it wasn't so bad. They could always make a new one. But if he lost both, they'd have to break open the box.

He walked out of the bank and down the street. He noted a sewer at the curb. He stopped uncertainly, feeling the keys in his pocket. Then he took them out and dropped them through the grille of the sewer.

After that, he hailed a taxi.

"All right," said Allan, after they gave the waitress their order. "Now tell me."

"Tell you what?"

"What hung you up in Venice. Why you threw up a good job to stay there. I want her name, address, telephone number, and . . . "

"It wasn't a girl."

270

"No? Then what *was* it?"

"Even if I told you, you wouldn't believe it."

"Tell me anyway."

He told Allan the whole story. His friend listened without interruption and progressively became more and more excited. And finally, Allan said:

"Jesus! What a hell of an experience. Man, what a *mystic* experience!"

David stared at him. "Then you believe me?"

Allan's face reflected disbelief at David's surprise.

"Of course I do. Are you kidding? I'm *into* reincarnation. So are a billion other people in the world, more or less. What's happened to you—well, I mean I just sit here and look at you, and what I see is a miracle! A revelation! Don't you realize it? You've been *chosen*. I've got to take this to our Leader."

"You mean Maharishi?"

"Who else?"

"Allan, let it die."

"What?"

"This is confidential. Just you and me."

"Are you crazy?"

"I mean it."

Allan stared at him incredulously. "Look, David, this is the Age of Enlightenment. Through our TM-Sidhi program, we're into all kinds of new things. Things that go beyond the normal TM process. We've trained people to lift themselves off the ground, to levitate; we've trained them to disappear before your eyes, to develop the senses to an extent you wouldn't believe. It all comes out of ancient Vedic knowledge. But according to Maharishi, these powers aren't superhuman, the way they were thought of in the old days. Anything and everything is within the normal range of man's ability, once you really master your own nature. Now, you've just proved that reincarnation through transcendental meditation is one of those new powers, maybe we can all reach—"

"Allan, wait a minute."

Fischer's eyes were shining through his thick lenses. He did not even hear David.

"Look, maybe we can break this first in a lecture at the Maharishi Academy for the Science of Creative Intelligence. Get Maharishi himself to come over and travel with you. You can tell the executive governors what happened, the people who teach the TM-Sidhi program, at the SCI Academies at the Cobb Mountain and Saboda Centers, out in California, and the Maharishi International University Faculty out in Fairfield, Iowa. And then, of course, at all the World Plan Centers—"

"Allan, forget it."

"What?"

"I don't want any part of it."

"But, Jesus, man, you don't seem to understand. Live your previous lives through transcendental meditation. This is fabulous. This is a deepening experience during the practice of the TM technique. And when we consider the other areas, the coherent states—"

"I'm out of TM, Allan."

"What?"

"I'm finished with it. I've had it. For good. I don't meditate any more."

"You're out of your mind. You don't know what else you might come up with."

"That's what I'm afraid of."

During the entire lunch Allan begged him, pleaded with him, to reconsider, change his mind. If they could spread the word around, maybe millions of other people would take up TM, maybe everybody. And if that happened, Maharishi's ideal would be finally consummated, the Age of Enlightenment would finally be here in all its glory, and we would have a true ideal society, a world without war, where each human being would be aware of and understand his inner self, his own karma, place himself in accord with the laws of nature, and become an ideal unit in the ideal society, and, finally, in the cosmos itself . . .

272

But still David said no.

After he left Allan, he went to a phone booth, dialed *Newsweek*, and got Cassie Knox on the phone.

She was delighted to hear from him and surprised that he was back from Iran so soon, and, of course, she'd love to see him again. She'd be jogging in the morning, in Central Park, as usual, and why not meet her and jog along? And he said: "Why not, indeed?" They'd start out from the monkey house at the zoo, as usual, and, while they were running, he could tell her all about Iran, what kind of a place it was.

After he hung up, he took a taxi to the Forty-second Street library and spent an hour reading up on the folkways and mores of modern Iran. Cassie Knox was the kind of girl who liked to ask questions, she had this reporter-researcher mind, so he had better be prepared.

It would be much more relaxing, he thought, to lie about Iran than to tell the truth about Venice.

About the Author

Max Ehrlich is the author of nine previous novels, including such widely known best sellers as *The Big Eye, First Train to Babylon, The Reincarnation of Peter Proud* (for which he also wrote the screenplay) and *The Cult.* All of his books have been translated into many foreign languages throughout the world.